For more than forty years,
Yearling has been the leading name
in classic and award-winning literature
for young readers.

Yearling books feature children's
favorite authors and characters,
providing dynamic stories of adventure,
humor, history, mystery, and fantasy.

Trust Yearling paperbacks to entertain,
inspire, and promote the love of reading
in all children.

Books by
# Paul Stewart & Chris Riddell

## The Edge Chronicles
*Beyond the Deepwoods*
*Stormchaser*
*Midnight over Sanctaphrax*
*The Curse of the Gloamglozer*
*The Last of the Sky Pirates*
*Vox*
*Freeglader*
*The Winter Knights*
*Clash of the Sky Galleons*

## Far-Flung Adventures
*Fergus Crane*
*Corby Flood*
*Hugo Pepper*

# The Edge CHRONICLES

## STORMCHASER

THE DEEP WOODS

THE TWILIGHT WOODS

THE EDGELANDS

The Edge.

# The Edge CHRONICLES

## STORMCHASER

### Paul Stewart & Chris Riddell

A Yearling Book

Published by Yearling, an imprint of Random House Children's Books
a division of Random House, Inc., New York

Text and illustrations copyright © 1999 by Paul Stewart and Chris Riddell

Originally published in Great Britain by Doubleday, an imprint of Random House Children's Books

Visit us on the Web! www.randomhouse.com/kids

Educators and librarians, for a variety of teaching tools, visit us at www.randomhouse.com/teachers

The Library of Congress has cataloged the hardcover edition of this work as follows:
Stewart, Paul.
Stormchaser / by Paul Stewart and Chris Riddell.
p. cm. — (The edge chronicles)
Summary: In his continuing adventures, Twig, now sixteen years old, joins the crew of his father's sky pirate ship and embarks on a dangerous mission to collect the powerful stormphrax, a substance that purifies water and also prevents the city of Sanctaphrax from floating away.
ISBN: 978-0-385-75070-7 (trade)—ISBN: 978-0-385-75071-4 (lib. bdg.)
[1. Fathers and sons—Fiction. 2. Fantasy.] I. Riddell, Chris. II. Title. III. Series.
PZ7.S84975St 2004
[Fic]—dc22
2004005170

ISBN: 978-0-440-42088-0 (pbk.)

Reprinted by arrangement with David Fickling Books

Printed in the United States of America

May 2008

10 9 8 7 6 5 4 3 2 1

First Yearling Edition

*For William and Joseph*

# ·INTRODUCTION·

Far far away, jutting out into the emptiness beyond, like the figurehead of a mighty stone ship, is the Edge. A broad, swollen river – the Edgewater – pours endlessly over the lip of rock at its overhanging point and down into the void below. Its source lies far inland, high up in the dark and perilous Deepwoods.

On the fringes of this great forest, where the clouds descend, lie the Edgelands, a barren wasteland of swirling mists, spirits and nightmares. Those who lose themselves in the Edgelands face one of two possible fates. The lucky ones will stumble blindly to the cliff edge and plunge to their deaths. The unlucky ones will find themselves in the Twilight Woods.

Bathed in their never-ending golden half-light, the Twilight Woods are enchanting – but also treacherous. The atmosphere there is intoxicating. Those who breathe it for too long forget the reason they ever came, like the lost knights on long-forgotten quests, who would give up on life – if only life would give up on them.

On occasions, the heavy stillness of the Twilight Woods is disturbed by violent storms which blow in from beyond the Edge. Drawn there like moths to a flame, the storms circle the glowing sky – sometimes for days at a time. Some of the storms are special. The lightning bolts they release create stormphrax, a substance so valuable that – despite the awful dangers of the Twilight Woods – it acts like a magnet to those who would possess it.

At its lower reaches, the Twilight Woods give way to the Mire. It is a stinking, polluted place, rank with the slurry from the factories and foundries of Undertown which have pumped and dumped their waste so long that the land is dead. And yet – like everywhere else on the Edge – there are those who live here. Pink-eyed and bleached as white as their surroundings, they are the rummagers, the scavengers.

Those who manage to make their way across the Mire find themselves in a warren of ramshackle hovels and rundown slums which straddle the oozing Edgewater River. This is Undertown. Its population is made up of all the strange peoples, creatures and tribes of the Edge crammed into its narrow alleys. It is dirty, over-crowded and often violent, yet Undertown is also the centre of all economic activity – both above-board and underhand.

It buzzes, it bustles, it bristles with energy. Everyone who lives there has a particular trade, with its attendant league and clearly defined district. This leads to intrigue, plotting, bitter competition and perpetual disputes – district with district, league with league, tradesman with rival tradesman. The only matter which unites all leaguesmen is their shared fear and hatred of the sky pirates who dominate the skies above the Edge in their independent boats and prey off any hapless leaguesmen whose paths they cross.

At the centre of Undertown is a great iron ring, to which a long and heavy chain – now taut, now slack – extends up into the sky. At its end is a great floating rock.

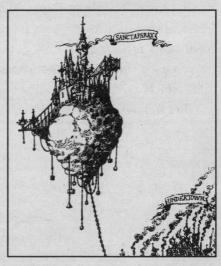

Like all the other buoyant rocks of the Edge, it started out in the Stone Gardens – poking up out of the ground, growing, being pushed up further by new rocks growing beneath it, and becoming bigger still. The chain was attached when the rock became large and light enough to float up into the sky. Upon it, the magnificent city of Sanctaphrax has been constructed.

Sanctaphrax, with its tall thin towers connected by viaducts and walkways is a seat of learning. It is peopled with academics, alchemists and apprentices – everyone has a title – and furnished with libraries, laboratories and lecture halls, refectories and common rooms. The subjects studied there are as obscure as they are jealously guarded and, despite the apparent air of fusty, bookish benevolence, Sanctaphrax is a seething cauldron of rivalries, plots and counter-plots and bitter faction-fighting.

The Deepwoods, the Edgelands, the Twilight Woods, the Mire and the Stone Gardens. Undertown and Sanctaphrax. The River Edgewater. Names on a map.

Yet behind each name lie a thousand tales – tales that have been recorded in ancient scrolls, tales that have been passed down the generations by word of mouth – tales which even now are being told.

What follows is but one of those tales.

# ·CHAPTER ONE·

# REUNION

It was midday and Undertown was bustling. Beneath the pall of filthy mist which hovered over the town, fuzzing the rooftops and dissolving the sun, its narrow streets and alleyways were alive with feverish activity.

There was ill-tempered haggling and bartering; buskers played music, barrow-boys called out unmissable bargains, beggars made their pitiful demands from dark, shadowy corners – though there were few who paused to place coins in their hats. Rushing this way and that, everyone was far too wrapped up in their own concerns to spare a thought for anyone else.

Getting from a to b as quickly as possible, being first to nail a deal, obtaining the best price while undercutting your competitors – *that* was what succeeding in Undertown was all about. You needed nerves of steel and eyes in the back of your head to survive; you had to learn to smile even as you were stabbing someone else in the back. It was a rough life, a tough life, a ruthless life.

It was an *exhilarating* life.

Twig hurried up from the boom-docks and through the market-place – not because he was in any particular hurry himelf, but because the frenzied atmosphere was contagious. Anyway, he had learned the hard way that those who don't adjust to the breakneck pace of the place were liable to get knocked down and tram-pled underfoot. Along with 'avoid all eye-contact' and 'do not display weak-ness', 'go with the flow' was one of the cardinal rules of Undertown.

Twig was feeling uncomfortably hot. The sun was at its highest. Despite being obscured by the choking, foul-tasting smoke from the metal foundries, it beat down ferociously. There was no wind and, as Twig dodged his way past the shops, stands and stalls, a bewildering mix of smells assaulted his nostrils. Stale woodale, ripe cheeses, burned milk and boiling glue, roasting pine-coffee and sizzling tilder sausages . . .

The spicy aroma of the sausages took Twig back, as it always did – back to his childhood. Every Wodgiss Night, in the woodtroll village where he had been brought up, the adults would feast on the traditional tilder sausage soup. How long ago that now seemed, and how far away! Life then had been so different: self-contained, ordered, unhurried. Twig smiled to himself. He could never return to that life. Not now. Not for all the trees in the Deepwoods.

As he continued across the market-place, the mouth-watering aroma of the sausages grew fainter and was replaced with a different smell – a smell which triggered a different set of memories altogether. It was the un-mistakable scent of freshly tanned leather. Twig stopped and looked round.

A tall individual with the blood-red skin and crimson hair of a slaughterer was standing by a wall. Hanging round his neck was a wooden tray overflowing with the leather talismans and amulets on thongs which he was selling – or rather *trying* to sell.

'Lucky charms!' he cried. 'Get your lucky charms here!'

No-one was paying him any heed, and when he went to tie the charms around the necks of the passers-by each attempt was greeted with an irritated shake of the head as the goblin or troll or whatever hurried past.

Twig watched him sadly. The slaughterer – like so many of the Deepwoods folk who had listened to rumours that the streets of Undertown were paved with gold – was finding the reality quite different. With a sigh, he turned and was about to move on when, at that moment, a particularly mean-looking cloddertrog in tattered clothes and heavy boots brushed past him.

'Lucky charm?' the slaughterer said cheerily and stepped forwards, leather thong at the ready.

'Keep your murderous red hands off me!' the cloddertrog roared and shoved the outstretched arms savagely away.

The slaughterer spun round and crashed to the ground. The lucky charms went everywhere.

As the cloddertrog stomped off, cursing under his breath, Twig hurried over to the slaughterer. 'Are you all right?' he asked, reaching down to help him to his feet.

The slaughterer rolled over and blinked up at him. 'Blooming rudeness,' he complained. '*I* don't know!' He looked away and began gathering up the charms and returning them to the tray. 'All I'm trying to do is scratch an honest living.'

'It can't be easy,' said Twig sympathetically. 'So far away from your Deepwoods home.'

Twig knew the slaughterers well. He had once stayed with them in their forest village, and to this day, he still wore the hammelhornskin waistcoat they had given him. The slaughterer looked up. Twig touched his forehead in greeting and reached down with his hand once again.

This time, with the last of the charms back in place, the slaughterer took a hold and pulled himself up. He touched his own forehead. 'I am Tendon,' he said. 'And thank you for stopping to see whether I was all right. Most folk round here wouldn't give you the time of day.' He sniffed. 'I don't suppose . . .' He checked himself.

'What?' said Twig.

The slaughterer shrugged. 'I was just wondering whether *you* might care to buy one of my lucky charms.' And Twig smiled to himself as, unbidden, the slaughterer selected one of the leather talismans and held it out. 'How about this one? It's extremely potent.'

Twig looked at the intricate spiral tooled into the deep-red leather. He knew that, for the slaughterers, the

individual designs on the
charms each had its own
significance.

'Those who wear this
charm,' the slaughterer
went on as he tied the thong
around Twig's neck, 'shall be
freed from fear of the known.'

'Shouldn't that be the
*un*known?' said Twig.

The slaughterer
snorted. 'Fear of the
unknown is for the fool-
ish and weak,' he said. 'I

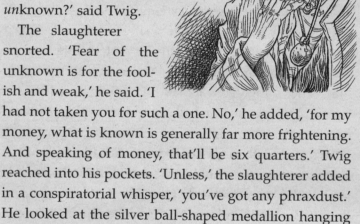

had not taken you for such a one. No,' he added, 'for my
money, what is known is generally far more frightening.
And speaking of money, that'll be six quarters.' Twig
reached into his pockets. 'Unless,' the slaughterer added
in a conspiratorial whisper, 'you've got any phraxdust.'
He looked at the silver ball-shaped medallion hanging
round Twig's neck. 'A speck would do.'

'Sorry,' said Twig, dropping coins into waiting blood-
red palm. 'I have none to spare.'

The slaughterer shrugged with resignation. 'Just a
thought,' he muttered.

With the latest charm nestling amongst the others he
had accumulated over the years, Twig continued on his
way through the labyrinth of tiny winding alleyways.

He was passing a pet shop – heavy with the odour of
damp straw and hot fur – when all at once, a small

vicious-looking
creature rushed
towards him, teeth
bared. Twig started
back nervously, then
laughed as it reached
the end of its leash
and began leaping up
and down on the
spot, grunting

excitedly. It was a prowlgrin cub, and it wanted to play.

'Hello, boy,' he said, crouching down and rubbing the frolicsome creature beneath its hairy chin. The prowlgrin gurgled with pleasure and rolled over onto its back. 'You big softie,' said Twig. He knew it wouldn't last. Fully-grown prowlgrins were both beasts of burden and the favoured guardbeasts of those with anything worth guarding.

'Hey!' came a rasping, yet insistent whisper. 'What are you wasting your time with that bag of leechfleas for? Come over here.'

Twig looked round. Besides the prowlgrin, the front of the ramshackle shop had countless other creatures on display: furry, feathered and scaled, as well as some of the lesser trolls and goblins which were chained to the walls. There wasn't one of them that looked as if it had just spoken.

'Up here, Twig,' the voice came again, more urgently now. A shiver ran up and down Twig's spine. Whatever *had* spoken also knew him. 'Over *here*!'

Twig looked up, and gasped. 'Caterbird!' he said.

'The very same,' the caterbird whispered, and shifted round awkwardly on its perch to face him. 'Greetings.'

'Greetings,' said Twig. 'But . . .'

'Keep your voice down,' the caterbird hissed, and its right eye swivelled round to the entrance of the shop. 'I don't want Flabsweat to know I can talk.'

Twig nodded, and swallowed away the lump in his throat. How had so noble a creature ended up in such squalid surroundings? The caterbird that had watched over Twig ever since he had been present at its hatching – who had dared to capture it? And why had it been placed in a cage barely larger than the poor creature itself so that it had to squat down on its perch, with its magnificent horned beak sticking out through the bars, unable to straighten up, unable to flap its wings?

'I'll soon have you out of there,' said Twig, pulling his knife from his belt. He thrust the thin blade into the key-hole of the padlock, and began jiggling it around feverishly.

'Hurry,' urged the caterbird. 'And for Sky's sake, don't let Flabsweat see what you're up to.'

'Any second now . . .' Twig muttered through clenched teeth. But the padlock remained stubbornly locked. 'If I can just . . .'

At that moment, the air suddenly resounded with a deafening CRACK! Twig immediately stopped what he was doing and spun round in alarm. He knew what had happened. It happened all the time. The emergency chains which helped to hold the floating city of Sanctaphrax in place were always breaking.

'Another one's gone!' someone screamed.

'Look out!' screeched another.

But it was already too late. The chain which had snapped was already tumbling back to earth with an incongruously gentle jingle-jangle. Down on the street, everyone was dashing this way and that, bumping into one another – getting nowhere.

The chain crashed down. A scream went up. Then silence.

As the dust settled, Twig surveyed the scene. The roof of the ironmonger's opposite had been stoved in. Two stalls were flattened. And there on the street lay an unfortunate creature, crushed to death by the weight of the falling metal.

Twig stared at the tattered clothes and familiar heavy boots. It was the cloddertrog. Perhaps you should have listened to the slaughterer after all, he thought, and fingered the amulet at his neck. Now it was too late. For the cloddertrog, luck had run out.

'Ah, me,' he heard the caterbird sigh. 'The situation is reaching crisis point, and that's a fact.'

'What do you mean?' Twig asked.

'It's a long story,' he said slowly. 'And . . .' He paused.

'What?' said Twig.

The caterbird remained silent. It swivelled one eye meaningfully round towards the entrance of the shop.

'Oy!' came a gruff voice. 'Are you intending to buy that bird, or what?' Sliding the knife up his sleeve as he did so, Twig turned. He was confronted by a heavy-set character who was standing with his legs apart and his hands on his hips.

'I . . . I just dodged in here when the chain broke,' he said.

'Hmm,' said Flabsweat, looking round at the damage that had been caused. 'A bad business it is, all this chain-breaking. And all for that bunch of so-called academics. What good do they ever do us? Parasites, the lot of them. You know what? If it was up to me, I'd cut *all* the chains and let Sanctaphrax fly off into open sky. And good riddance!' he added bitterly, as he patted his glistening head with a dirty handkerchief.

Twig was speechless. He'd never heard anyone talk ill of the academics of the floating city before.

'Still,' Flabsweat went on, 'at least none of my property's been damaged, eh? *This* time. Now, are you interested in that bird or not?' he asked wheezily.

Twig glanced back at the bedraggled caterbird. 'I was looking for a talker.'

Flabsweat chuckled mirthlessly. 'Oh, you'll get nothing out of that one,' he said scornfully. 'Thick, it is. Still, you're welcome to try . . . I could let you have it for a very reasonable price.' He turned abruptly. 'I'm with another customer at the moment,' he called back. 'Give me a shout if you need any help.'

'Thick, indeed!' the caterbird exclaimed when Flabsweat had gone. 'The cheek! The audacity!' Its eye swivelled round and focused on Twig. 'Well, don't just stand there smirking,' it snapped. 'Get me out of here – while the coast is clear.'

'No,' said Twig.

The caterbird stared back at him, nonplussed. It cocked its head to one side – as far as the cage would allow. 'No?' it said.

'No,' Twig repeated. 'I want to hear that "long story" first. "The situation is reaching crisis point", that's what you said. I want to know why. I want to know what's happened.'

'Let me out, and then I'll tell you everything,' said the caterbird.

'No,' said Twig for a third time. 'I know you. You'll fly off the moment I unlock the cage door, and then I won't see you again till Sky knows when. Tell me this story first, and *then* I'll set you free.'

'Why, you insolent young whelp!' the caterbird shouted angrily. 'And after everything I've done for you!'

'Keep your voice down,' said Twig, looking round nervously at the doorway. 'Flabsweat will hear you.'

The caterbird fell still. It closed its eyes. For a moment, Twig thought that it was going to remain stubbornly silent. He was on the point of relenting, when the caterbird's beak moved.

'It all started a long time ago,' it began. 'Twenty years, to be precise. When your father was little older than you are now.'

'But that was before you were even born,' said Twig.

'Caterbirds share dreams, you know that,' it replied. 'What one knows, we all know. And if you're going to interrupt the whole time . . .'

'I'm not,' said Twig. 'Sorry. I won't do it again.'

The caterbird humphed irritably. 'Just see that you don't.'

# ·CHAPTER TWO·

# THE CATERBIRD'S TALE

'Picture the scene,' the caterbird said. 'A cold, blustery, yet clear evening. The moon rises over Sanctaphrax, its towers and spires silhouetted against the purple sky. A lone figure emerges from the bottom of a particularly ill-favoured tower and scurries across the cobbled court-yard. It is an apprentice raintaster. His name, Vilnix Pompolnius.'

'What, *the* Vilnix Pompolnius?' Twig blurted out. 'Most High Academe of Sanctaphrax?' Although he had never seen the lofty academic, his reputation went before him.

'The very same,' said the caterbird. 'Many of those who attain greatness have the humblest of origins – in fact he used to be a knife-grinder in Undertown. But Vilnix Pompolnius was always ruthlessly ambitious, and never more so than on that night. As he hurried on, head down into the wind, towards the glittering spires of the School of Light and Darkness, he was plotting and scheming.'

Twig shuddered, and the fur of his hammelhornskin waistcoat bristled ominously.

'For you see,' the caterbird explained, 'Vilnix had the ear – and an indulgent ear, what's more – of one of the most powerful Sanctaphrax scholars at that time. The Professor of Darkness. It was he who had sponsored Vilnix through the Knights' Academy. And when Vilnix was later dismissed for insubordination, it was he who had secured his place in the Faculty of Raintasters rather than see him cast out of Sanctaphrax completely.'

The caterbird took a breath, and continued. 'Once inside the opulence of the professor's study, Vilnix held up a glass beaker of liquid dramatically. "The rain coming in from over the Edge is becoming more acidic," he said. "This is due to an increase in the number of sourmist particles in the raindrops. It was thought you might be interested," he added slyly.

'The Professor of Darkness *was* interested. Very interested. The presence of sourmist particles could presage the arrival of a Great Storm. "I must consult with the windtouchers and cloudwatchers," he said, "to determine whether they have also identified signs of an approaching Great Storm. Good work, my boy."

'Vilnix's eyes gleamed; his heart missed a beat. Things were going better than he had hoped. Taking care not to arouse his suspicions, he drew the old professor on. "A Great Storm?" he said, innocently. "Does this mean that a Knight Academic will be sent in search of more stormphrax?"

'The professor confirmed that it did. He tapped the papers in front of him. "And not before time, either, if these figures are correct," he said. "The great rock which Sanctaphrax stands upon is still growing – larger and larger, more and more buoyant . . ." His voice trailed away. He shook his head in despair.

'Vilnix watched him out of the corner of his eye. "And you need more stormphrax in the treasury to weigh it down – to . . . to . . ."

'The professor nodded vigorously. "To preserve the equilibrium," he said, and sighed. "It is so long since a Knight Academic returned with fresh supplies of stormphrax."

'A smile played over Vilnix's curled lips. "And which knight is to be sent on this occasion?" he asked.

'The professor snorted. "The Professor of Light's protégé. Quintinius . . ." He frowned. "Quintinius . . . oh, what's his name?"

'Vilnix winced. "Quintinius *Verginix*," he said.'

'My father!' Twig exclaimed, unable to keep quiet a moment longer. 'I didn't realize he knew the Most High Academe. Nor that he was ever in the Knights' Academy . . .' He paused thoughtfully. 'But then there's much I don't know about his life before he became a sky pirate,' he added.

'If you'd just hold your tongue for a moment,' the caterbird said impatiently, 'then perhaps . . .' It was cut short by the sound of frantic yelping which came from inside the shop.

The next moment, Flabsweat appeared at the doorway, white as a sheet and babbling on about how a vulpoon – a straggly bird of prey with a viciously serrated beak and razor-sharp talons – had just slipped its tether and laid into a hapless lapmuffler.

'Is it all right?' asked Twig.

'All right?' Flabsweat wheezed. 'The lapmuffler? No it's *not* all right. Guts everywhere, there are. And you can get good money for a lapmuffler. I'll have to fetch the animal-quack,' he muttered. 'Get it stitched up again.' He looked at Twig, as if seeing him for the first time. 'Are you trustworthy?' he asked.

Twig nodded.

'Hmm,' Flabsweat mumbled. 'Well, since you're still here, would you mind watching the shop while I'm gone? There could be something in it for you.'

'That's fine,' said Twig, trying not to sound too eager.

The moment Flabsweat was out of earshot, the cater-bird immediately asked once more to be set free. But Twig was adamant. 'All in good time,' he said. 'After all, there's nothing worse than a tale which ends half way through its telling.'

The caterbird grumbled under its breath. 'Where was I, then? Ah, yes. Vilnix and your father . . . The pair of them entered the Knights' Academy on the very same morning and yet, from that first day, Quintinius Verginix outshone all the other young hopefuls – Vilnix included. In swordplay, archery and unarmed combat, he was unmatched; in the sailing of the stormchasers – the sky ships especially designed to chase the Great Storms – he was peerless.'

Twig beamed proudly, and imagined himself chasing a Great Storm. Pitching and rolling as the ship locked on to the whirling wind and then breaking through to the stillness within . . .

'Pay attention!' hissed the caterbird.

Twig looked up guiltily. 'I am!' he protested.

'Humph!' said the caterbird dubiously, its neck feathers ruffling. 'As I was saying, the professor explained to Vilnix that, if the Great Storm *was* confirmed, then – as tradition demanded – Quintinius Verginix would be knighted and despatched to the Twilight Woods. Sky willing, he would return with stormphrax.

'Vilnix smiled that smile of his. Inscrutable, reptilian. Now, at last, the time had come to touch upon the subject he had wanted to enquire about all along. "This . . . stormphrax," he said, in as off-hand a manner as he could manage. "When I was in the Knights' Academy, it was often talked about as the most wonderful substance that ever existed. We were told that the shards of stormphrax are in fact pure lightning," he continued, his voice oily, treacherous. "Can this possibly be true?"

'The Professor of Darkness nodded solemnly, and when he spoke again it was as though he was reciting from an ancient text. "That which is called stormphrax," he proclaimed, "is created in the eye of a Great Storm – a mighty maelstrom which is formed far beyond the Edge once every several years, which blows in on parched and sulphurous winds, which howls and sparks as it crosses the sky towards the Twilight Woods. There, the Great Storm breaks. It delivers a single mighty lightning bolt that scorches through the heavy twilight air and plunges into the soft earth beneath. In that instant it turns to solid stormphrax, gleaming in the half-light. Honoured is he who should witness such a sight."

'Vilnix's eyes gleamed greedily. Pure lightning! he thought. What power must each piece of stormphrax contain. He looked up. "And ... errm ... what does it look like exactly?"

'The professor's expression became dreamy. "Of unsurpassed beauty," he said. "A crystal that fizzes, that glows, that sparks ..."

'"And yet it is heavy," said Vilnix. "Or so I learned. But how heavy?"

'"In the twilight of its creation it is no heavier than sand. Yet in the absolute darkness of the treasury at the centre of Sanctaphrax, a thimbleful weighs more than a thousand ironwood trees," the professor told him. "It provides the counter-balance to the buoyancy of the rock itself. Without it, the floating city would break its moorings and fly off into open sky . . ."

'Vilnix scratched his head theatrically. "What I don't understand is this," he said. "If the crystals and shards are so heavy, then how is the stormphrax brought through the darkness of the tunnels to the treasury in the first place?"

'The Professor of Darkness surveyed the youth gravely. Perhaps,' said the caterbird, interrupting his own story, 'just for a moment, he doubted the motives of the young apprentice. I'm not sure. Nor can I say what finally decided him to entrust Vilnix with the information. But entrust him, he did. It was a decision which was to change the course of history in Sanctaphrax. "It is transported in a light-box," he explained, "with the light it emits calibrated to approximate twilight itself."

'Vilnix turned away in order to hide his glee. If a light-box could be used to get the stormphrax in, then surely, he reasoned, it could also be used to get some out. "Perhaps I could see some for myself?" he suggested tentatively.

'"Absolutely not!" the Professor of Darkness barked – and Vilnix knew he had gone too far. "None may set eyes upon stormphrax," the professor said. "None save the Knights Academic and the guardian of the treasury –

who happens to be myself. It is blasphemy for unworthy eyes to feast upon the purity of stormphrax," he ranted. "An action, Vilnix, punishable by death."'

The caterbird paused dramatically. 'At that moment, the wind abruptly changed. The floating rock of Sanctaphrax drifted to the west and jerked violently as all the chains went taut.

'"I understand," said Vilnix humbly.

'"Ah Vilnix," the professor continued more gently. "I wonder if you truly do understand. There are many out there who covet stormphrax for themselves. Unscrupulous windtouchers and traitorous cloudwatchers who would not think twice at observing . . . at touching . . ." A violent shudder passed through his body. "At *experimenting* on stormphrax – if they thought it would serve their own ends."'

The caterbird fell silent for a moment before continuing with his tale. 'Early the following morning,' it said, 'the treasury guard would have seen a gangly figure creep furtively along the corridor from the treasury – had he not been dozing at his post. There was a light-box clutched in the intruder's bony hands. Inside the box were several fragments of stormphrax.'

Twig gasped. Vilnix *had* stolen some.

'Vilnix scurried back to the Apprentices' Laboratory at the top of the Raintasters' Tower,' the caterbird continued. 'Triumphantly he placed the box down in front of an eagerly waiting group of young raintasters and, with a flourish, opened the lid. The crystals of stormphrax sparkled and flashed like nothing they had seen before. "Pure lightning," said Vilnix. "If we can unleash and harness its energy then we'll become the most powerful academics Sanctaphrax has ever known."

'Hour after hour the raintasters worked, yet no matter what they tried – be it dissolving, freezing, melting or mixing the crystals with other substances – none discovered how to unlock the power of the stormphrax.

'Outside the window, the sun went down. The light turned a golden orange.

'Suddenly overcome with frustration, Vilnix raised the pestle and brought it down hard, crushing the fragment in his fury. A moment later, he was overcome with remorse. He had destroyed the priceless stormphrax.'

The caterbird's eye narrowed. 'Or so he thought at first. When he looked more carefully, though, Vilnix saw the result of his action. The crystals had turned to a sepia powder which moved in the bottom of the bowl like quicksilver. "I don't know what it is," Vilnix told the others, "but let's make some more."

'A second shard was taken. It was placed in a second mortar. A second pestle was raised. Outside, the light faded. Then, with the exception of Vilnix himself, who was busy pouring his own liquid dust into a jar, all the apprentices gathered round. The pestle was brought down and – BOOM!'

Twig started back in surprise.

'The power of the lightning had been unleashed all right,' the caterbird snorted. 'But with the direst of consequences. The explosion ripped through the tower, reducing half of it to smouldering rubble; it rocked Sanctaphrax to its core and jarred the ancient Anchor Chain to the very edge of breaking. The apprentices were all killed in the blast. All, that is, save one.'

'Vilnix Pompolnius,' Twig whispered.

'Precisely,' said the caterbird. 'There he lay, on the floor, barely alive but still clutching the jar to his chest. The scent of almonds hung in the air. Dazed and confused, Vilnix stared down at the stormphrax dust. What had gone wrong this second time? he wondered. What had happened?

'As he pulled himself up on his elbows, a drop of blood fell from a gash in his cheek and into the jar. The instant it made contact with the dust, the thick, red blood turned to crystal-clear water . . .'

The expression on the caterbird's face grew deadly serious. 'Crisis now hung over lofty Sanctaphrax,' it said solemnly. 'Thanks to the arrogant young raintaster's folly, the ancient chain was now perilously close to breaking point. Worse still, the theft of the stormphrax had left the treasury depleted. With the buoyancy of the rock increasing every day, and less to weight it down, the upward pressure on the rock became intolerable.

'There was just one glimmer of hope: the wind-touchers and cloudwatchers had confirmed that a Great Storm was indeed approaching. Accordingly, an Inauguration Ceremony was hurriedly arranged. Quintinius Verginix was to be knighted and would set off to chase the Great Storm to the Twilight Woods in search of stormphrax.

'Meanwhile,' the caterbird continued, 'Vilnix lay in his sick bed, his mind working furiously. He might have failed to harness the power of the lightning, but he realized that the stormphrax dust he'd created was itself miraculous – a single grain dropped into the foulest water instantly purified it. What would the inhabitants of filthy, fetid Undertown not give for his wonderful dust? "Anything," he whispered greedily. "Anything at all!"

'Without waiting to be discharged, he left his hospital ward and returned to the dilapidated tower of the rain-tasters – or rather rain*taster*, since he was the only one left. There, he busied himself. Everything had to be ready for the great day.

'Finally that day arrived. The sun rose, and shafts of light streamed in through the eastern arch of the Great Hall where the Sanctaphrax council was already assembled.

'The Professors of Light and Darkness – in white and black robes respectively – sat at the front of the hall

behind a table, upon which were a sword and a chalice. Before them, seated in rows, were the academics of Sanctaphrax. Every discipline was represented: the College of Cloud, the Academy of Wind, the Institute of Ice and Snow; the airsifters, the mistgraders, the fog-probers ... And, on crutches, the single remaining member of the Faculty of Raintasters.

'A tall, powerfully built young knight crossed the floor and knelt down in front of the Professor of Light. "By the powers invested in me – oh, thirst for knowledge, oh, sharpness of wit," the professor announced, raising first the chalice and then the sword, "I offer up for your approval Quintinius Verginix of the Knights' Academy."

'The professor looked down at the kneeling figure. "Do you, Quintinius Verginix, swear by all that is wise, that you will serve the Order of Knights Academic with heart and mind, forswearing all loyalties other than to Sanctaphrax."

'Quintinius trembled. "I do," he said.'

Twig's heart swelled with pride. My father! he thought.

'"And do you swear also that you will dedicate your life to the finding of stormphrax? That you will chase the Great Storms? That ..." The professor breathed in, slowly, deeply. "That you will not return until and unless you have completed your sacred quest?"'

The caterbird turned and fixed Twig with its unblinking gaze. 'His father – your grandfather – Wind Jackal, was a sky pirate captain. How furious Quintinius had been with him when the old fellow had offered him up for service at the Knights' Academy, for he had wanted to follow in his footsteps. Yet now ... Now! Words could not describe how honoured he felt at receiving the highest accolade that Sanctaphrax could bestow. "Quintinius," he heard the professor gently say, "do you swear?"

'Quintinius Verginix raised his head. "I do!" he said.

'The Professor of Light then leaned forwards and handed the chalice to Quintinius. "Drink!" he said. Quintinius raised the chalice to his lips. The Professor of Light took up the sword, held it high above his head, and waited for Quintinius to drain the chalice. And waited and waited ... But Quintinius remained motionless, unable to drink the thick, foul-smelling liquid.

'All at once, there was a flurry of movement in the rows of benches. It was Vilnix, leaping up noisily onto his crutches and making his way to the front of the hall.

'The Professor of Darkness sat forwards uneasily in his throne. What was the young fool doing now? he wondered. He watched Vilnix raise one of his crutches and tap the chalice lightly. "The good waters of the Edgewater River are no longer what they used to be," he chuckled, then turned to address the hall. "So, isn't it time we stopped fooling ourselves? All this nonsense about Knights Academic. About 'stormchasing'. About 'sacred' stormphrax'." He sneered unpleasantly. "When did a Knight Academic last return? Tell me that? What has happened to all those others?"

'A murmur went round the hall. Garlinius Gernix? Lidius Pherix? Petronius Metrax? Where were they now? The murmuring increased. "Seven years ago, the last Knight Academic set sail," Vilnix went on, "Screedius Tollinix, his name . . ."

'"It was eight years ago," someone cried out.

'"Nearly nine," called another.

'Vilnix smiled slyly. He knew he had got them. "Nearly nine years," he announced, his voice echoing round the hall. He turned to Quintinius Verginix and pointed accusingly. "And we are pinning all our hopes on *him*!" He paused dramatically. "Why should he succeed where others have – so tragically – failed?"

'Just then, the Great Hall lurched violently. "Nine years!" Vilnix cried out again. "We need to do something now!" The hall lurched a second time. "But what?" Dust fell from cracks in the ceiling. "The answer is simple, my friends," Vilnix announced. "We must build more chains."

'There was a gasp, then the hall fell still. The plan was indeed simple. It was also outrageous. There had only ever been one chain: the Anchor Chain.

'A senior reader from the Faculty of Air Studies was the first to break the silence. "The production of chains would mean more factories, more foundries, more forges," he said. "The Edgewater River is already polluted." He nodded towards the chalice, still clutched in Verginix's hands. "We run the risk of making the water completely undrinkable."

'All eyes turned to Vilnix, who smiled benevolently. Then, making a mental note to reward the senior reader with a full professorship for his question, he hobbled back to Verginix and seized the chalice. With his free hand, he pulled a silver ball-shaped medallion from his gown and dipped it into the muddy liquid. Instantly, the  water turned crystal clear. He returned the chalice to Verginix, who sipped. "It's sweet," he said. "Pure. Clean. It's like the water from the Deepwoods springs."

'The Professor of Light grabbed the chalice and drank, too. He looked up, eyes narrowed. "How is this possible?" he demanded.

'Vilnix returned the professor's gaze impassively. "It is possible because of an amazing discovery," he said. "*My* amazing discovery." He tapped the medallion. "Inside this pretty bauble is a substance so powerful that a single speck is enough to provide a person with drinking water for an entire year." He turned to the rows of incredulous academics. "This stor . . ." He stopped himself. "This substance, which I call *phraxdust* in honour of our beloved floating city, signifies a new beginning. Now we can ensure the future of Sanctaphrax by building those chains we so badly need, safe in the knowledge that we will never go thirsty."

'A cheer resounded around the hall. Vilnix lowered his head modestly. When he looked up again, his eyes were blazing with the excitement of impending victory. "My associates in the League of Free Merchants are merely awaiting the go-ahead to get started on the chains," he said. A smile flickered over his lips. "Naturally," he said, "they will deal only with the Most High Academe – the *new* Most High Academe, that is."

'He swung round and stared at the Professors of Light and Darkness. "For what would you have – this pair of buffoons who, between them, have brought Sanctaphrax to the very edge of destruction with their arcane rituals and pointless traditions? Or will you have someone who offers change, a fresh start, a new order?"

'Cries of "a fresh start" and "a new order" began to echo round the Great Hall. It lurched again. "And a new Most High Academe – Vilnix Pompolnius," the soon-to-be Professor of Air Studies proclaimed. The others took up the chant. Vilnix closed his eyes and bathed in their adulation as the chanting grew louder.

'Finally, he looked up. "Let your will be done!" he cried. "I, your new Most High Academe of Sanctaphrax, shall speak with the leaguesmen. The chains will be built. And Sanctaphrax, teetering on the brink of oblivion, will be saved!"'

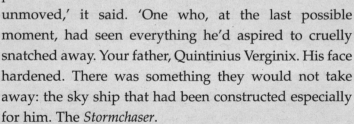

The caterbird looked sadly at Twig. 'One person alone remained unmoved,' it said. 'One who, at the last possible moment, had seen everything he'd aspired to cruelly snatched away. Your father, Quintinius Verginix. His face hardened. There was something they would not take away: the sky ship that had been constructed especially for him. The *Stormchaser*.

'He spat with disgust and strode across the floor. At the door, he paused, turned. "If I, Quintinius Verginix cannot prove myself as a Knight Academic, then I shall prove myself as Cloud Wolf, the sky pirate," he bellowed. "And I make you this promise, Vilnix Pompolnius. You and your treacherous friends in the leagues will rue this day for so long as you shall live."

And with that, he left.'

The caterbird shook its head sadly. 'Of course, nothing is ever that simple,' it said. 'Despite your father's parting words, it was many moons before his defiant promise came true. His first ill-fated voyage almost saw the end of both him and his ship – indeed the only good that came of it was his initial meeting with the Stone Pilot. He was forced to lay low, to store the *Stormchaser* in a safe berth and take up a position on a league ship until he had gained sufficient money and inside information of the Leagues to try again.' Its eye swivelled and narrowed. 'The league captain he ended up serving was the notorious Multinius Gobtrax . . .'

'It was upon his ship that *I* was born,' said Twig thoughtfully. 'But what about Sanctaphrax itself?'

The caterbird snorted. 'For all Vilnix's fine words of *a fresh start* and *a new order*, the situation rapidly worsened. Nowadays, as you know, the Undertowners labour like slaves in the foundries and forges, making chains and weights to support the Anchor Chain. They manage to keep Sanctaphrax in place – but only just. It is a never-ending task. And all the while, the waters of the Edgewater River are becoming more and more polluted. It is only because of the particles of phraxdust, supplied to the loyal leaguesmen by Vilnix Pompolnius, that Undertown hasn't already choked to death on its own filth.'

Twig shook his head in dismay. 'And Vilnix?' he asked. 'What does he get out of it all?'

'Wealth and power,' the caterbird replied simply. 'In return for drinkable water, the leagues shower Vilnix and his new Faculty of Raintasters with everything they could possibly want – and more. Just so long as the specks of phraxdust keep coming.'

'But surely the situation cannot last for ever,' said Twig. 'When the phraxdust runs out Vilnix Pompolnius will have to take more stormphrax from the treasury.'

The caterbird nodded. 'That's precisely what he does do,' he said. 'And the Professor of Darkness is powerless to stop him. What's more, the production of more phrax-dust has proved elusive. Despite a thousand attempts – many tragic – no-one has been able to reproduce the results of that first experiment.'

'But it's crazy!' said Twig. 'The more stormphrax that's taken from the treasury, the more chains they need to manufacture. The more chains that are manufactured, the worse the pollution in the water gets. And the worse the pollution in the water, the more phraxdust they need to purify it!'

'It's a vicious circle,' said the caterbird, 'that's what it is. A terrible, vicious circle. And twenty years after that momentous meeting in the Great Hall, the situation is looking bleaker than ever for both Sanctaphrax and Undertown. Wrapped up in their own concerns, both the raintasters and the leaguesmen remain blind to what is going on around them. But if nothing is done – and done soon – then it is only a matter of time before everything falls apart.'

'But what *can* be done?' said Twig.

The caterbird shrugged and turned his head. 'That is not for me to say.' It swivelled a purple eye round towards him. 'Right,' it said, 'my story is complete. *Now*, will you release me?'

Twig started guiltily. 'Of course,' he said, and retrieved the knife from his sleeve. He began jiggling the narrow blade about in the padlock again. There was a soft click. The lock was undone. He unclasped the padlock and pulled the door open.

'OY!' came an angry cry. 'You said you were trustworthy! What in Open Sky do you think you're doing?'

Twig spun round and gasped with horror. It was Flabsweat, back at last with the animal-doctor, and bearing down upon him like a madman.

'I can't . . .' he heard the caterbird complaining. 'Help me, Twig.'

Twig looked back. The caterbird had managed to get its head and one wing out of the cage, but the door was small, and its other wing was twisted back and jammed. 'Go back in and try again,' Twig instructed.

The caterbird did as it was told, folded its wings up and thrust its head back outside. Flabsweat was almost upon them, a heavy club swinging at his side. Twig reached up and, with his hands round the creature's neck and shoulders, pulled gently. Flabsweat raised the club. The caterbird pushed its legs hard against the perch.

'Come on!' Twig urged it desperately.

'Almost there . . .' the caterbird strained. 'I . . . Made it!' It flapped its wings experimentally – once, twice – then launched itself off from the edge of the cage and soared up into the air, apparently none the worse for its confinement.

It was time for Twig to make himself scarce, too. Without looking round, he turned on his heels and sped away into the thronging street. As he set off, the club glanced against his shoulder. A second earlier, and it would have smashed his skull.

Faster and faster Twig ran, barging through the crowds, elbowing dawdlers out of his way. Behind him, Flabsweat screamed with rage.

'Thief! Scoundrel! Netherwicket!' he roared. 'CATCH HIM!'

Twig ducked down into a narrow alley. The shouting grew fainter, but Twig kept going, faster than ever. Past pawnbrokers and tooth-pullers, barbers and inns, round a corner – and slap-bang into the arms of his father.

Cloud Wolf shook him roughly by the shoulders. 'Twig!' he bellowed. 'I've been looking for you everywhere. We're ready to set sail. What have you been up to?'

'N . . . nothing,' Twig faltered, unable to return Cloud Wolf's furious gaze.

High in the sky, behind his father's head, Twig saw the caterbird flapping off into the setting sun – past Sanctaphrax, out of Undertown, and away. He sighed enviously. The caterbird might be gone, but its doom-laden words remained with him. *A vicious circle, that's what it is. If nothing is done then it is only a matter of time before everything falls apart.*

And for a second time, Twig found himself wondering, But what *can* be done?

## ·CHAPTER THREE·

# CRIES AND WHISPERS

### i
### In the Twilight Woods

It was twilight. It was always twilight in the woods, with the sun permanently setting. Or was it rising? It was difficult to tell. Certainly none who entered the Twilight Woods could ever be sure. Most, however, felt that the golden half-light between the trees whispered of endings not beginnings.

The trees, majestically tall and always in full leaf, swayed in a gentle breeze which endlessly circled the woods. They, like everything else – the grass, the ground, the flowers – were coated in a mantle of fine dust which glittered and glistened like frost.

Yet it was not cold. Far from it. The breeze was balmy, and the earth itself radiated a soothing warmth which rippled through the air above so that everything swam slightly before the eyes; nothing was quite in focus. Standing in the Twilight Woods was like standing under water.

There was no birdsong, no insect-rustle, no animal-cry, for none of these creatures inhabited the woods. Yet, to those with ears to hear, there were voices – and not simply the whisperings of the trees. They were real voices – muttering, mumbling, occasionally crying out. One was close by.

'Hold steady, Vinchix,' it said wearily, though not without hope. 'Nearly there. Hold steady, now.'

The voice came from high up in the air, where a wrecked sky ship was skewered on a jagged treetop, its broken mast pointing accusingly up at the sky out of which it had dropped. Dangling from a harness was a knight, seated upon his prowlgrin charger and silhouetted against the golden sky. Inside the rusted armour, their bodies were skeletal. Yet both the knight and his mount were alive, still alive.

The visor creaked, and the ghostly voice repeated its words of encouragement, words of command.

'Nearly there, Vinchix. Hold steady!'

# In the Palace of the Most High Academe

The chamber – or Inner Sanctum, as it was known – was truly sumptuous. The floors were carpeted with snow-white fur, the ceiling embossed with gold, while those areas of wall not lined with bookcases were panelled with blackwood and silver, and encrusted with precious stones. Ornaments cluttered every surface – porcelain vases and ivory figurines, ornate carvings and intricate time-pieces.

A crystal chandelier sparkled from the centre of the room, unlit, but glinting in the sunlight – shooting darts of brilliance all around the room. On the silver panels, they flickered; on the polished tables, the cabinets, the grand piano; on the portraits and mirrors – and on the gleaming pate of the Most High Academe of Sanctaphrax himself, who was stretched out on an ottoman next to the long arched window, fast asleep.

He looked out of place in the opulent surroundings. The black gown he wore was faded, and there were sandals on his feet – modest, scuffed. Likewise, his angular body and sunken cheeks spoke of a life of abstinence rather than indulgence; his shaven head, of humility and rigour – yet also a degree of vanity. After all, why else would a person have his personal mono-gram – **ViP** – stitched into the hem of his hair-shirt?

A high-pitched rasping vibrated throughout the chamber. The person stirred and rolled onto his side. His

hooded eyes snapped
open. The rasping sound
came again, louder than
before. He sat up and
peered through the window.

Situated at the top of one
of the tallest, and certainly
the most magnificent tower
in Sanctaphrax, the Inner
Sanctum offered breathtaking
views across Undertown and
beyond. The Most High
Academe looked down.
Between the billowing clouds
of smoke, he could just make
out half a dozen or so
Undertowners busy securing
the latest chain to the side of
the great floating rock.

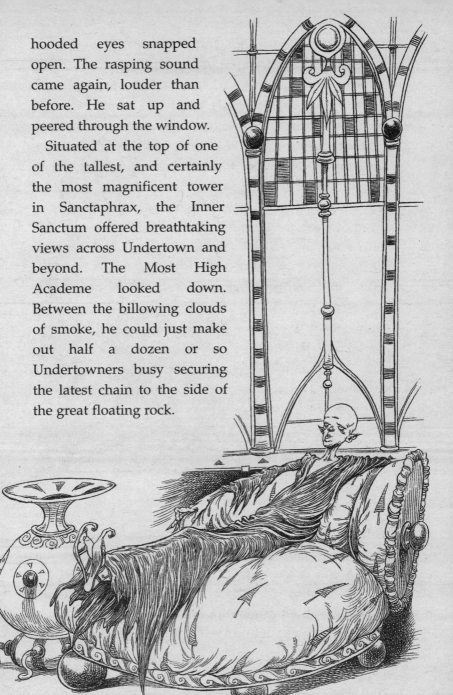

'Splendid,' he yawned, and climbed stiffly to his feet. He stretched, scratched, rubbed a hand absentmindedly over his head, and yawned again. 'Things to be done.'

He strode over towards a massive ironwood chest which stood in the corner of the room, pulled a heavy iron key from the folds of his robes and crouched down. At sundown, he was to have a meeting with Simenon Xintax, the current Leaguesmaster. Before then, he wanted to weigh the remaining phraxdust and calculate just how long the precious specks would last.

The lock released with a soft click, the lid creaked open and the Most High Academe stared down into the gaping darkness within. He bent down, retrieved a glass phial, held it up to the window – and sighed.

Even *he* could see the liquid dust was all but gone.

'A problem, certainly,' he muttered, 'but not yet an emergency. Better get it weighed, though. Work out just how many particles of phraxdust remain. Bargaining with Xintax from a point of ignorance would be fatal . . .' He wriggled round irritably. 'But first I have got to do something about this intolerable itching.'

Thankfully, thoughtful to the last, Minulis his manservant, had remembered the back-scratcher. A pretty thing it was, with a solid gold handle and claws of dragon ivory. The Most High Academe squirmed with pleasure as he scraped it up and down his back, reminded – as he always was – that the greatest pleasures in life are often the simplest. He lay the scratcher down and – deciding to postpone his calculations a little longer – poured himself a glass of wine from the decanter which Minulis had also thought to bring.

He walked across the room and stopped in front of a full-length mirror, smiled, straightened up and lifted his head. 'To you, Vilnix Pompolnius,' he said, raising his glass. 'The Most High Academe of Sanctaphrax.'

At that moment, the drilling began again – louder than ever. The floating rock trembled, the Inner Sanctum rocked and the mirror shook. The Most High Academe was so startled that he let the glass slip from between his fingers. It broke with a muffled *clink* and the spilt wine spread out over the white fur like blood.

The Most High Academe turned, and stepped away in disgust. As he did so, he heard a breathy whooshing sound behind him, followed by an almighty crash. He froze. Turned back. And there, lying on the floor in a thousand pieces, was the mirror. Crouching, he picked up a piece of glass and turned it over in his hand.

What was it his grandmother used to say? *A broken looking-glass, a sorrow come to pass.* He stared at the dark eye staring back at him from the jagged fragment, and winked. 'It's a good job *you're* not superstitious,' he said, and cackled with laughter.

# iii
# In the Mire

The leader of the gnokgoblins – a short, stocky female by the name of Mim – sniffed the air, fingered the collection of talismans and amulets around her neck and stepped forwards. She winced as the soft mud oozed up between her stubby toes.

Screed Toe-taker watched her scornfully. 'Still think you can make it across the Mire on your own?' he said.

Mim ignored him and waded on. *Squellp, squellp, squellp* went the pale sticky mud as it covered first her ankles, then her calves, then her knees. She stopped and looked up. The Mire seemed to stretch out for ever in front of her. Even if she, by some miracle, could make it

across to the other side, she knew that neither old Torp nor the young'uns would stand a chance.

'All right,' she said, and turned angrily – sinking down still further in the process. 'Perhaps we *could* be doing with a guide after all.' She hitched her skirt up. The mud crept higher. 'Help us out of here,' she said.

Screed stepped forwards and held out a bony white hand. Like the Mire which was his home, every inch of his body had been bleached the colour of dirty sheets. He pulled the goblin back to safety, and stared down at her, hands on hips.

The goblin rummaged inside her bag. 'Fifty, per person,' she said. 'That's what you said. Which makes . . .' She counted out the coins. 'Five hundred in all.'

Screed shook his head. 'The price has gone up,' he said, his voice nasal, mocking. 'A hundred each. That's what it's going to cost you now.'

'But that's all our savings,' she gasped. 'What are we ever supposed to live on when we do make it to Undertown?'

Screed shrugged. 'That's your problem,' he said. 'I'm not forcing you to come with me. If you can cross the Mire with its sinking-mud and poisonous blow-holes – not to mention the muglumps, oozefish and white ravens that would rip you apart as soon as look at you ... Well, it's your choice.'

Mim stared glumly at the rest of her family group, huddled together on the bank. The choice was simple, she realized. Either they arrived in Undertown with nothing, or they didn't arrive at all.

'A thousand it is,' she sighed, handing over the money. 'But your price is very high, so it is.'

Screed Toe-taker snatched the money and dropped it into his pocket. He turned away, muttering under his breath. 'My price is higher than you could ever imagine, dear lady.' And he set off into the bleached and sticky landscape.

The family of goblins collected up their sacks of belongings.

'Come on then,' Screed called back impatiently. 'Look lively. Keep together. Walk where I walk. And don't look back.'


## iv
## In the Tower of Light and Darkness


The Professor of Light was angry. 'Accursed chains, accursed drilling, accursed Vilnix Pompolnius,' he growled between clenched teeth. 'Must we now destroy Sanctaphrax in order to save it?' He heaved himself up, with an armful of books, and began returning them to the shelves.

It was always the same. Every time a new chain was attached to the floating rock, the vibrations wreaked havoc in his humble study. Priceless apparatus was damaged, invaluable experiments ruined – and his entire library of books ended up on the floor.

With the last book back in place, the professor returned to his desk. He was just about to sit down when he noticed something out of the corner of his eye. Something most unwelcome. At that moment, however, there was a knock on the door and the Professor of Darkness burst in. 'We must talk,' he said.

The Professor of Light didn't move. 'Look,' he said glumly.

'What?'

'There,' he said, pointing. 'Light!'

The Professor of Darkness laughed. 'You should be pleased,' he said. 'Light is, after all, your field of study and expertise.'

'As yours is darkness,' the Professor of Light snapped. 'Or rather, the *absence* of light. But there is a place for everything. And just as the darkness in the heart of your erstwhile protégé, Vilnix Pompolnius, is misplaced, so too is light appearing through cracks in the middle of my wall.' He turned back and poked at the mortar. 'See that,' he said. 'It's all crumbling away.'

The Professor of Darkness sighed miserably. 'My study's just as bad,' he said.

The first thing Vilnix had done when he became Most High Academe, was to take the palatial School of Light and Darkness for himself, while relegating the two professors and their departments to the dilapidated Raintasters' Tower. The explosion had caused bad structural damage. Each time a chain was attached to the rock, that damage increased. It was merely a matter of time before the tower collapsed completely.

'Well, it can't go on like this,' said the Professor of Light. 'Which is why . . .'

'Which is why we need to talk,' the Professor of Darkness butted in.

'Which is why,' the Professor of Light continued, 'I have already spoken to someone about how one might change the situation.'

The Professor of Darkness stared at his colleague with a mixture of admiration and resentment. Despite their reduced circumstances, the old rivalry between the two academics remained. 'You have already spoken to whom?' he demanded.

'Mother Horsefeather,' came the reply.

'Mother Horsefeather!' The Professor of Darkness was astounded. 'That greedy old bird-woman. She'd sell her own eggs if the price was right. Do you seriously think we can trust her?'

'Oh, yes,' said the Professor of Light. 'We can trust her to do everything in her power to deceive us. That knowledge will be our strength.'

## V
# In the Backstreets of Undertown

'In here,' said Slitch, stopping abruptly next to a ramshackle hut on his left. He unlocked the door, and disappeared inside. His companion followed him. He pushed the door to and waited while the gnokgoblin located the lamp and lit it. 'My word,' Slitch shuddered, as he turned round and the pale light filled the room. 'You slaughterers *are* red.'

Tendon shuffled about awkwardly. 'Have you got any phraxdust, or what?' he said. 'If you haven't . . .'

'The best phraxdust in Undertown,' Slitch assured him. 'Potentially.'

'Potentially?'

'I have acquired some black-market stormphrax,' he explained. 'All you have to do is grind it down and, Hob's your goblin!'

Tendon stared at him impassively. 'You must think I'm daft,' he said at length. 'Stormphrax explodes when you try and grind it. Everyone knows that. His high-and-mighty Acadimwit is the only one with the secret . . .'

'I, too, now have that secret,' said Slitch. He took a bowl down from a shelf and placed it on a small table. Then he pulled a wad of velvet from his inside pocket, carefully unfolded it and removed a glistening, sparkling shard of stormphrax, which he held up between his middle-finger and thumb – the others all being missing – and placed it gently down in the bowl.

Tendon remained dubious. 'What's the secret, then?'

'This,' said Slitch, removing a leather pouch from his belt. He loosened the drawstring for Tendon to see inside.

'But what is it?' he said.

'Powdered deadwood bark,' said Slitch conspiratorially. 'The finest money can buy.'

Tendon pulled back nervously. It was the stuff Undertown doctors used to anaesthetize their patients for an operation.

'The numbing qualities of the deadwood counteract the volatility of the stormphrax,' Slitch explained. 'The explosion is *paralysed*, so to speak.'

'You're sure about that?' said Tendon.

'Oh, for Sky's sake!' said Slitch impatiently. 'Didn't you tell me you were sick of spending all your hard-earned cash on drinking water? Didn't you say you'd do *anything* to get hold of some phraxdust of your own. The deadwood will work, I assure you,' he said as he sprinkled a liberal quantity into the bowl. 'There will be no explosion and you, my friend, will have phraxdust to last you for the rest of your life.'

Tendon fingered the charms around his neck anxiously. Despite his misgivings, however, the gnokgoblin's offer proved too tempting to resist. He paid over the hundred quarters they had agreed upon, picked up the pestle and raised it above his head. With the money safely in his pocket, Slitch scuttled off to the far end of the hut, and crouched down behind a metal stove.

'Strike now!' he cried. 'It *will* work!'

And Tendon, gripping the handle as tightly as his sweaty hands would allow, brought the pestle sharply down with all his strength.

The explosion blew the roof of the hut right off. Tendon was hurled back against the far wall where he collapsed, a lifeless heap.

Slitch crawled out of his hiding place and climbed shakily to his feet. He looked down at the body of the dead slaughterer.

'Or then again,' he sighed, 'maybe it won't.'


## vi
## In the Bloodoak Tavern

Mother Horsefeather sat at a table by the door of the heaving Bloodoak tavern. Perched on a bar-stool beside her was Forficule, the nightwaif she employed. The pair of them were watching the rowdy groups of drinkers plunge their tankards into the communal trough of frothy woodale, one after the other. The illicit brewery concealed in the cellar was a nice little earner – particularly when the weather was so hot.

The door opened and three leaguesmen swaggered in. Mother Horsefeather clacked her beak with distaste. 'A good evening to you,' she said, avoiding their gaze. She removed three tankards from the shelf behind her and placed them on the table. 'That'll be twenty quarters apiece.'

'You can drink as much as you like,' the first leaguesman – a regular to the Bloodoak – explained to the others. 'Is that not right, Mother Horsefeather?'

Mother Horsefeather scowled. 'Indeed it is,' she said. 'But remember the rules.' She nodded over to a sign nailed to the wall. *No swearing. No fighting. No vomiting on the premises.*

'We need no reminding,' said the leaguesman, as he handed her a single gold coin worth twice the asking price. 'Keep the change, dear lady,' he said, and winked.

Mother Horsefeather stared down at the till. 'Thanking you kindly, sire,' she said, and slammed the drawer shut. Only when he had turned away, did she look up. You worm-ridden lump of hammelhorn dung, she thought bitterly.

'Now, now,' said Forficule gently, his huge bat-like ears twitching. Mother Horsefeather swivelled her head round and glared furiously at the nightwaif.

'*Heard* that, did you?' she snapped.

'I hear everything,' Forficule replied. 'As you well know. Every word, every whisper, every thought – for my sins.'

Mother Horsefeather snorted. The feathers around her neck were standing on end, her yellow eyes glinted. 'Well he is!' she said sourly, and nodded towards the table of leaguesmen. 'They all are. With their fine clothes, big tips and fancy manners. Hammelhorn dung, the lot of them!'

Forficule tutted sympathetically. He understood his employer's loathing of the leaguesmen. Because of their alliance with Vilnix Pompolnius – building chains in return for phraxdust – their dominance in the drinking-water market had left them unassailably powerful. If it wasn't for her black-market dealings with the sky pirates, Mother Horsefeather would have gone under long ago.

'Ah, the sky pirates,' Forficule sighed. 'Those intrepid

skyfaring brigands who will kow-tow to no-one. Where would we be without them?'

'Where indeed?' Mother Horsefeather nodded, her neck feathers finally lying down smooth. 'Speaking of which, Cloud Wolf and his crew should be back soon. I hope to goodness he's had as profitable a trip as he led me to believe. Otherwise . . .' The conversation she'd had with the Professor of Light abruptly came back to her, and an idea appeared, as if from nowhere. Her eyes twinkled. 'Unless . . .'

Forficule, who had been listening in to her thoughts, chuckled. 'Heads you win, tails he loses, eh?'

Before she had a chance to reply, the Bloodoak tavern suddenly rocked with the force of a nearby explosion. Forficule clutched at his ears and squealed with pain.

'Lawks-a-mussy!' Mother Horsefeather cried out, and the ruff of feathers shot back upwards. 'That sounded close!' As the dust settled, Forficule removed his hands, and shook his head from side to side. His massive ears fluttered like two enormous moths.

'Two more poor fools trying to grind their own phraxdust,' he said sadly. He cocked his head to one side and listened intently. 'The dead one is Tendon, a slaughterer.'

'I remember him,' said Mother Horsefeather. 'Often in here, he is – was. Always stank of leather.'

Forficule nodded. 'The survivor's name is Slitch,' he said, and shuddered. 'Ooh, a horrible piece of work, he is. He'd tried mixing stormphrax with deadwood dust and got Tendon to do his dirty work for him.'

Mother Horsefeather frowned. 'Everyone is so desperate to get hold of phraxdust,' she said. Her yellow eyes sparkled malevolently. 'If anyone's to blame for what happened,' she added, nodding her beak towards the table of rowdy leaguesmen, 'it's them! Oh, what I wouldn't give to wipe that smug expression off their loathsome faces once and for all!'

# ·CHAPTER FOUR·

# THE CARGO OF IRONWOOD

It was late afternoon and, having successfully con-cluded a deal with some woodtrolls for a massive consignment of ironwood, the crew of the *Stormchaser* were heading back to Undertown. The atmosphere on board the sky pirate ship was buoyant, and Twig – the hero of the hour – was feeling particularly pleased with himself.

Although he hadn't personally known any of the woodtrolls they'd encountered, the fact that he'd been brought up in a woodtroll village meant that Twig was familiar with their ways. He knew when their *nos* meant *yes*. He knew when to haggle and, more importantly, when to stop – for if a woodtroll is offered too little for his wood, then he will take offence and refuse to sell no matter what. When Twig saw the tell-tale signs in their faces – a pursing of the lips and twitching of their rubbery noses – he had nodded towards his father. The deal was as good as it possibly could be.

Afterwards, to celebrate, Cloud Wolf had cracked open a barrel of woodgrog and handed round tots of the fiery liquid to each member of his motley crew. 'To a job well done,' he proclaimed.

'A job well done!' the sky pirates roared back.

Tem Barkwater, a hairy giant of an individual, slapped Twig on the back and squeezed his shoulder. 'Without this lad's knowledge of the Deepwoods folk, we would never have got the wood at such a price,' he said and raised his glass. 'To Twig!'

'To Twig!' the sky pirates chorused.

Even Slyvo Spleethe the quartermaster, who seldom had a good word to say to anyone, spoke generously. 'He did indeed do well,' he conceded.

Only one person failed to join in the congratulations: Cloud Wolf himself. In fact, when Tem Barkwater had proposed his toast, the captain had turned away abruptly and returned to the helm. Twig understood why. None of the crew knew that he was Cloud Wolf's son. To avoid any accusations of favouritism, the captain preferred it that way. Accordingly, he treated the lad more harshly than the other crew members and never betrayed any affection he might feel.

Understanding the reason for Cloud Wolf's surliness was one thing. Liking it, however, was another. Every slight, every injustice, every harsh word cut Twig to the quick and left him feeling that his father was ashamed of him. Swallowing his pride now, Twig joined Cloud Wolf on the bridge.

'When do you think we'll be back?' he asked tentatively.

'Nightfall,' said Cloud Wolf, as he locked the wheel and made minute adjustments to the hanging weights. 'If the winds remain favourable, that is.'

Twig watched his father in awe. Sky ships were notoriously difficult to sail, yet to Cloud Wolf it came as second nature. He understood his ship as though it was a part of him. Having heard the caterbird's story, Twig knew why. 'I guess you learned all about sky sailing and . . . and stormchasing in the Knights' Academy . . .'

Cloud Wolf turned and stared at him curiously. 'What

do you know about the Knights' Academy?' he demanded.

'N . . . nothing much,' Twig faltered. 'But the caterbird told me . . .'

'Pfff!' Cloud Wolf said dismissively. 'That scraggy blabbermouth! It is better to live in the present than dwell on the past,' he said sharply. And then, clearly eager to change the subject, he added, 'It's high time *you* learned the rudiments of skysailing.'

Twig's heart fluttered. He had been with the sky pirates now for more than two years. Like them, he wore one of the heavy pirate longcoats with its numerous hanging accoutrements – the telescope, the grappling iron, the compass and scales, the drinking vessel . . . Like them, his front was protected by an ornately tooled leather breastshield, while on his back was a set of parawings. In all that time, however, Twig's duties on board had been restricted to the most menial of tasks. He scrubbed. He cleaned. He was the all-purpose gofer. Now, it seemed, that was to change.

'The flight-rock, when cold, gives us natural lift,' Cloud Wolf explained. 'Balance, forward thrust and manoeuvring have to be achieved manually. Through these,' he said, and pointed to two long rows of bone-handled levers, each set at a different angle.

Twig nodded keenly.

'These levers here are connected to the hanging weights,' he said. 'The stern-weight, prow-weight, starboard hull-weights, small, medium and large; port hull-weights, ditto, mid-hull, peri-hull, neben-hull, and

klute-hull-weights . . .' he said, rattling off the names.
'And *these* levers on the other side are attached to the
sails. Foresail, aftsail, topsail,' he said, tapping the levers,
each in turn. 'Mainsails – one and two – skysail, staysail,
studsail, boomsail, spinnaker and jib. Got that? It's just a
matter of keeping everything in balance.'

Twig nodded uncertainly. Cloud Wolf stood back.
'Come on then,' he said gruffly. 'Take the wheel, and let's
see what you're made of.'

At first, it was easy. The adjustments had already been
made and Twig merely had to grip the wooden wheel to
hold a steady course. But when a sudden gust from the
north-east caused the ship to dip, the task suddenly
became more complicated.

'Up the medium starboard hull-weight,' the captain instructed. Twig panicked. Which lever was it? The eighth or the ninth from the left? He grasped the ninth and yanked. The *Stormchaser* tipped to one side. 'Not *that* much!' Cloud Wolf snapped. 'Up the staysail a tad and down the large port hull-weight . . . The *port* hull-weight, you idiot!' he roared, as the sky ship tipped over still further.

Twig yelped with terror. He was going to crash the boat. At this rate, his first attempt at skysailing would also be his last. He clung on to the helm grimly – brain feverish, hands shaking, heart thumping fit to burst. He mustn't let his father down. Pulling himself forwards, he seized the ninth lever for a second time. This time he moved it gently, downing the weight only a couple of notches.

And it worked! The boat righted itself.

'Good,' the captain said. 'You're developing the touch. Now, up the skysail,' he instructed. 'Down the prow-weight a fraction, realign the small and medium starboard hull weights and . . .'

'League ship to starboard!' Spiker's strident voice cried out. 'League ship to starboard – and approaching fast.'

The words echoed round Twig's head. He felt short of breath; he felt sick. The rows of levers blurred before his eyes. One of them would almost certainly make the sky ship accelerate forwards – but which one? 'League ship getting closer,' Spiker announced. And Twig, in his blind panic, broke the first rule of sky ship sailing. He let go of the helm.

The wheel spun back viciously the moment his sweaty hands loosened their grip, sending him skittering across the deck. Instantly, the sails crumpled, and the *Stormchaser* went into a sudden spinning descent.

'You halfwit!' Cloud Wolf roared. He seized the wheel and, bracing himself against the deck, frantically tried to stop it turning. 'Hubble!' he bellowed. 'Here. Now!'

Twig was just stumbling back to his feet when Hubble brushed past him. It was only the most glancing of blows, but the albino banderbear was a colossal mountain of a creature – and Twig went flying.

The next moment, the spinning stopped. Twig looked up. The wheel was clasped, motionless, in the banderbear's massive paws. And the captain, freed up at last, was running his hands over the levers – now here, now there – as surely as an accordion-player darting over the keys.

'League ship, one hundred strides and closing,' called Spiker. The captain's silent playing continued. 'Fifty strides! Forty . . .'

All at once, the *Stormchaser* leapt forwards. The crew roared their approval. Twig staggered to his feet at last, muttering heartfelt thanks to Sky above. They'd made it.

Then Cloud Wolf spoke. 'There's something wrong!' he said quietly.

Wrong? thought Twig. What could be wrong? Hadn't they escaped with their illicit cargo of ironwood after all? He squinted behind him. Yes, there was the league ship, miles away!

'Something *very* wrong,' he said. 'We've got no lift.'

Twig stared at Cloud Wolf in horror. His stomach felt empty. Was this some kind of joke? Had he chosen this moment to tease him like a father? One look at the man's ashen face as he jiggled, jerked and yanked at a lever with more and more force confirmed that he had not.

'It's . . . it's the bl . . . blasted stern-weight,' he spluttered. 'It's jammed.'

'League ship gaining once more,' Spiker called out. 'And from the flag I'd say the Leaguesmaster himself was on board.'

Cloud Wolf spun round. 'Hubble,' he said, but then

had second thoughts. The massive creature was ill-suited to clambering over the hull. As were Tem Barkwater and Stope Boltjaw. And the oakelf, Spiker, though willing, would never be strong enough to release the great iron weight. Slyvo Spleethe would have been ideal if he wasn't such a coward. While Mugbutt, the flat-head goblin, though fearless in battle and everything else, was too stupid to remember what he was supposed to do. 'I'd better see to it myself,' he muttered.

Twig leaped forwards. 'Let me,' he said. 'I can do it.' Cloud Wolf looked him up and down, his thin lips tightly pursed. 'You need to stay here, at the levers,' Twig went on. 'For when I've released it.'

'League ship at two hundred strides,' Spiker called.

Cloud Wolf nodded briefly. 'All right,' he said. 'But be sure not to let me down.'

'I won't,' said Twig grimly, as he hurried off to the back of the ship. There he seized a tolley-rope and pulled himself up onto the rail. A flash of forest green blurred past him far, far below.

'Don't look down!' he heard Tem Barkwater shouting to him.

Easier said than done, thought Twig as he lowered himself carefully onto the hull-rigging, which hugged the bottom of the ship like cobwebs. The further down and round he went – slowly, carefully – the more upside down he became. The wind tugged his hair and plucked at his fingers. But he could see the stern-weight now – all tangled up in a loop of pitched rope.

He kept on, whispering words of encouragement to himself as he went. 'Just a little bit further. Just a teeny bit more.'

'How's it going?' he heard his father call.

'Nearly there,' he shouted back.

'League ship back on one hundred strides, and closing,' came Spiker's latest update.

Trembling with anticipation, Twig reached forwards, and pulled the clump of rope hard to one side. The weight should be swinging free. If he could just . . . He inched forwards and pushed the back of the huge knot with the heel of his hand. Suddenly it gave, the rope came loose, the weight swung down and . . . fell completely away. Twig gasped in absolute horror as the huge, round circle of iron tumbled off through the air, down to the forest below.

'What have you done?' came a voice. It was Cloud Wolf, and he sounded furious.

'I . . . I . . .' Twig began. The sky ship was rolling from end to end and reeling from port to starboard, completely out of control. It was all Twig could do to hang on. What *had* he done?

'You've only gone and released the rudder-wheel!' Cloud Wolf yelled. 'For Sky's sake, Twig! I thought that Mugbutt was stupid!'

Twig quaked under the barrage of insults and recriminations. Scalding tears welled in his eyes, tears he couldn't wipe away for fear of losing his grip. Then again, he thought miserably, wouldn't it be better simply to let go, to disappear? Anything, rather than face his father's wrath.

'Twig! Can you hear me, lad?' came a second voice. It was Tem Barkwater. 'We're going to have to ditch our cargo. That means opening the hull-doors. You'd better get yourself out of there sharpish!'

Ditch the cargo! Twig's heart sank and his tears flowed more freely than ever. The ironwood which had taken so much effort – and money – to acquire would have to go. And all because of him.

'Come on!' Tem screamed.

Twig climbed feverishly back along the hull-rigging, hand over hand, foot over foot, until he was climbing upright once more. He looked up. Tem Barkwater's huge red hand was reaching down for him. He grasped it gratefully and gasped as he was pulled back onto the deck. 'Right-ho, cap'n!' Tem cried.

Twig went to smile his thanks, but the sky pirate had already turned away, unable to meet his gaze. No cargo meant no wages. And, though squalid, Undertown was not the place to be with neither money nor the means to make it.

'Open the hull-doors!' Cloud Wolf commanded.

'Aye-aye, cap'n,' came the voice of Stope Boltjaw from the hold. Then, from deep within the bowels of the ship, there came the clanking of chains, followed by a rumbling *thud-thud-thud.*

Twig looked away guiltily. It was the ironwood logs tumbling, one after the other, through the gap beneath the hull as the doors were slowly cranked open. He glanced over the side. As he did so, the rest of the load was abruptly discharged. A strange and deadly precipitation, it tumbled back down to the Deepwoods from where it had come.

On seeing what was taking place just in front of them, the league ship immediately gave up the chase and swooped down after the falling logs. A load that size was not to be sniffed at. Twig's misery was complete. The *Stormchaser*'s loss had turned to the league ship's gain.

'Can't we go down and battle it out with them?' Twig asked. 'I'm not afraid.'

Cloud Wolf turned on him with a look of utter contempt. 'We have no rudder-wheel,' he said. 'No control. It's only the flight-rock keeping us skyborne at all.' He turned away. 'Raise the mainsheets,' he bellowed. 'Square the bidgets – and pray. Pray like you've never prayed before. An untimely squall and it won't be just the cargo we lose. It'll be the *Stormchaser* itself.'

No-one spoke a word as the sky ship limped back to Undertown. It was the slowest and most nail-biting trip that Twig had ever endured. Darkness had fallen by the time the fuzzy lights of Sanctaphrax came into view. Below it, Undertown seethed and gagged beneath a heavy pall of smoke. And still the silence continued. Twig felt wretched. It would have been better if the sky pirates had ranted and raved, called him every name under the Sky – anything but this deathly hush.

There were patrol boats around, but none took any notice of the crippled sky ship as it headed in towards the boom-docks. With its hull-doors still open, the craft clearly had nothing to hide.

Cloud Wolf steered the *Stormchaser* into its concealed berth, Stope Boltjaw dropped anchor, and Spiker jumped down onto the raised jetty to secure the ship's tolley-ropes to the tether-rings. The crew disembarked.

'Outstanding, Master Twig!' Slyvo Spleethe hissed as he passed him by. Twig shuddered, but the comment was only to be expected. Spleethe had never liked him. Worse, by far, were the averted eyes of the others. He shuffled miserably after them towards the gangplank.

'Not you, Twig,' said Cloud Wolf sharply. Twig froze. Now he was for it! He turned round, hung his head – and waited. Only when the last sky pirate had departed, did Cloud Wolf speak.

'That I should live to see the day when my son – my own son – should scupper a sky ship,' he said.

Twig swallowed hard, but the tears would not go away. 'I'm sorry,' he whispered.

'Sorry? What good is sorry?' Cloud Wolf thundered. 'We've lost the ironwood, the rudder-wheel – we almost lost the *Stormchaser* itself. And I still might.' His eye glinted like hard flint. 'I'm ashamed to call you my son.'

The words struck Twig like a blow to the back of the neck. 'Ashamed to call me your son?' he said and, as he spoke, his distress turned to anger. He looked up boldly. 'So, what's new?' he demanded.

'How dare you!' Cloud Wolf raged, his face turning purple.

But Twig did dare. 'You've never acknowledged to anyone, ever, that you're my father,' he said. 'Does that mean you've always been ashamed of me, ever since the moment we first found each other? Does it? Well, does it? Tell me it does and I'll leave, now.'

Cloud Wolf remained silent. Twig turned to go.

'Twig!' said Cloud Wolf. 'Wait.' Twig stopped. 'Turn and face me, boy,' he said. Twig turned slowly round. He stared up at his father defiantly.

Cloud Wolf stared back, a twinkle in his eye. 'That was well said,' he told him. 'You are right. I have not acknowledged who you are on board the ship. But not for the reason you suppose. There are those who would mutiny given half a chance, and take the *Stormchaser* for themselves. If they found out what . . .' He paused. 'How important you are to me – for you *are* important to me, Twig. You should know that.'

Twig nodded and sniffed. The lump in his throat was back.

'If they found that out, it would put your own life in the gravest danger.'

Twig let his head hang. How could he ever have doubted what his father felt for him? Now *he* was the one who felt ashamed. He looked up and smiled sheepishly. 'Can I stay, then?' he said.

Cloud Wolf's face creased up with concern. 'I meant it when I said I still might lose the *Stormchaser*,' he said.

'But how?' said Twig. 'Why? It's your sky ship, isn't it? I thought you took it on the day of your inauguration.'

Cloud Wolf snorted. 'It costs a lot to keep a sky ship

aloft,' he said. 'And ever since that infestation of wood-bugs, the *Stormchaser* has been in debt up to the top of her pretty caternest. I was depending on the ironwood to pay off some of the money I owe. No,' he sighed, 'if any-one owns the *Stormchaser*, it's Mother Horsefeather. She's the one who finances us. And rakes off most of the profits into the bargain,' he added with a scowl. 'And now I can't pay her, she might well decide to take back what's rightfully hers.'

Twig was appalled. 'But she can't,' he cried.

'Oh, but she can,' said Cloud Wolf. 'What's more, she'd make sure I never got credit anywhere else. And what is a sky pirate captain without a sky ship, Twig? Eh? I'll tell you. Nothing. That's what he is. Nothing at all.'

Twig turned his head away, distraught. His father – once the finest Knight Academic Sanctaphrax had ever seen, now the greatest sky pirate in the Edge – was staring ignominy in the face. And he, Twig, was to blame. It was *all* his fault.

'I'm . . .'

'Just don't say you're sorry again,' Cloud Wolf inter-rupted. 'Come on. Let's go and get this over with,' he said gruffly. 'I just hope the old buzzard's not in too greedy a mood. And remember,' he said, as he strode off towards the gangplank, 'when we're sat down talking with Mother Horsefeather in the Bloodoak tavern, you be careful what you say – or even think. I swear the walls in there have ears!'

# CHAPTER FIVE

# THE BLOODOAK
# TAVERN

*Creak, creak, creak*, the tavern sign protested as it swung to and fro in the gathering wind. Twig glanced up and flinched. The sign was – as might have been expected – an artist's impression of a bloodoak, a terrible flesh-eating tree. And a very good impression it was, too, Twig admitted with a shudder. The glistening bark, the glinting mandibles – every time he saw the picture of the tree, he could almost *smell* the rank, metallic stench of death oozing from it.

For Twig knew all about bloodoaks. Once, lost in the Deepwoods, he had fallen victim to a particularly gruesome specimen. It had swallowed him whole and would have eaten him alive had it not been for his hammelhornskin waistcoat, which had bristled at the danger and jammed in the monster's throat. Trembling at the memory, he asked himself why anyone would want to name a tavern after so disgusting a creation.

'Are you going to stand there gawping all night?' Cloud Wolf snapped impatiently as he pushed past his son. 'Let's go in.'

As he threw the door open – BOOF! – a burst of energy exploded from the room. Heat. Noise. Light. And a heavy cocktail of smells, both fragrant and foul. Twig reeled backwards from the blast. No matter how many times he visited the Bloodoak tavern, he would never get used to the shock of that first moment.

The tavern was like a miniature version of Undertown itself, reflecting the incredible diversity of the place. There were flat-head and hammer-head goblins; oakelves, mobgnomes, black-dwarfs and red-dwarfs; trolls and trogs of every shape and every size. There were leaguesmen and sky pirates, tinkers and totters, raggers and royners, merchants and mongers ... It seemed to Twig, as he stared in through the open door, that there was not a single Edge creature, tribe or profession not represented in the throbbing room.

The cloddertrog on the door recognized Cloud Wolf at once. He informed them that Mother Horsefeather was 'somewhere hereabouts' and waved them through. Sticking close to him as Cloud Wolf carved a route across the room, Twig tried hard not to knock anyone's drinks as he went. Flat-heads were notoriously volatile and throats had been slit for far less than a tankard of spilled woodale before now. Jostled and crushed in the sweaty, steaming surge of bodies, it occurred to Twig that *the Bloodoak* was exactly the right name for the tavern after all.

The owner of the tavern was over by the rear exit. She looked up as Cloud Wolf approached.

'Mother Horsefeather,' he said. 'I trust I find you well.'

'Well enough,' came the guarded reply.

She turned and stared down at Twig questioningly.

'Ah yes,' said Cloud Wolf. 'This is Twig. Twig, Mother Horsefeather. I want him to sit in on our meeting.'

Twig trembled under the ferocious gaze of the creature

in front of him. Of course, he'd seen Mother Horse-feather before, but always at a distance. Close up, she was imposing, intimidating.

As tall as Cloud Wolf himself, she had beady yellow eyes, a sharp hooked beak and a ruff of crimson feathers around her neck. Her arms, too, were fringed with feathers which, since she was standing with her taloned hands clasped together, hugged her like a purple and orange shawl. Twig found himself wondering whether, under the voluminous yellow dress, her whole body was covered with the same magnificent plumage.

All at once, he became aware of someone sniggering to his right. He turned. And there, perched on a bar-stool, was a slight, almost luminous creature, grinning from ear to huge bat-like ear.

Mother Horsefeather raised a feathery eyebrow and glared at Twig menacingly. 'This is Forficule,' she said, and returned her unblinking gaze to Cloud Wolf. 'He, too, will be present during our little talk,' she told him.

Cloud Wolf shrugged. 'It's all the same to me,' he said, then added as if Forficule were not there, 'What is it? Looks like the runt of an oakelf litter.'

Mother Horsefeather's beak clacked with sudden amusement. 'He's my little treasure-weasure,' she whispered. 'Aren't you, Forfy? Right then,' she announced to the rest. 'Follow me. We'll find it much easier to talk in the quiet of the back room.' And with that, she turned on her talon-toes and disappeared through the door. Cloud Wolf and Twig followed her, with Forficule bringing up the rear.

The room was hot, airless, clammy; it smelled of decay. And as Twig took his place at the small, square table, he felt increasingly uneasy. To his left was his father; to his right, Mother Horsefeather; while opposite him sat Forficule, eyes shut, ears trembling. The fur of his hammelhornskin waistcoat prickled beneath Twig's fingers.

Mother Horsefeather placed her scaly hands in front of her, one on top of the other, and smiled at Cloud Wolf. 'Well, well,' she said pleasantly. 'Here we are again.'

'Indeed,' said Cloud Wolf. 'And may I say how hale and hearty you are looking tonight, Mother Horsefeather – and how much yellow suits you.'

'Oh, Wolfie!' she said, preening despite herself. 'You old flatterer!'

'But I mean every word,' Cloud Wolf insisted.

'You, too, are as dashing as ever,' Mother Horsefeather clucked admiringly.

Twig looked at his father. It was true. In his ornate sky pirate regalia – with its ruffs and tassels and gleaming golden buttons – Cloud Wolf looked magnificent. Then, with a sudden shiver, Twig recalled how angry his father's face had turned when he had let go of the helm; when the *Stormchaser* had gone into a downward spin. How he had cursed when their precious cargo of iron-wood had tumbled down out of the sky.

He looked up. Forficule was staring at him intently. *Be careful what you say – or even think*, that was what his father had told him. Twig stared back at the quivering-eared nightwaif and shivered with anxiety.

'The rudder-wheel, eh?' he heard Mother Horse-feather saying. The pleasantries were clearly over. 'It sounds important.'

'It is,' Cloud Wolf agreed.

'And therefore costly?'

Cloud Wolf nodded.

'Well, I'm sure we can come to some agreement,' she said brightly. 'So long as the quality of the ironwood lives up to my expectations.'

Twig felt the blood drain from his face as the enormity of what he had done suddenly struck home. Because of him, the *Stormchaser* would never fly again. His heart pounded loudly. And when Forficule leaned across and whispered to Mother Horsefeather behind his hand, it pounded louder still.

The bird-woman's eyes gleamed. 'So, Wolfie,' she said, '*will* it live up to my expectations, do you think?' She leaned forwards and thrust her beak into his face. 'Or is there something you'd like to tell me?' she demanded, her voice suddenly clipped and hard.

'Tell you? I . . .' he began, scratching behind his eye-patch. 'That is . . .' He glanced round at his son. Twig had never seen him look so weary, so *old* before.

'Well?' Mother Horsefeather demanded.

'We did have rather an unfortunate set-back,' Cloud Wolf agreed. 'But nothing that can't be put right on our next voyage . . .'

'You seem to forget,' she interrupted brusquely, 'that you owe me ten thousand already. And that's before interest. Plus, of course, the cost of a new rudder-wheel . . .' She paused dramatically, and began preening her neck feathers carelessly. 'I'm not sure there should *be* a next voyage.'

Twig shrivelled up inside.

'Unless,' she went on slyly, 'it is on my terms.'

Cloud Wolf did not flinch. 'And those terms would be?' he said calmly.

Mother Horsefeather pulled herself to her scaly feet and turned around. She clasped her hands behind her. Cloud Wolf and Twig stared at her back expectantly. A half-smile played over Forficule's lips.

'We go back a long way, Cloud Wolf; you and I,' she said. 'Despite your current, unfortunate financial problems, you are still the finest sky pirate captain there is – after all, it was hardly your fault that the *Stormchaser* became riddled with woodbugs.' She stepped forwards. 'Therefore it is to you that I come with what will surely prove to be your greatest challenge. If you are successful, your debts will be cancelled at a stroke.'

Cloud Wolf eyed her mistrustfully. 'And what's in it for you?'

'Oh, Wolfie, Wolfie,' she said, and cackled with

laughter. 'You know me so well.' Her beady eyes glinted. 'A great deal, that's all I am prepared to say for now.'

'But . . .'

'Save your questions until I have explained,' Mother Horsefeather interrupted sharply. She breathed in. 'I have been approached,' she said, 'by the P . . .'

Forficule coughed loudly.

'. . . by . . . a Sanctaphrax academic,' Mother Horsefeather continued. 'He wishes to get his hands on some stormphrax – lots of it – and he will pay hand-somely for the privilege.'

Cloud Wolf snorted. 'If he needs stormphrax, then why doesn't he simply raid the treasury,' he said. 'From what I've heard, everyone else does these days.'

Mother Horsefeather stared at him impassively. 'It is to replenish the depleted stocks in the treasury that the stormphrax is needed,' she said. 'Too much has been taken for phraxdust already,' she continued, glancing down at the silver medallion around her own neck. 'Not that anyone has actually been successful – but if nothing is done, then the floating rock will break its moorings and Sanctaphrax will drift off. Into open sky. For ever.'

'Pah,' Cloud Wolf spat. 'Sanctaphrax. What good has that place ever done me?'

Mother Horsefeather clucked with irritation. 'Sanctaphrax is an integral part of all our lives,' she snapped. 'Its scholars are the weather-diviners, the map-makers, the sifters of mists and phantasms that come in from beyond the Edge. It is they who read the patterns which bring order from chaos. Without them,

Undertown itself could not exist. You, of all people, Wolfie, should understand this.'

'I know only that Sanctaphrax stole the years of my prime and then cast me out,' Cloud Wolf said.

Mother Horsefeather's eyes sparkled. 'You felt cheated – you still do,' she said. 'And rightly so.' She paused. 'That is why I offer you now the possibility to avenge yourself on the usurpers.'

Cloud Wolf stared back at her, as it finally occurred to him what the devious bird-woman was after. 'You mean you want me to sail to the Twilight Woods in search of fresh stormphrax,' he said.

'I *mean*,' said Mother Horsefeather, 'that I am giving you a second chance. You will be able to utilize all that training you were given in the Knights' Academy; you will show that Cloud Wolf is more than a mere cut-throat and outlaw. At long last,' she said as she puffed out her breast feathers, 'the magnificent *Stormchaser* will be used for the purpose it was originally built. Not lugging ironwood around like some glorified tug-ship. But stormchasing!'

Twig's heart thrilled at the sound of the word. Stooorm-cha-sing! he whispered, savouring every syllable. He smiled excitedly. *Stoooooooorrm-cha-sing*.

The next moment, any dreams he might have had were shattered. 'Out of the question,' Cloud Wolf snapped.

'Oh, but Wolfie,' Mother Horsefeather wheedled, 'think of the acclaim that will be heaped upon your head when you arrive back triumphant, with enough storm-phrax to weigh down the floating rock of Sanctaphrax for a thousand years. Think of the glory – think of the *power*,' she added softly.

Twig willed his father to agree. Cloud Wolf shook his head.

'For, of course, with the treasury weighted down once again,' Mother Horsefeather went on, 'the accursed link between the raintasters and the leaguesmen will at last be broken.' Her eyes glinted. 'New alliances will have to be forged – a new hierarchy established. Think how high in the pecking-order you could find yourself. You and me, Wolfie. Just you and me, up there at the top.'

But still Cloud Wolf remained unmoved. 'Many long years have gone by since I left the Academy,' he said. 'And the *Stormchaser* is not the sky ship she once was . . .'

'Wolfie! Wolfie!' Mother Horsefeather chided him. 'Such false modesty! Quintinius Verginix was the most outstanding knight the Academy had ever seen, and the skills you learned there have been honed to razor sharp-ness as Cloud Wolf, the finest sky pirate captain ever.' Twig heard his father snort. 'And as for the *Stormchaser*,' she went on, 'we will have it repaired, realigned, re-furbished – the works. She will fly as she has never flown before.'

For a moment, Twig thought this would sway it. Surely his father would be unable to resist such an offer. Cloud Wolf smiled and played with his waxed side-whiskers.

'No,' he said. He scraped the chair noisily backwards and stood up from the table. 'And now if you'll excuse me . . .'

Mother Horsefeather began scratching at the floor in a sudden fury. 'Excuse you?' she screeched. 'No I will *not* excuse you.' Her voice grew more and more shrill. 'You have no choice! I have something you need – and you have something I need. You *will* do what I say!'

Cloud Wolf merely chuckled to himself as he made for the door. In an uncontrollable rage, Mother Horsefeather flapped and thrashed about. The table tipped over. The chairs went flying. Twig, dodging back out of her way, caught sight of Forficule. He was staring intently at the door, ears quivering and a smile twitching at the corners of his mouth.

'You're finished!' Mother Horsefeather was screaming. 'Finished! Do you understand? I'll see you never so
much as set foot on a sky ship again. I'll . . .'

There was a muffled knock. Mother Horsefeather
froze. The door opened. 'You!' she exclaimed.

'My lord,' Cloud Wolf gasped, and fell to his
knees.

Twig stared at the newcomer in confusion. He was old – very old – with
long white hair and a stout staff to
aid his unsteady gait. With his broken sandals, his fingerless gloves
and his patched and threadbare gown, he looked as
wretched as any alley-
vagrant. Yet there
was his father
kneeling
d o w n
before
him.

Twig turned to Forficule for an explanation, but the nightwaif had moved away. It was up on the table, urgently whispering into Mother Horsefeather's ear behind its pale and bony hand. Twig would have given anything to know what was being said but, strain as he might, he could hear nothing but a conspiratorial *hssp-psss-psss*.

Twig groaned, returned his attention to his father – and groaned again. If he had been disappointed by Cloud Wolf's reaction to Mother Horsefeather's proposal, then he was mortified to find his father still kneeling.

Will you stand up and fight? he wondered bitterly. Or do you intend to remain on your knees for ever?

# ·CHAPTER SIX·

# SCREED TOE-TAKER

The journey across the Mire was proving to be as harsh as anything Mim had ever experienced. And if the leader of the gnokgoblin family was finding the going tough, then the others were all but at the end of their strength. Mim's concern was growing more acute with every passing minute.

Screed had given strict instructions that they should all keep together, yet the further they went on across the endless muddy wasteland, the more separated they were becoming.

Mim squelched back and forth along the long straggling line as fast as the gluey mud would allow. From the young'uns up at the front to old Torp, who was bringing up the rear, and back again, she went – offering words of encouragement as she passed.

'Not far, now,' she assured them. 'Nearly there.' The

rank, stagnant stench of the Mire grew stronger. 'Forget where we are now and keep your thoughts on the wonderful place for which we're bound – a place of plenty, a place of opportunity, a place where goblins are respected and the streets are paved with gold.'

The gnokgoblins smiled back at her weakly, but none made any attempt to reply. They didn't have the energy. Even the young'uns, who had started out so enthusiastically – gambolling ahead like lambs – were now dragging their feet painfully slowly. Mim knew it would not be long before the first of her party gave up completely.

'Hey!' she cried out to the gaunt figure up ahead. 'Slow down a bit.'

Screed turned. 'Now what?' he snapped irritably.

Mim strode towards him. The burning sun beat down ferociously. Screed waited for her to catch up, hands on hips, leering. 'We need a rest,' she panted.

Screed looked her up and down, then squinted up at the sky. 'We keep on till sundown,' he said. 'Then we'll rest for the night. It's too dangerous travelling by darkness – what with the sinking-mud and poisonous blow-holes . . .'

'Not to mention the muglumps, oozefish and white ravens,' Mim interrupted tartly. 'Not that we've encountered any so far.'

Screed pulled himself up to his full height, and stared down his nose at her scornfully. 'Forgive me,' he said, his voice loaded with sarcasm, 'I was under the impression that you employed me as a guide to *avoid* these dangers.

If I'd only *known* you wanted to see them for your-selves . . .'

Mim looked down sheepishly. 'I'm sorry,' she said. 'It's just . . . Well, some of us are finding it difficult to keep up with the pace you're setting.'

Screed glanced back along the line of goblins. 'You paid for a two-day crossing,' he said sharply. 'Any longer than that and it'll cost you.'

'But we haven't got any more money,' Mim cried out.

Screed's yellow teeth gleamed against the bleached paleness of his lips. 'Like I say,' he said, turning and walking away. 'It'll cost you.'

Darkness had fallen by the time Screed Toe-taker called it a day. He stopped on an outcrop of rocks and placed the lantern down. 'We'll stop here,' he called back through cupped hands.

One by one, the goblins started to arrive.

'Keep that infant still!' Screed shouted at a young female with a squawling babe-in-arms. 'It'll attract every muglump for miles around.' He lifted the lantern and peered back the way they'd come. 'And where are the others?' he snapped. 'Just my luck if they've already gone and got themselves lost.'

'No, look! Over there!' one of the young'uns cried, and pointed back towards a curious, squat figure which was shuffling towards them out of the low, swirling mist. As it grew closer, the one figure became three. It was Mim, trudging purposefully on with a youngster on her back and an arm around old Torp.

Screed smiled. 'All present and correct,' he said.

Buoyed up by the gleeful cheers of the others, Mim staggered across that last stretch of sucking quicksilver mud and up onto the rocky outcrop. Old Torp released himself from her supporting arm and sat down. 'Well done, old-timer,' she whispered breathlessly. 'You made it.' She pulled the sleeping youngster from her back, laid him gently down on the ground and covered him with a blanket. Then, groaning with the effort, she pulled herself upright and looked round.

'Well, it's certainly not the most comfortable place I've ever spent the night,' she said. 'But it's dry. And that's the main thing. So, thank you, Screed, for bringing us to this place.'

'My pleasure,' he said, ignoring the sullen faces of the others – it was, after all, an expression he had seen a thousand times before. 'And now,' he said, 'you must all get some sleep.'

The gnokgoblins didn't need telling twice. Within seconds, all of them were rolled up in their blankets, like a row of woolly cocoons – all, that is, except for Mim. 'And yourself?' she asked Screed.

'Me?' he said loftily, as he perched himself on the top of the tallest rock. 'Oh, don't you worry about me. I have little need of sleep.' He gazed round the flat landscape, glinting and glistening like burnished silver beneath the moon. 'Besides, someone has to keep watch.'

Mim was reassured. Despite what she'd said earlier, she hadn't liked the sound of the muglumps, oozefish or white ravens one tiny little bit. She wished Screed a good night, snuggled up between two of the young'uns and, by the time dark clouds rolled over the moon a couple of minutes later, she was, like all the others, fast asleep.

Screed listened to the rasping chorus of snoring and smirked to himself. 'Sleep well, little dwarves,' he whispered, 'or goblins – or whatever you are.'

He brought the lantern nearer as the clouds rolled in, and pulled a knife from his belt which he began sliding gently back and forwards over the smooth rock. Occasionally he would spit on the metal, and inspect the blade in the yellow light. Then off he went again, slowly, methodically – *whish, whish, whish* – until every point along the blade was sharp enough to split a hair in two.

Woe betide the creature that thought it could get the better of him. Screed stood up, lantern in one hand, knife in the other. Woe betide *any* who fell into his clutches.

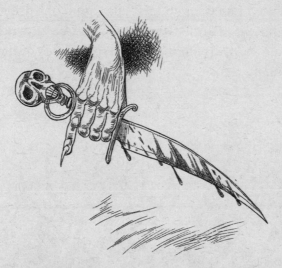

Abruptly, the clouds rolled back, and the bright moon shone down on the grisly scene, turning everything to black and white.

White blankets. Black blood.

White bony body, lurching on into the mud. Black shadow, stretching back across the rocks.

White ravens, already scavenging. Black deeds. Monstrous deeds.

With his leather bag full of bloody booty clasped in his bony hand, Screed Toe-taker picked his way across the Mire. Far away in front of him, the moon glinted on the wreck of a sky ship which lay half-buried in the mud like a giant skeleton. Unblinking, Screed kept his eyes fixed on the glinting ribs of the broken hull. Closer and closer

he came. Not once did he falter. Not once did he look
back.

'At last,' Screed muttered as he made it to the wreck.
He glanced round for any tell-tale sign of intrusion and,
when he was satisfied there was no-one and nothing
there, he scuttled into the shadowy recesses of the lop-
sided shipwreck.

·  If some intruder *had* taken the opportunity to in-
vestigate the place during its owner's absence, he, she or
it would have been left shaking with disbelief at the
horrors the ship concealed. The dank air, for a start, was
thick with the pungent stench of death. And then there
were the walls – studded their length and breadth with
mummified toes, nailed to the wood.

There were big toes, small toes, hairy toes, scaly toes,
toes with razor-sharp talons, toes with claws, toes with
webbing – all of them shrivelled and black. And these

were just a fraction of the total number – the select few –
for at the far end of the hull in a massive wedge-shaped
drift, were thousands upon thousands more.

Screed sloshed his way along the sky ship. He didn't
register the gory trophies lining the walls, neither did he
notice the awful stench; to Screed Toe-taker, the wreck of
the *Windcutter* simply smelled of home.

He hung the lantern on a hook above a huge chest of
ironwood and glass, opened the lid, crouched down and
set to work. One by one he pulled the severed toes from
his bag and, like an insane manicurist, scraped beneath
the nails with a small file. Tiny particles of dust – some
glistening white, some tinged with sepia – dropped
down into the chest with the rest. And when he was
satisfied that every speck had been removed, he tossed
the toes on to the great heap with the others.

Finally done, Screed stared down with dreamy contentment into the chest. It was more than three-quarters
full of the toe-nail scrapings. 'Oh, my beea-oootiful
looty-booty,' he whispered. 'One day you will fill the
chest, right up to the top. One day soon, Sky willing.
And on that wondrous day, then maybe – just maybe –
shall my quest be at an end.'

Screed stood up, slammed the lid shut, and stepped
outside. The long night was over. To his left, the tell-tale
purple clouds of a gathering storm were rolling in from
the retreating darkness. To his right and far away in the
distance, was a sky ship, silhouetted against the rising
sun.

Both were coming closer.

# ·CHAPTER SEVEN·

# ASSENT AND BETRAYAL

Mother Horsefeather watched uneasily as the ancient figure approached Cloud Wolf. She knew from bitter experience that it could be disastrous to allow the different parties – the supply and demand, so to speak – to meet. Far better to remain in the middle: fixing the deal, pulling the strings. And yet, as Forficule had pointed out, since she had singularly failed to persuade Cloud Wolf to embark on the journey, the newcomer was their only hope.

He leaned forwards and tapped Cloud Wolf with his staff. 'Arise, Quintinius Verginix,' he said.

Twig watched his father climb to his feet and look up. He saw his eyes gleaming with reverence, with respect, and at that moment, Twig knew with absolute certainty who the old, shabbily dressed person must be. It was his father's erstwhile patron and mentor, the Professor of Light.

'It has been a long time, Quintinius,' he said. 'The finest Knight Academic in a hundred generations, you were – yet . . .' He paused and looked at Twig, seeing him for the first time. 'Who is this, Horsefeather?' he demanded.

'The lad is with me,' Cloud Wolf answered for her. 'Anything you have to say to me can be said in front of him.'

'Are you sure?' the professor asked.

'Quite sure,' said Cloud Wolf, polite yet firm.

The Professor of Light nodded resignedly. 'We failed you, Quintinius Verginix. I appreciate that. Now, we come to you, cap in hand. We need your help.'

Watching his father shuffling about under the professor's penetrating gaze, Twig was reminded of himself. And when Cloud Wolf spoke, it was his own faltering tones that Twig heard in his voice.

'I . . . errm . . . that is . . . Mother Horsefeather has already outlined the . . . the problem.'

'Indeed,' said the professor, surprised. 'Then you will understand the gravity of the situation – or should that be the *lack of gravity* of the situation,' he added, chuckling at his little joke.

Cloud Wolf smiled weakly. 'Sanctaphrax is truly in danger then?' he said.

'It could break free of its moorings at any moment,' the professor said. 'We must have fresh supplies of storm-phrax.'

Cloud Wolf listened in silence.

'The windtouchers and cloudwatchers have already

confirmed that a Great Storm is imminent,' the professor continued. 'By the time it arrives, someone must be ready to chase it to the Twilight Woods so that he might retrieve the stormphrax it creates. And that someone, my dear Quintinius Verginix,' he said, 'is you. There is not another soul alive equal to the task. Will you help us or will you see Sanctaphrax cast for ever into open sky?'

Cloud Wolf stared back impassively. Twig couldn't begin to guess the thoughts spinning round his head. Yes? Or no? Which was the answer to be?

Then Cloud Wolf gave the slightest of nods to the Professor of Light's proposal. Twig's heart pounded with excitement. No matter how minimal the response, his father had accepted.

They were to go stormchasing.

On the other side of the door with his ear pressed against the wood, someone else was excited to hear of the proposed voyage to the Twilight Woods. It was Slyvo Spleethe, the *Stormchaser's* quartermaster. He listened carefully to the plans being made, memorizing each and every detail mentioned. There were those who would pay well for such information.

At the sound of chairs being pushed back, Spleethe pulled away from the door and slipped back into the bar-room. He couldn't be caught eavesdropping now. The good captain would discover soon enough that his plans had been overheard.

By Undertown standards, the Leagues Chamber was luxurious – that is, there were floorboards rather than trodden earth underfoot and there was glass in the majority of the windows. Most of the room was taken up with a giant ring-shaped table, at which were seated all the senior leaguesmen who had been available at such short notice.

In the circular hole at the centre of the table was a swivel stool. And upon this sat Slyvo Spleethe.

Simenon Xintax, the Leaguesmaster, rapped loudly on the table with his gavel. 'Order!' he bellowed. 'Order!!'

The Leagues Chamber fell silent, and all eyes turned towards him. Xintax arose from his chair.

'Tricorn mitres on!' he said, and there was a flurry of activity as each of the leaguesmen picked up their head-gear and put it into place. Xintax nodded approvingly. 'I declare open this emergency session of the Undertown League of Free Merchants,' he announced. 'Let the questioning commence.'

The leaguesmen remained silent, waiting for Xintax, as chairperson, to frame the first question, the most important question – the question that would set the tone for all subsequent questions. For truth, as the leaguesmen were well aware, was a slippery thing. It had to be approached with care if it was not to change into something completely different.

Xintax took his seat. 'If we were to ask you, Slyvo Spleethe, whether you be – an honest individual,' he began, in the contorted form that tradition demanded, 'how would you verily reply?'

Spleethe gulped. Now that's a difficult one, he thought. Certainly he intended to answer the leaguesman's questions honestly. But as to whether he himself was honest, well, an honest person would not have been eavesdropping in the first place. He shrugged, and wiped away the droplets of sweat from above his top lip. 'It's like this, you see . . .' he began.

'You will answer the question with a yes or a no,' Xintax interrupted. 'You will answer *all* questions with a yes or a no. Nothing more, nothing less. Is that quite clear?'

'Yes,' said Spleethe.

Xintax nodded approvingly. 'So, I repeat. If we were to ask you, Slyvo Spleethe, whether you be an honest individual, how would you verily reply?'

'No,' said Spleethe.

A ripple of surprise went round the table. Then all the leaguesmen thrust their arms up into the air. 'I. I. I. I,' they called, each one trying to grab the chairperson's attention.

'Leandus Leadbelly, Gutters and Gougers,' he said.

Leandus, a short angry-looking character with one dark eyebrow which ran the width of his heavy brow, nodded towards Spleethe. 'If we were to ask you whether you have information concerning your captain, Cloud Wolf, the former Quintinius Verginix, how would you verily reply?'

Spleethe swivelled round to face his questioner. 'Yes,' he said.

'Farquhar Armwright,' said Xintax. 'Gluesloppers and Ropeteasers.'

'If we were to ask you whether the *Stormchaser* was currently skyworthy, how would you verily reply?'

'No,' said Spleethe, swivelling back again.

'Ellerex Earthclay, Melders and Moulders.'

'If we were to ask you whether, should the need arise, you would be prepared to kill one of your fellow crew-members, how would you verily reply?'

Spleethe breathed in sharply. 'Yes.'

And so it continued. The leaguesmen put their questions and Spleethe answered them. One after the other after the other. There was no order to the questions – at least, if there was, then Spleethe was blind to it. As far as he was concerned it would have made far more sense if he'd been allowed to tell them precisely what he'd over-heard. But no. The interrogation continued, with the questions coming thicker and faster as the time went on.

Little by little, the entire story was revealed – and not just the bare facts. By pursuing the information so obliquely, the leaguesmen managed to build up a picture, complete in every single detail – and, with it, the knowledge of precisely what to do.

Simenon Xintax arose for a second time. He raised his arms. 'The questioning be concluded,' he said. 'If we were to ask you, Slyvo Spleethe, to swear allegiance to the Undertown League of Free Merchants, forswearing all other ties and pledging obedience to our will, how would you verily reply?'

Spleethe's head was in a whirl. From the questions they had framed, he guessed that untold wealth was on offer. Plus a sky ship of his own. *Plus*, most important of all, league status. But he also knew precisely what was expected of him – and for such a feat, Spleethe wanted more than wealth. He wanted power.

'I answer this question with a question of my own, be it permitted,' he began. Xintax nodded. 'If I were to ask you whether, for the successful conclusion of this hazardous endeavour, I might become the new Leaguesmaster of the Undertown League of Free Merchants, how would *you* verily reply?'

Xintax's eyes narrowed. He had learned much about Slyvo Spleethe through the questioning. The quartermaster, he knew, was a greedy creature, treacherous and self-important – his question came as no surprise. 'Yes,' he answered.

'In that case,' Spleethe smiled, 'my answer be also yes.'

On hearing his reply, the leaguesmen all climbed solemnly to their feet, clutched their tricorn mitres to their breasts and hung their heads. Simenon Xintax spoke for them all.

'We have asked, you have answered, and a deal has been struck,' he said. 'But be sure of this, Spleethe. If you should attempt to dupe, deceive or double-cross us, we shall not rest until you have been hunted down and destroyed. Do you understand?'

Spleethe stared back grimly. 'Yes,' he said. 'I understand. But be aware, Xintax, that what is true for the woodboar is also true for the sow. Those who cross *me* do not live long enough to tell the tale.'

Back in the stuffy room behind the bar of the Bloodoak tavern, a mood of optimism held sway. Once business had been concluded – with the flurry of double-hand-shakes that ritual required – Mother Horsefeather had rung a bell to summon her servants. It was time for the feast which had been prepared to celebrate the success-ful conclusion to the deal.

The food was delicious and plentiful, and the woodale flowed freely. Twig sat in contented silence, listening with only half an ear as the others talked on and on. *Stormchasing. Stormchasing.* It was all he could think about, and his heart thrilled with anticipation.

'I still think it was very forward of you to assume that we'd come to an agreement,' he heard Cloud Wolf chuckling as he tucked into his succulent hammelhorn steak.

'Who is to say I would not have provided a meal even if we had not?' Mother Horsefeather said.

'I say so,' said Cloud Wolf. 'I know you, Mother Horsefeather. *'If you do anything for nothing, do it for yourself* – isn't that how the saying goes . . .?'

Mother Horsefeather clacked her beak with amuse-ment. 'Oh, Wolfie!' she said. 'You are a one!' She rose to her feet and lifted her glass. 'Since, however, the matter *has* been settled to everyone's satisfaction, I would like to propose a toast. To success,' she said.

'To success!' came the enthusiastic response.

The Professor of Light turned to Cloud Wolf. 'I am so very glad you have consented,' he said warmly. 'After all, I would not have liked to entrust so valuable a cargo to a lesser person.'

'You mean the stormphrax,' Cloud Wolf said. 'We've got to find the stuff first.'

'No, Quintinius, not the stormphrax,' the professor said, and laughed. 'I was talking about myself, for I shall be accompanying you. Together, with your skill and my knowledge, we shall return with enough stormphrax to end the current madness of chain-building once and for all.'

Cloud Wolf frowned. 'But won't Vilnix be suspicious should he get wind of it?'

'That's where *we* come in,' Mother Horsefeather said, and nodded towards the nightwaif. 'Tomorrow morning, Forficule will pay a visit to Sanctaphrax to announce the Professor of Light's tragic accident and untimely death.'

'I see that, between you, you've thought of everything,' said Cloud Wolf. 'There is, however, one last thing *I* have to say.' He turned to Twig.

'I know, I know,' Twig laughed. 'But it's all right. I promise I won't mess up on this voyage – not even once.'

'No, Twig, you will not,' said Cloud Wolf sternly. 'For you are not coming with us.'

Twig gasped. His face fell; his heart sank. How could his father say such a thing? 'B . . . but what will I do? Where will I go?' he asked.

'It's all right, Twigsy,' he heard Mother Horsefeather saying. 'It's all been sorted. You're to stay with me...'

'No, no, no,' Twig muttered, hardly able to take in what was happening. 'You can't do this to me. It's not fair...'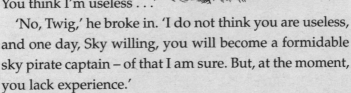

'Twig!' his father barked. 'Be still!'

But Twig could not be still. 'You just don't trust me, do you?' he shouted. 'You think I'm no good at anything. You think I'm useless...'

'No, Twig,' he broke in. 'I do not think you are useless, and one day, Sky willing, you will become a formidable sky pirate captain – of that I am sure. But, at the moment, you lack experience.'

'And how will I gain that experience if you leave me behind?' Twig demanded. 'Besides,' he said hotly, 'no-one alive has any experience of stormchasing. Not even you.'

Cloud Wolf did not rise to the bait. 'I have made my decision,' he said calmly. 'You can accept it with good grace, or you can rant and rave like a child. Either way, you are not coming, and that is an end to it.'

# CHAPTER EIGHT

# DEPARTURE

'Setting sail?' Tem Barkwater exclaimed.

'That's what the Stone Pilot reckons,' said Spiker.

'But that's admirable news,' said Tem. 'Why, three days ago, after all the trouble with the ironwood, and then losing the rudder-wheel like that, I had truly feared that the *Stormchaser* might never set sail again. Yet now look at her – all fixed and ready, and raring to go. I en't never seen the brasses gleam so bright.'

'And it's not just the brasses,' said Stope Boltjaw. 'Haven't you noticed the sails and ropes? And the rigging? Brand spanking new, the lot of them.'

'And the weight-workings have been tuned to perfection as well,' said Spiker.

'We must be about to embark on something very important,' said Tem Barkwater, stroking his beard thoughtfully.

'You don't need to be a genius to work that one out,' said Stope Boltjaw. 'The question is, what?'

Tem shook his head. 'I'm sure the cap'n'll tell us when he's good and ready,' he said.

'Aye, well,' said Stope Boltjaw. 'If we *are* to set sail then we'd do well to leave now, under the cover of darkness.'

'On the contrary,' said Tem Barkwater. 'We should bide our time and wait until morning.'

'What, and set off in full view of the leagues patrols?' said Stope Boltjaw. 'Have you taken leave of your senses?'

'Not I, Stope,' Tem retorted. 'It is you who has forgotten that, with the *Stormchaser* as she now is, we could outrun any and every league ship they might care to send after us.'

'Yes, but . . .' Stope protested.

'And anyhow,' Tem Barkwater went on, 'the Mire is a treacherous place at the best of times – crossing it in darkness is madness. What with them poisonous blow-holes erupting all round about. And nowhere to attach the grappling-irons in a storm. Not to mention that it's impossible to see where the sky ends and the ground begins. I remember once – I couldn't have been much more than a lad at the time – we were on our way back from . . .'

He was interrupted by Spiker. 'It's the captain,' he hissed. 'And he's not alone.'

Tem Barkwater fell silent, and he, Stope Boltjaw and Spiker turned to greet the two figures climbing the gangplank.

'Cap'n,' said Tem warmly. 'Just the person I wanted to see. Perhaps you could settle a little dispute for us. Stope, here, maintains that . . .'

'No, Tem, I can't,' Cloud Wolf snapped. He peered round into the darkness. 'Where's Hubble?'

'Below deck, cap'n,' said Tem. 'With Mugbutt. I believe the pair of them are helping the Stone Pilot make his final adjustments to the new rudder-wheel.'

Cloud Wolf nodded. 'And Spleethe?'

The sky pirates shrugged. 'Spleethe, we haven't seen,' said Tem Barkwater. 'We lost him in Undertown. He must still be on shore.'

Cloud Wolf turned on him furiously. 'He what?' he roared. 'How many times do I have to tell you that Slyvo Spleethe is never *ever* to be left to his own devices? Who knows what he might be up to now?'

'One minute he was with us in the Bloodoak,' Stope Boltjaw explained. 'The next minute he was gone.'

Cloud Wolf shook his head in disbelief. 'Spleethe is our quartermaster,' he explained to the Professor of Light. 'A slippery character with a mutinous heart. I've half a mind to set sail without him. Trouble is, he's good at his job. And with Twig staying behind, that'll put us at two crewmen down.' He shook his head. 'I can't risk it.'

'Twig's staying behind?' Tem Barkwater said, surprised. 'Has the lad fallen ill?'

'No, Tem, he has not,' Cloud Wolf said angrily. 'Though it is no concern of yours *what* has happened to him.'

'But . . .'

'Enough!' he shouted. 'I will not have such insubordination in front of our guest.' He turned to the Professor of Light. 'Now, if you'd like to follow me, sire, I'll show you to your quarters myself.'

'Thank you, I should like that,' the professor said. 'There are a few last-minute calculations I need to work on before we set sail.'

'Quite, quite,' said Cloud Wolf, and ushered the professor away before he could say too much about the proposed voyage.

The three sky pirates looked at one another in confusion. Who was this old character? Why was Twig not coming with them? And where *were* they going? Cloud Wolf suddenly spun round. 'Idle speculation is the pastime of the fool,' he remarked, causing them all to look down guiltily at the deck. 'You will inform me the moment Spleethe returns,' he said.

'Aye-aye, cap'n,' came the reply.

Twig stared down miserably into his glass of woodfizz. Mother Horsefeather had poured the drink long ago – 'to raise his spirits' as she'd commented to Forficule. Now it was warm and flat.

All round him, the drunken revelry continued at full-throttle. There was raucous laughter and loud swearing; tales were told, songs were sung, violent arguments broke out as the flat-head and hammer-head goblins became increasingly volatile. At the stroke of midnight, a lumpen she-troll started up a snake dance and, within minutes, the whole tavern was squirming with a long line of individuals, winding its way round and round the room.

'Oy, cheer up, mate,' Twig heard. 'It might never happen.'

He turned and found himself face to face with a grinning mobgnome standing beside him. 'It already has,' he sighed.

Puzzled, the mobgnome shrugged and returned to the dance. Twig turned back. He placed his elbows on the bar, rested his head in his hands with his fingers clamped firmly over his ears and closed his eyes.

'Why did you have to leave me here?' he whispered. 'Why?'

Of course, he knew what his father would reply. 'I'm only thinking of your well-being' or 'One day, you'll thank me for this' or, worst of all, 'It's all for your own good.'

Twig felt his sadness and regret shifting, by degrees, to anger. It was not good for him; not good at all. Life on the *Stormchaser* was good. Being with his father, after so long a separation, was good. Sailing the skies in pursuit of wealth and riches was good. But being placed in the charge of Mother Horsefeather in her seething, seedy tavern while the *Stormchaser* and its crew set off on so wonderful a voyage was unutterably bad.

Torturing himself all the more, Twig thought of everything he was missing. He imagined how it must feel to be sucked along in the wake of a Great Storm. He tried to envisage the single lightning bolt as it froze in mid-air and turned to solid stormphrax. And he asked himself what it must be like inside the notorious Twilight Woods. For, although the *Stormchaser* had often passed above them, none of the Sky Pirates had ever risked venturing down.

Would they be like the Deepwoods of his childhood? he wondered. Endless, luxuriant forest. Teeming with life. Filled with all manner of trees, from humming lullabees to the flesh-eating bloodoaks, and home to countless tribes and villagers and creatures of every kind . . .

Or were they indeed as mysteriously treacherous as the legends described? A place of endless degeneration. A place of confusion and delusion. A place of madness. *That* was how the storytellers spoke of the Twilight Woods, as they passed their tales on, word of mouth, down the generations.

Twig sighed. Now he would never know. What should have been the greatest adventure of his life had been snatched cruelly away by his own father. Even if it had been done for his own safety, because he was, as Cloud Wolf had put it, 'important to him'; even if that *was* the case, the fact remained that to Twig, it felt like a punishment.

'And it's just not fair!' he complained.

'What is not fair?' came a voice at his elbow. Twig started. If it was the ridiculous grinning mobgnome trying to get him to dance again, he would give him what for! He swung round angrily.

'Spleethe!' he said.

'Master Twig,' said Spleethe, his narrow lips curling to reveal a set of stained and crooked teeth. 'I thought it was you. Just the person I was looking for – though it saddens me, of course, to see you so down in the mouth,' he added.

Twig frowned. 'You were looking for *me*?' he said.

'Indeed I was,' Spleethe purred as he rubbed his chin thoughtfully, and Twig swallowed queasily at the sight of the quartermaster's hand, with its missing fingers and mess of puckered skin. 'You see, I couldn't help noticing that you were present during the discussions between the good captain and the bird-woman.'

'What if I was?' said Twig suspiciously.

'It's just that, well . . . although, naturally, the captain has filled me in on all the details of our little venture . . .'

Twig was surprised. 'He has?'

'Of *course* he has,' Spleethe said. 'Chasing the Great Storm to the Twilight Woods. The quest for the sacred stormphrax . . . I know it all. It's just that . . . One's memory, you understand . . . That is . . .'

Spleethe was fishing. The Leaguesmaster had demanded even more of him than he'd expected – taking the *Stormchaser*, killing Cloud Wolf, delivering the stormphrax. His task would be difficult and he had kicked himself for leaving the Bloodoak tavern so hastily before. After all, if he was to be successful, he needed to know *everything* about the meeting – including the part which took place after his departure.

'Silly of me, I know,' he continued slyly, 'but I cannot for the life of me remember how Cloud Wolf said the meeting was concluded.'

Twig's reaction took the quartermaster by surprise.

'Concluded?' he said angrily. 'I'll tell you how it was concluded. I was told to remain here, in Undertown, with Mother Horsefeather, while the rest of you go sailing off to the Twilight Woods.'

Spleethe's brow furrowed. 'Remain here?' he repeated softly. 'Tell me more, Master Twig,' he said. 'Open up your heart.'

Struggling to fight back the tears, Twig shook his head.

'But Master Twig,' Spleethe persisted, his voice whiny and wheedling, 'a problem shared is a problem halved. And of course, if there's anything that *I* can do, anything at all . . .'

'It's the captain,' Twig blurted out. 'He says he's worried about my safety, but . . . but . . . I don't believe him. I can't believe him. He's ashamed of me, that's what it is!' he sobbed. 'Ashamed to have such a gangly, blundering oaf for a son.'

Slyvo Spleethe's eyebrows shot upwards with surprise. Cloud Wolf, the lad's father? Now that *was* interesting – very interesting indeed – and his head spun with ways in which he could use this latest piece of information to his advantage. Composing himself, he laid his hand on Twig's shoulder.

'The captain has a good heart,' he said softly. 'And I am sure he has your best interests in mind. Yet . . .'

Twig sniffed, and listened.

'Yet there is a fine line between being protective and being *over*-protective,' he said. 'Why, the trip to the Twilight Woods would be the making of you.'

Twig scowled. 'Not now it won't,' he muttered. He shook Spleethe's bony hand off his shoulder, and turned away. 'Why don't you just go?' he said.

For an instant, a smile flickered at the edge of Spleethe's mouth; then it was gone. 'Master Twig,' he said. 'I do not intend to return to the *Stormchaser* alone. I believe – and here I must speak frankly – I believe that Cloud Wolf has erred in his judgement. Of *course* you must accompany us on our Twilight Woods adventure. This is my plan,' he said, and brought his face close to Twig's. His breath was stale and sour. 'We will smuggle you aboard. You can stow away below deck in Mugbutt's berth – no one will ever suspect you of hiding there.'

Twig continued to listen in silence. It all sounded too good to be true. Yet he knew well enough that Cloud Wolf would find him eventually. There would be trouble when he did!

'It'll all be fine, you'll see,' Spleethe's nasal wheedling continued. 'When the time is right I myself shall reveal your presence to Cloud Wolf. I'll talk him round. I'll make him see sense. You just leave it all to me.'

Twig nodded. Spleethe squeezed Twig's elbow with his hard bony fingers. 'Come on, then, let's go,' he said. 'Before I change my mind.'

*

All was not well on board the *Stormchaser*. The crew stood nervously by while their captain paced up and down the quarterdeck, purple with rage.

The Professor of Light – freshly kitted out with a pirate longcoat and parawings – had informed the captain that the Great Storm could strike 'at any minute'. That was several hours ago. Yet the sky ship had still not set sail.

Cloud Wolf ceased his pacing, seized the side rail and bellowed into the night. 'SPLEETHE, YOU MISERABLE EXCUSE FOR A MANGY SKYCUR, WHERE ARE YOU?'

'At your service, cap'n,' came a familiar voice.

Cloud Wolf spun round to see the quartermaster emerging from the aft-hatch. He stared in disbelief. 'Spleethe!' he spluttered. 'You're here!'

'I thought you called me,' he said, innocently.

'I've been calling you for three hours or more!' Cloud Wolf raged. 'Where have you been?'

'With Mugbutt,' Spleethe replied. 'A wound to his foot has become infected. Septic and swollen it is. The poor creature was quite delirious.'

The captain breathed in sharply. It seemed he had found his quartermaster only to lose his finest fighter. Mugbutt was fearless in any battle and had got them out of more scrapes than Cloud Wolf cared to remember.

'How is Mugbutt now?' he asked.

'I've left him sleeping,' said Spleethe. 'Sky willing, he will be back to his old self when he wakes.'

Cloud Wolf nodded. Setting sail for the treacherous Twilight Woods without Mugbutt was a risk. And yet, with the Great Storm imminent, it was a risk he had to take.

He raised his head. 'Gather round,' he called. 'I have something important to tell you all.'

The sky pirates listened, open-mouthed, as Cloud Wolf outlined the plans. 'Stormchasing,' Tem Barkwater whispered reverently.

'The Twilight Woods,' Spiker shuddered.

Cloud Wolf continued. 'And our quest will be, as it ever was, to retrieve stormphrax for the treasury of Sanctaphrax.'

'Stormphrax!' Slyvo Spleethe – feigning surprise – exclaimed with the rest.

'Yes, stormphrax,' said Cloud Wolf. 'That is why the Professor of Light is travelling with us. He understands its properties. He will ensure we travel safely with our precious cargo.'

Spleethe frowned. So *that* was who the newcomer was. If only he'd known before.

'Right then, you scurvy skycurs,' Cloud Wolf announced. 'To your posts. We set sail at once.' While the sky pirates scurried this way and that, Cloud Wolf strode to the helm. 'Release the tolley-ropes,' he cried.

'Aye-aye,' Spiker called back. 'Tolley-ropes, released.'

'Unhook the grappling-irons!'

'Grappling-irons, unhooked.'

'And weigh anchor.'

As the heavy anchor was winched up, the *Stormchaser* leapt from its moorings and up into the sky.

'Come on, my lovely,' Cloud Wolf whispered to his sky ship as it bucked and lurched, responding to the lightest touch of the weight and sail levers. 'My, but you're frisky once more. Just like you were when you were first built. Forgive me for all the times I used you as a common tugship. I had no choice. But now, my wonderful chaser of storms, your time has come.'

As the dawn broke – and keeping both Tem Barkwater *and* Stope Boltjaw happy – the *Stormchaser* sailed majestically out of Undertown, unchecked. Wispy wings of pink and orange fanned out across the morning side of the sky. A moment later, the sun appeared above the horizon on the starboard side. It rose slowly, bright red and tremulous.

Cloud Wolf sighed impatiently. The weather looked unpromisingly good. What *had* happened to the Great Storm that the windtouchers and cloudwatchers had predicted; that the Professor of Light himself had confirmed?

Just then, Spiker let out a yell from his look-out. 'Storm to port!' he cried.

The captain spun round and peered into the distance. At first, he could make out nothing unusual in the featureless darkness of the receding night. But then there was a flash. And another. Short, dazzling bursts of light in the shape of a circle – a circle which, when the lightning faded, still remained. Black on indigo. Growing larger with every passing second.

The lightning flashed again, and Cloud Wolf saw that it was not a circle, but rather, a ball – an immense fizzing, crackling ball of electrical energy, darkness and light combined, which was rolling headlong across the sky towards them.

'It's the Great Storm,' he roared, above the howl of the rising wind. 'Unfurl the mainsail, batten down the hatches and rope yourselves securely. We're going stormchasing!'

# ·CHAPTER NINE·

# STORMCHASING

It had seemed like a good idea at the time, stowing away on the sky ship. Now Twig was not so sure. As the *Stormchaser* pitched and tossed, he retched emptily. Sweat beaded his ice-cold forehead; tears streamed down his burning cheeks.

Mugbutt sniggered unpleasantly. 'Feeling queasy?' he sneered. 'Too rough for you, is it?'

Twig shook his head. It wasn't the flight that was making him ill, but having to breathe the warm, fetid air he was sharing with the goblin. No flat-heads were known for their cleanliness, and Mugbutt was a particularly filthy specimen. He never washed, his bed of straw was wet and fouled, and remnants from the meat he had gleaned from the dinner table lay all around in various stages of decomposition.

Covering his nose with his scarf, Twig breathed in

deeply. Slowly, the nausea subsided, and with it the awful clamouring in his ears. He breathed in again.

Outside, he could hear the familiar noises of Undertown as the *Stormchaser* sped through the busy boom-docks, over the early-morning markets and past the foundries and forges. Bargains, banter, hog-squeal and hammer-blow; a cackle of laughter, a chorus of song, a muffled explosion – the intricate cacophony of life in Undertown which, even this early in the day, was already in full swing.

Soon, the sounds faded away and were gone, and Twig knew they must have left the bustling town and were heading out across the Mire. Now he could hear the *Stormchaser* itself. The creaking, the groaning; the hissing of air as it rushed past the hull. From below him, came the squeaking and scratching of the ratbirds that lived in the bowels of the sky ship; from above – if he strained – the murmur of voices.

'Oh, how I wish I could be up there with them,' Twig whispered.

'And face the captain's wrath?' Mugbutt growled. 'I don't think so.'

Twig sighed. He knew the flat-head was right. Cloud Wolf would surely skin him alive when he discovered that he had been disobeyed. Yet remaining hidden below deck was torture. He missed the feel of the wind in his hair, of soaring through the air, with the places of the Edge spread out below like an intricate map, and above the yawning expanse of endless open sky.

All through the childhood he'd spent in the Deepwoods, Twig had longed to rise up over the forest canopy and explore the sky above. It was as if, even then, his body had known that this was where he belonged. And perhaps it had. After all, Cloud Wolf, himself, had said on more than one occasion that sky-piracy was 'in the blood' – and with such a father . . .

Twig could hear him now, bellowing commands, and he smiled as he imagined the crew hurrying to obey him. For Cloud Wolf kept a tight ship. He was harsh, but just, and it was to his credit that, with him as its captain, the *Stormchaser* had suffered fewer casualties than any other sky pirate ship.

It was, however, the harshness of his justice which now kept Twig cowering in the flat-head's berth, too nervous to appear until Slyvo Spleethe had spoken up for him. He had no option but to wait.

'Storm to starboard, and advancing,' came Spiker's shrill cry. 'Three minutes to contact, and closing.'

'Belay that skysail,' roared Cloud Wolf. 'And check all winding-cleats.'

As the sky ship pitched abruptly to the left, Twig clutched hold of the main stanchion and clung on tightly. He knew the turbulence was a mere foretaste of what was to come. Normally at this point, with a storm so close, the *Stormchaser* would descend, drop anchor and remain there until it had passed. But not today.

Today, the sky ship would greet the storm up in the sky. It would tack closer and closer, until it was drawn into the hurricane-force slip-stream and be whisked away. Ever faster the *Stormchaser* would fly, inching its way round to the head of the storm. Then, when Cloud Wolf judged the moment to be right, it would spin round and pierce the outer shell of the maelstrom.

This was the most dangerous moment of all. If the *Stormchaser* flew too slowly, it would break up in the violent air. If it flew too fast, then there was always the risk that they would pass straight through the storm, emerge on the other side and watch helplessly as the Great Storm continued without them. In either event, their quest for stormphrax would be over.

No, Twig had heard that there was only one way to penetrate the inner calm of a Great Storm safely, and that was to hold the sky ship at a thirty-five degree angle against the windspin – at least, that was the theory. Yet, as the sky ship bucked and turned and Twig held on for grim death, the *Stormchaser* struck him as absurdly small and fragile for so daunting a task, no matter what angle they chose.

'One minute to contact, and counting,' Spiker shouted above the oncoming roar.

'Secure that spinnaker!' Cloud Wolf screamed. 'And Spiker, get down from the caternest, NOW!'

Twig had never heard such urgency in Cloud Wolf's voice before. What must it look like, he wondered, this Great Storm which filled his father – the esteemed Quintinius Verginix – with so much terror and awe? He had to see for himself.

Hand over hand, he pulled himself along a crossbeam towards the hull. Although there were no portholes down this deep in the sky ship, the cracks between the curving planks of lufwood were, in places, wide enough to see through. Wedge-shaped chinks of light sliced through the gloom. Reaching the hull at last, Twig knelt down and peered into the cracks.

Below him, he saw the featureless wasteland of the Mire stretching out in every direction. The white mud rippled in the wind, as if the entire wasteland had been transformed into a vast ocean. And there, to complete the illusion, was a ship.

'Except it's not sailing,' Twig muttered as he squinted at the distant shipwreck. 'And probably never will again.'

As the *Stormchaser* sped onwards, Twig realized that the ship had not been abandoned. There was someone there: a tall, thin figure, brandishing his fist at the sky. As colourless as his surroundings, he was well camouflaged. Twig wouldn't have noticed him at all had it not been for the bright lightning of the approaching storm glinting on the dagger clenched in his fist.

Was it the storm he was cursing? Twig wondered. Or was it the sight of the *Stormchaser* itself, passing over-

head, that had filled the curious bleached individual with such anger?

The next instant, both he and the shipwreck were gone. Lightning-dazzle briefly lit up the flat-head's disgusting quarters. The air crackled and hissed. Twig struggled to his feet and peered through a chink higher up the hull, wincing as the onrush of air stung his eyes. He wiped his tears away on his sleeve and squinted back through the gap in the wood.

'Sky above!' he cried out.

Directly in front of the sky ship, and obliterating everything else from view, was a rolling, tumbling, heaving wall of furious purple and black. The noise of the blast was deafening – like a never-ending explosion. Louder still, was the creak and groan of the *Stormchaser* itself.

As Twig maintained his gaze, so more lightning was discharged. It streaked across the curving surface of the Great Storm like a network of electric rivers, and imploded in circles of pink and green.

The din grew louder than ever; the lightning, brighter still. And all the while, the *Stormchaser* shook and rattled as the seconds to impact ticked unstoppably past. Twig wrapped both arms around the beam to his left, and tensed his legs.

Five . . . four . . . three . . .

*Wheeeiiiiiiiiii* whistled the wind, its high-pitched whine rising to an ear-splitting scream.

Two . . .

The sky ship had never travelled so fast before. Twig clung on for dear life as it hurtled onwards.

One . . . And . . .

*WHOOOMPH!!*

Like a falling leaf in an autumn gale, the *Stormchaser* was abruptly seized and whisked off by the spinning wind. It listed hard to port with a fearful lurch. Twig was torn from the beam and hurled back across the straw-strewn floor.

'Aaaii!' he cried out as he flew through the air. He landed heavily, with a thud; his head jerked sharply back and struck the side of Mugbutt's berth with a loud *crack*.

Everything went black.

Mugbutt looked down and smirked. 'That's it, *Master* Twig,' he said, 'you stay here by my side where I can keep an eye on you.'

Above deck, it was all the captain and his crew could do to keep the *Stormchaser* airborne. While Hubble held the wheel in his powerful grasp, Cloud Wolf's fingers played over the keyboard of levers.

Twenty years it was since he had studied in the Knights' Academy; twenty years since he had learned about the finer points of stormchasing – and twenty years is a long time in which to forget. As Cloud Wolf raised this weight a fraction and lowered that sail a tad, it was instinct rather than memory that guided him.

'Stormchasing!' he murmured reverently.

On and on, they were drawn, whistling across the sky in the slip-stream of the Great Storm. Slowly, slowly and little by little, Cloud Wolf used the dry, turbulent currents to inch his way along the outer edge of the storm and on towards the front.

'Whoa, there, my beauty,' he whispered to the *Stormchaser*. 'Easy now.' Tentatively, he lowered the prow-weight – a fraction of a degree at a time. The sky ship bowed forwards.

'Raise the mainsail!' he ordered. Tem Barkwater and Stope Boltjaw stared at one another in confusion. What madness was this to raise the mainsail in such a wind? Surely they had misheard. 'RAISE THAT ACCURSED MAIN-SAIL, BEFORE I HAVE YOU SKY-FIRED!' the captain raged.

Tem and Stope Boltjaw leapt to it. And as the sail flapped and billowed, Cloud Wolf offered up a little prayer that he would be virtuous for ever more – if the sailcloth would just hold.

'Now, let's see,' he muttered through clenched teeth as he returned his attention to the weight-levers. 'Up with the peri-hull-weights, and down with the port hull-weights, small . . .' The *Stormchaser* trembled. 'Medium . . .' It leaned to the left. 'And large . . .'

As the third weight was lowered, the *Stormchaser* – still held in place by the raised mainsail at the front of the driving storm – began slowly to turn. Cloud Wolf stared down at his compass. Bit by bit the sky ship was shifting round to the thirty-five degree angle required to penetrate safely to the centre of the storm.

Forty-five degrees, he read off. Forty. Thirty-seven . . . Thirty-six . . .

'LOWER THE MAINSAIL!' he bellowed.

This time neither Tem Barkwater nor Stope Boltjaw needed telling twice. They unhitched the rope. The sail fell. The sky ship slowed, and was instantly swallowed up by the dense billowing clouds of purple and black. They were entering the Great Storm.

The air was blinding, choking. It crackled and fizzed. It smelled of ammonia, of sulphur, of rotten eggs.

All around them, the wind thrashed and battered. It pummelled the hulls and threatened, at any moment, to snap the creaking mast in two.

'Just a little further, my lovely one,' Cloud Wolf urged the *Stormchaser* gently. 'You can do it. You can bring us safely to the centre of the Great Storm.'

Even as he spoke, however, the sky ship shuddered as if to say, no, no it could not. Cloud Wolf threw an anxious glance at the compass. It was back at forty-five degrees. The wind was hitting them full on. The juddering grew more violent. Much more, and the sky ship would be shaken to pieces.

With trembling hands, Cloud Wolf raised the three starboard hull-weights as high as they would go. The *Stormchaser* swung back. The fearful judders subsided.

'Thank Sky,' Cloud Wolf said, as he seized the opportunity to wipe the sweat from his brow. He turned to Hubble by his side. 'Hold tight,' he instructed. 'Any second now and . . . YES!' he yelled – for at that moment, the compass point swung round to thirty-five degrees and the *Stormchaser* plunged through the violent, violet storm and into the eerie stillness within.

'RAISE THE MAINSAIL!' he bellowed, his voice echoing as if he was standing in a huge cavern. If they were not to fly out the far side of the storm, the sky ship's momentum would have to be brought under control. The sail should – if he had remembered his studies accurately – act like a brake. 'RAISE *ALL* THE SAILS!'

At first nothing seemed to happen to the sky ship as it continued to hurtle on towards the back of the storm. The flashing fingers of lightning which fanned out before them, came closer and closer. Tem Barkwater, Stope Boltjaw, Spiker and the others leaped to the ropes – even the Professor of Light joined in. Together, they hoisted the sails up, one after the other after the other. And as the sail-sheets rose, so the *Stormchaser* finally slowed down.

Before they came to a complete standstill, Cloud Wolf lifted the port hull-weights, lowered the starboard hull-weights and – when they had turned right about – pulled the prow-weight back to its original position.

Now facing the way the Great Storm itself was travelling, the *Stormchaser* sailed on within it. All around him, Cloud Wolf could hear the excited cheering of his crew. But he knew better than to celebrate too soon. Pin-point accuracy was essential if the *Stormchaser* was to maintain its position – one weight too low, one sail too high, and the sky ship would hurtle to one side of the storm and be spat into open sky.

'Hold a steady course, Hubble,' the captain said. 'And Spiker,' he called, 'how long before we cross into the Twilight Woods?'

' 'Bout twelve minutes,' the oakelf called back.

Cloud Wolf nodded grimly. 'I want you all – each and every one – to keep a watchful eye for the lightning bolt,' he commanded. 'If we are to retrieve the stormphrax, we must see exactly – and I *mean* exactly – where it lands.'

Back below deck, Twig slithered this way and that over the hard, wooden floor as the *Stormchaser* continued to pitch and toss. Every jolt, every jerk, every judder which was felt above deck, was magnified a hundredfold by the time it reached the bowels of the sky ship where he lay. Yet all the while Twig had not stirred. It was only at that moment when the *Stormchaser* finally pierced the wild outer edges of the turbulent storm that his eyelids had fluttered.

He became aware of voices behind him. Hushed and plotting voices: familiar voices. Taking care to remain as still as possible, Twig listened.

'. . . and I don't think the captain will put up much of a fight when he discovers what will happen to his captive son if he does,' Slyvo Spleethe was whispering. 'So, for the time being, Mugbutt, I want you to keep him down here.'

'Down here,' the flat-head whispered back.

'Until I come for him,' said Spleethe. He paused. 'I'll have to choose my moment very carefully.'

'Very carefully,' Mugbutt repeated.

'After all, stormchasing is a hazardous business,' Spleethe continued. 'I shall wait until Cloud Wolf has retrieved the stormphrax – before disposing of him.' He laughed unpleasantly. 'Let him do all the hard work, and then reap the rewards.'

'The rewards,' said Mugbutt.

'And what rewards they are to be!' Spleethe said. 'Captain of a sky pirate ship *and* Leaguesmaster! You stick with me, Mugbutt,' he added breathlessly, 'and you shall have wealth and power beyond your wildest dreams.'

'Wildest dreams,' the flat-head chuckled.

'And now I must leave you,' said Spleethe. 'I don't want the captain to become suspicious. And remember, Mugbutt. Keep Twig well guarded. I'm depending on you.'

As the sound of the receding footsteps faded away, Twig trembled with horror. What a fool he had been to listen to so shiftless a rogue. The quartermaster was intent on mutiny and – if he had understood him correctly – was planning to use Twig against his father to ensure that his wicked plans bore fruit.

Somehow, before that happened, he would have to warn Cloud Wolf – even if it did mean having to confront his father's wrath.

He opened one eye slightly, and peered out at the ferocious flat-head goblin. The question was, how?

## ·CHAPTER TEN·

# CONFESSION

A sound, unfamiliar to the Inner Sanctum, echoed round the gold-embossed ceiling of the chamber. It was the sound of humming. Although utterly tuneless, it bounced along with unmistakable joy and optimism.

The servants – and there were many who tended to the Inner Sanctum and its important occupant – were under strict instructions to maintain complete silence at all times. And music of any kind – humming, singing, whistling – was particularly frowned upon. Only the week before, old Jervis – a loyal servant for more than forty seasons – had been caught crooning a lullaby under his breath. (He had recently become a great-grandfather.) For this moment of mindless contentment he was dismissed on the spot.

It was not, however, a servant humming now. The sound came from the thin lips and pudgy nose of the

Most High Academe of Sanctaphrax. For Vilnix Pompolnius was feeling exceedingly pleased with himself.

'Hmm, hmm, hmmm. Pom pom pom pom,' he continued as he busied about. 'Pom pom pom . . .' He paused and chuckled as the details of the previous evening came back to him. He had been dining with Simenon Xintax, and a most illuminating meal it had proved to be.

As a rule, the Leaguesmaster was far from his favourite dinner guest. He was, as far as Vilnix Pompolnius was concerned, an ill-mannered oaf – he slurped his soup, he chewed with his mouth open, and he belched loudly after every course. Yet it served Vilnix well to keep him sweet. If it wasn't for the support he received from the leagues, his own grip on power would soon evaporate.

As always, Xintax had eaten and drunk too much. Not that Vilnix objected. In fact he positively encouraged the Leaguesmaster's gluttony, piling seconds and thirds onto his plate and keeping his glass constantly topped up with Xintax's favourite woodbrew. After all, as his grandmother had so often said, *a full stomach and a loose tongue oft go hand in hand*. The Leaguesmaster's tongue had started to loosen during dessert. By the time the cheese and crackers were served, he was practically babbling.

'Mother Horsefeather, she's the one, she... *bwurrrp*... 'Scuse me!' He paused to wipe his mouth on his sleeve. 'She's only gone and organized a trip to the Twilight Woods, hasn't she? Her, the Professor of Light, and a sky pirate captain – can't remember his name just now ... Anyway, they're all in it together. They're ... *bwulchh* ... Whoops.' He giggled. 'They're planning on returning with a whole cargo of stormphrax,' he explained and pressed his finger to his lips conspiratorially. 'It's meant to be a secret,' he said.

'Then how have you come by this information?' Vilnix Pompolnius demanded.

Xintax tapped his nose knowingly with his finger. 'A cry in the spew,' he slurred and giggled again. 'I mean, a spy in the crew. Spleethe. Told us everything, he did.' Then he had leaned forwards, seized Vilnix chummily by the sleeve and grinned leerily up at his face. 'We're going to be rich beyond belief.'

'Pom pom pom pom,' Vilnix hummed, as the words came back to him. Rich beyond belief! At least, he thought, *one* of us is.

At that moment, there was a respectful knock at the door and the tousled head of his personal manservant, Minulis, appeared. 'If you please, your Most High Academe,' he said, 'the prisoner has been prepared and awaits your attention.'

'Ah, yes,' Vilnix nodded, and smiled unpleasantly. 'I shall be there, directly.'

As Minulis closed the door behind him, Vilnix rubbed his hands together gleefully. 'First Xintax spilling the beans, now this Forficule character dropping into our lap – my my, Vilnix, aren't *we* the lucky Most High Academe!'

He strode across the room to the mirror – the new mirror – and looked at himself. Unlike its predecessor, this mirror had not been hung. Instead, it leaned up against the wall at an angle. It was safer – it was also more flattering. His reflection smiled back at him.

'Oh, no,' he chided. 'That will never do. Whatever should the nightwaif think if I entered the Hall of Knowledge in so effervescent a mood? Prepare yourself, Vilnix,' he said dramatically, and let his dressing-gown fall to the floor. 'Make yourself ready.'

And doing what he always did before an important encounter, the Most High Academe of Sanctaphrax dressed himself up in the specially fashioned garments of high office – clothes which would help focus his mind, heighten his senses and darken his mood.

First, he pulled on the hair-shirt over his bare, scaly skin. Then, wincing as the protruding nails dug into the soles of his feet, he stepped into his sandals and bound them tightly. Next, he rubbed a stinging unguent over his freshly shaven head, and lowered the steel skull-cap onto his head until the internal spikes pressed into his scalp. Last of all, he took his shabby roughspin gown, swung it over his shoulders and raised the hood.

With each item of clothing he put on, the Most High Academe's good humour gradually drained away. By

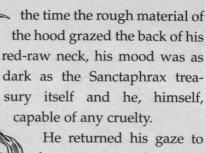

the time the rough material of the hood grazed the back of his red-raw neck, his mood was as dark as the Sanctaphrax treasury itself and he, himself, capable of any cruelty.

He returned his gaze to the mirror and glared approvingly at his reflection. Seldom, if ever, had Vilnix Pompolnius looked so gaunt, so imposing. He arched one eyebrow.

'So, Forficule, my little messenger bird,' he said. 'I am ready for you now. How I am looking forward to hearing you sing!'

The Hall of Knowledge – as the interrogation chamber was euphemistically known – was situated at the top of a tower in the west-wing of the vast palace. The only access was through a concealed door in the upper corridor, and up a circular stone staircase.

With every step he climbed, the nails in his sandals dug sharply into his feet. By the time he reached the top, Vilnix Pompolnius was cursing under his breath. He threw the door open and strode inside. 'Where is the horrible little pipsqueal, then?' he demanded.

Minulis trotted over, closed the door and ushered the Most High Academe across the room. Despite its airy position, the windowless chamber was as dark and dank as any dungeon. The only light came from the two flaming torches fixed to the wall, and a golden glow which gleamed on the array of polished pokers, pincers, and pliers laid out ready.

Forficule himself was seated in an upright chair, so large it seemed almost to be swallowing him up. His ankles were bound, his wrists had been tied to the arm-rests, and his neck secured to a head-support by a leather strap: he could not move. As Vilnix Pompolnius approached him, Forficule glanced up. An icy shiver ran the length of his body.

'Ah, *there* you are,' said Vilnix. 'So good of you to drop by.' He sneered. 'I trust you're sitting comfortably.'

As he moved closer, Forficule shuddered. Behind the harmless words were thoughts no person should ever have.

'I understand you are a nightwaif,' Vilnix continued.

'No, no,' said Forficule, and laughed nervously. 'Many have made the same mistake. I am an oakelf,' he said. 'The runt of the litter.'

Vilnix Pompolnius sighed as the spikes of the steel skull-cap bit into his scalp. 'You will have noticed the interesting design of the chair,' he continued, running his fingers over the concave bowl of burnished silver which was fixed over Forficule's head. 'It amplifies sound,' he said, and flicked it lightly.

The metal chimed and Forficule, whose head had been secured at the point where the sound waves collided, winced with pain.

'I would advise you *not* to lie to me,' said Vilnix, and flicked the metal bowl a second time.

'I . . . I don't understand. Why have you brought me here?' Forficule trembled as the ringing in his ears slowly subsided. 'I came to Sanctaphrax from Undertown, in all good faith, to inform you about the tragic death of the Professor of Light . . .'

'Forficule, Forficule,' Vilnix purred. 'This is not good.'

He turned away and selected a pair of pincers. Forficule quivered with horror as he overheard precisely what the Most High Academe was thinking of doing with them. Worse and worse the imagined tortures became, until Forficule could stand it no more.

'Stop it!' he pleaded, his ears fluttering with distress.

Vilnix spun round, pincers in one hand, tapping them in the other. 'Oakelf, eh?' he said.

Forficule sniffed. 'I *am* a nightwaif,' he confessed.

Vilnix Pompolnius nodded. 'That's better,' he said,

and added – in his thoughts alone – from now on, I want the truth and nothing but the truth. He brandished the pincers, and imagined them smashing hard against the metal bowl above the chair. Do you understand me?

'Yes,' said Forficule simply.

'Now, who sent you?'

'I came of my own accord,' said Forficule.

Without saying a word, Vilnix strode up to him, and struck the bowl sharply. Forficule howled with pain.

'No, no,' he whimpered.

'Then tell me who?' barked Vilnix.

'Mother Horsefeather,' said Forficule. 'She thought you ought to know – the professor being an academic of Sanctaphrax, and all. He . . . he was in her tavern – the Bloodoak – when he had a . . . a seizure. Keeled over, he did. We did everything we could to revive him.'

'But, nevertheless, you failed,' Vilnix said.

'Sadly, yes,' said Forficule.

Vilnix narrowed his eyes. 'And where is the good professor's body now?' he asked.

'I . . . errm . . . that is, with it being so hot and all, Mother Horsefeather thought he should be buried as soon as possible.'

'You have interred a professor of Sanctaphrax in the ground?' Vilnix gasped. 'Do you not know that it is the right of every academic of our great floating city to have his body ceremonially laid out in the Stone Gardens, where the white ravens will pick his bones? How else is his spirit to rise up to open sky?'

'I . . . we . . .'

'But then, of course, the situation will not arise,' said Vilnix thrusting his head forwards into Forficule's face until his shining skull-cap grazed the tip of the night-waif's nose. 'Because he isn't dead. Is he?'

'Yes, yes,' said Forficule. 'He is.'

Vilnix straightened up abruptly, raised the pincers and slammed them against the metal bowl. 'Lies! Lies! Lies! Lies!' he screamed in time to the deafening hammer blows. 'And more and more and *more* lies!'

After seven blows, he let his arm fall limp. 'Now will you tell me the truth,' he said.

Forficule didn't answer. Although he had seen the angry lips move, he hadn't heard a single word above the pounding, crackling, screeching cacophony of noise inside his head. It was several minutes before he could make out any sounds again, and even then, the echoing din continued in the background.

'THIS IS YOUR FINAL CHANCE!' Vilnix was bellowing.

Forficule lowered his gaze. He shivered miserably. There was a saying among the fragile nightwaifs. *Better dead than deaf.*

'All right,' he whimpered. 'I'll tell you everything I know.'

And that was what he did. He told Vilnix every detail of the meeting which had taken place in the back room of the Bloodoak tavern. Of the entrance of the Professor of Light, and how the sky pirate captain had fallen to his knees. Of the plan the three of them had hatched up. Of the Professor of Light's decision to accompany the sky pirates on their quest to the Twilight woods.

'The treacherous cur,' Vilnix spat. 'And this captain?' he said. 'Has he a name?'

'Cloud Wolf,' said Forficule promptly. 'Though the Professor of Light addressed him by a different name.'

'Which was?'

'Quintinius Verginix,' came the reply.

Vilnix nodded. 'Now, there's a name to conjure with,' he said thoughtfully.

The nightwaif's thorough, if belated, confession had proved very interesting to Vilnix Pompolnius. Not only did it confirm what he suspected about the Professor of Light, but he now also knew that Xintax had lied to him the night before. *No-one* could forget the name of Cloud Wolf – the sky pirate captain was infamous. The Leaguesmaster himself must be planning something underhand.

Vilnix chuckled to himself. There were many other ambitious leaguesmen who would be only too happy to strike a deal with the Most High Academe.

He turned back to Forficule. 'And this youth you mentioned,' he said. 'This Twig. What is he to the assembled gathering?'

Forficule swallowed. Although he hadn't known Twig long, he had liked what he heard in the boy's head. His thoughts were decent and honest, loyal and true. He would hate to think that something he said might mean that the boy came to harm.

Vilnix dangled the heavy pincers in front of his face. Forficule nodded, as much as the leather strap would allow, and continued. 'He is a crew-member on board the *Stormchaser*,' he said.

'And?' said Vilnix Pompolnius, sensing he was on to something.

'He was born and raised in the Deepwoods,' he said.

'And?'

Forficule shuddered. If he made it clear that Twig was not relevant to the plan, perhaps the youth would be left in peace. 'He is not to accompany the pirates on this particular trip,' he said. 'He is to stay with Mother Horsef . . .'

Vilnix cut him short. 'There is something you're not telling me,' he said, and raised the pincers threateningly.

Forficule looked down. Tears welled up in his eyes. He was not a bad creature – but neither was he brave. The pincers hovered in the torchlight next to the metal bowl. Better dead than deaf.

'He . . . he is . . .' he faltered. 'That is . . . Cloud Wolf is his father.'

Vilnix breathed in sharply. 'A son,' he hissed. 'Quintinius Verginix has a son. And he has left him behind,' he smirked. 'How very careless.' He turned to Minulis. 'We must introduce ourselves to the lad forthwith,' he said. 'We shall invite him back here to Sanctaphrax, to await the return of his valiant father.'

He turned back to Forficule. 'What a splendid little bargaining chip you have given us,' he said, as he returned the heavy pincers to the shelf. 'I can't tell you how grateful we are.'

Forficule felt wretched. His attempt to protect Twig had failed, and now the youth was in mortal danger. And yet – Sky forgive him! – he couldn't help but be relieved that the Most High Academe seemed so pleased with the information.

'Am I free to go, then?' he asked.

Vilnix looked round at him, and smiled. Forficule stared back, hoping. With his head still echoing from the deafening noise of metal crashing on metal, he was unable to hear the dark thoughts lurking behind the Most High Academe's smiling face.

'Free to go?' Vilnix Pompolnius said at last. His eyes twinkled. 'Oh, yes. Quite free.'

Forficule gasped for joy.

Vilnix nodded to Minulis. 'Unbind him and throw him out,' he said. Then, as the hair-shirt itched and the spikes and nails dug into the Most High Academe's head and feet, he added, 'But first, cut off his ears.'

# ·CHAPTER ELEVEN·

# THE EYE OF THE STORM

Twig lay some way from Mugbutt's filthy straw-covered quarters. He was still pretending to be unconscious. Each time the *Stormchaser* pitched and tossed he would roll over a little further, hoping that the flat-head would assume it was the movement of the boat shifting him across the floor. Slowly – painfully slowly – he was manoeuvring himself towards the staircase. One chance at escape, that was all he would get.

Stupid! Stupid! Stupid! he told himself. Not only had he disobeyed his father, but he'd left him at the mercy of treacherous mutineers – just as Cloud Wolf had feared might happen.

The sky ship lurched sharply to the left and Twig rolled over twice. The stairs were getting closer.

It was so obvious that Spleethe was up to no good, Twig continued angrily to himself. He never liked you.

You should've realized why he was being so friendly! 'Oh, Sky above,' he murmured. 'What have I done?'

The sky ship listed to starboard and Twig had to brace himself against the floor to stop himself being propelled back to Mugbutt's berth. Through the crack in his eyelids he watched the flat-head snuffling through the soiled straw for any bits of meat he might have missed.

Disgusting creature, he thought, and trembled. And a formidable fighter . . .

At that moment, the *Stormchaser* reared up like a prowlgrin charger, tilted abruptly to port and dropped in the sky. With his heart in his mouth, Twig rolled the last few yards towards the bottom of the stairs. There he hesitated and looked back. The sky ship reared up a second time and there was a loud crash as Mugbutt lost his balance and tumbled to the floor.

Now! Twig said to himself. Get out while you can.

He leapt to his feet, gripped the wooden rails fiercely and climbed the steep set of stairs as quickly as his trembling legs would allow.

'OY!' Mugbutt bellowed, when he realized what was happening. 'Where are you going?'

Twig didn't wait to reply. 'Come on!' he urged himself desperately. He was halfway up the stairs, yet the hatch at the top looked no nearer. 'Come *on!*'

Already, Mugbutt had climbed to his feet, vaulted over the bars which enclosed his berth and was racing headlong towards him. Six more steps he had to go, and Mugbutt was there at the bottom. Five . . . four . . . Twig could feel the entire staircase tremble as the heavy

flat-head hurried up behind him. Three . . . two . . .

'Nearly there,' Twig muttered. 'One more step and . . .'
All at once, he felt the horny hand of the flat-head goblin
grasping at his ankle. 'No!' he screamed and kicked back
with both legs.

Shoving the hinged hatch open with shaking hands,
Twig launched himself up and pulled himself through

the narrow opening. He knelt down beside the hole. Mugbutt's spatula fingers appeared at the rim. Twig leaned forwards, seized the hatch door and slammed it down with all his strength.

There was an agonizing cry. The fingers disappeared from view and from below the hatch came the muffled sound of Mugbutt tumbling back down the staircase. Twig had done it! He'd escaped – yet already, he could hear the flat-head pounding back up the stairs.

With his heart thumping, Twig slid the heavy bolts across the hatchway and, to make doubly sure, heaved a huge barrel of pickled tripweed across the floor until it came to rest on the hatch door. Then, leaping to his feet, he headed for the next flight of stairs – the flight which would take him up on to the deck itself. As he began climbing, the sound of furious hammering and cursing exploded behind him.

Let the hatch hold, Twig prayed. Please!

Up on deck and completely unaware of the drama that had been unfolding below them, the captain and crew of the *Stormchaser* were struggling to keep the sky ship air-borne as the mighty ball of cloud crackled and flashed across the sky.

'Double bind the tolley-ropes,' Cloud Wolf bellowed as the Great Storm hurtled on towards the Twilight Woods. It was essential that he maintain the *Stormchaser*'s position at its very centre. 'Draw in the studsail. Untangle those jib lines!'

The atmosphere was, in every sense, electric. Tiny filaments of hissing blue light fuzzed the outline of the sky ship. They fizzed. They sparked. They danced on every surface, from bowsprit to rudder-wheel, masthead to hull. They danced on the sails, the ropes, the decks. And they danced on the sky pirates themselves – on their beards, their clothes, their fingers and toes; setting their entire bodies tingling.

Tem Barkwater was turning a handspike. 'Can't say as I like this over-much,' he grumbled as the sparking blue light played all round his hands.

Stope Boltjaw looked up from the skysail he was busy repairing. 'It's *ah* playing ha-*ah*-voc with my *ah* jaw,' he gasped.

Tem grinned.

'It's not *ah* fu-*ah*-nny!' he complained.

'But it is!' Tem Barkwater chuckled as his shipmate's lower jaw continued to open and close with a will of its own.

Years earlier, Stope Boltjaw had lost his lower jaw during a fierce battle between his sky pirate ship and two league ships. A notoriously ruthless leaguesman by the name of Ulbus Pentephraxis had crept up on him with his hunting axe, and struck him a savage blow which had caught him sideways on, just below his ear.

When he recovered, Stope had fashioned a replacement from a piece of ironwood. So long as he remembered to keep the bolts well oiled, the false jaw served him well enough – at least, it had done up until now. From the moment the *Stormchaser* penetrated the Great Storm, the curious electrical force had caused it to gape wide and slam shut, time and again – and there was nothing Stope Boltjaw could do to stop it.

'How *ah* much longer *ah* is this going on?' he groaned.

'Till we get to the Twilight Woods, I reckon,' said Tem Barkwater.

'Which will be in approximately . . . nine minutes,' Spiker called down from the rigging.

'Nine minutes,' Slyvo Spleethe repeated gleefully under his breath. The quartermaster, who had been sent to check that the mooring-cleats were holding up, but was now leaning against the poop-deck handrail gazing idly into the hypnotic swirl of the clouds all round them, glanced round.

'Keep it up, Quintinius Verginix,' he sneered. 'Complete your journey to the Twilight Woods. Recover the stormphrax. Then I shall make my move. And woe betide anyone who . . .' He gasped. 'What in Sky's name?'

The sight of Twig, standing in the doorway of the little cabin above the staircase, filled Spleethe with an uncontrolled rage. If Cloud Wolf should also see him, then all would be lost. Without a moment's thought, Spleethe dashed off towards him.

Twig looked about him in a state of bewildered excitement. His narrow escape from the flat-head goblin had left him breathless and edgy. Now, as he took in his surroundings, his heart clamoured more urgently than ever.

The air was purple; it smelled of sulphur, of burnt milk. All around the sky ship, the enveloping clouds boiled and writhed and crackled with blinding lightning. His body tingled as tentacles of blue light wrapped themselves around him, causing every hair to stand on end.

*This* was stormchasing!

The crew were feverishly busy, with Hubble, the ferocious albino banderbear, tethered to the helm, and Cloud Wolf fully occupied with the sail and weight levers as he struggled to maintain both speed and lift. What a time to have to reveal that he had stowed away on board; what a moment to have to break the news of the impending mutiny.

'Yet I have no choice,' Twig muttered grimly. Already, he could hear the wooden hatchway splintering below him. It was only a matter of time before Mugbutt emerged on board. Twig knew that if he didn't speak up now then his father would surely end up dead. He shuddered miserably. 'And it'll all be my fault!'

Bracing himself for the short yet perilous journey from stair-head to helm, Twig was about to set off when a heavy hand slammed down on his shoulders and yanked him back. An ice-cold blade pressed hard at the base of his neck.

'One move, one sound, *Master* Twig, and I'll slit your throat,' Spleethe hissed. 'Understood?'

'Yes,' Twig whispered.

The next instant, he heard a click behind him and found himself being shoved roughly into a store-cupboard filled with buckets and mops, lengths of rope and spare sailcloth. He tumbled backwards and landed heavily in the corner. The door slammed shut.

'Five minutes and counting!' the oakelf's strident voice announced.

Twig climbed shakily to his feet and pressed his ear against the locked door. He could just make out two voices speaking in conspiratorial whispers above the continuing roar and rattle. One was Spleethe's. The other was Mugbutt's.

'I'm not to blame,' the flat-head was whining. 'He'd escaped before I had a chance to stop him.'

'You should have kept him tied up,' came Spleethe's irritated reply. 'Curse that Twig!' he said. 'Someone's bound to find him before the stormphrax has been retrieved ...'

'I could finish him off now,' Mugbutt suggested coldly.

'No,' said Spleethe. 'We need him alive, not dead.' He growled with mounting rage. 'The meddlesome little whelpersnapper has forced my hand and that's a fact. But all is not lost, Mugbutt. Come on. Let's see if we can't turn the situation to our advantage after all.'

As the pair of them departed, Twig felt his heart hammering harder than ever. There he was inside a Great Storm, hurtling on towards the Twilight Woods in search of stormphrax. Finally he was doing what, for so long, he had only dreamed about. And yet, because of him, the dream had become a waking nightmare.

Above him, Spleethe and Mugbutt had made it to the helm. He could hear Spleethe's voice – though not what he said. Twig swallowed nervously and hammered on the door.

'Let me out!' he cried. 'Tem! Spiker! Boltjaw! Oh, why won't you hear me? Let me...'

At that moment Cloud Wolf shouted out. 'What?' he bellowed. 'But this is mutiny!'

Twig shuddered, and hung his head. 'Oh, Father,' he whimpered. 'If we ever get out of this alive will you ever forgive me?'

Confronted by the captain's rage, Spleethe remained icily calm. Apart from his eyes, which glinted beadily behind the steel rims of his glasses, his face betrayed not a hint of emotion.

'Not mutiny,' he said, as he drew his sword from its sheath. 'Merely a redistribution of power.'

Hubble growled ominously.

'This is leaguesman's chatter,' Cloud Wolf snorted. 'Has it really come so far, Spleethe?'

Just then, the *Stormchaser* lurched to the left, and abruptly lost speed. The rear of the storm raced up to meet them. Cloud Wolf lowered the stern weight and raised both the fore and aft sails. The sky ship leapt forwards again.

He turned back to Spleethe. 'Do you seriously imagine for a moment that you could sail the *Stormchaser*? Eh?'

Spleethe hesitated for a moment.

'You are a fool, Spleethe!' Cloud Wolf continued. 'What use have the leagues for stormphrax? Tell me that! It is phraxdust they need, and no-one knows the secret of how to make it safely.'

'On the contrary,' Spleethe replied. 'The League of Free Merchants is prepared to pay highly for a cargo of stormphrax. Very highly indeed. And since you are so reluctant to deliver it to them, then *I* shall. I think you'll find the others are behind me when they realize how much is at stake.'

Mugbutt made a move forwards. Hubble's ears fluttered. Cloud Wolf's hand gripped the hilt of his sword.

'Sky above!' the captain exclaimed. 'Did you not hear me? The leagues have no use for stormphrax. They simply wish to prevent it from reaching the treasury of Sanctaphrax – for if that happened, the floating city would again become stable and their lucrative alliance with the raintasters would fall apart.'

Slyvo Spleethe tightened his grip on his flashing sword.

'They have tricked you, Spleethe. They *want* you to fail.'

'You're lying!' Spleethe screamed, and turned to Mugbutt. 'He's lying!'

Cloud Wolf seized the opportunity. He drew his sword and threw himself at Slyvo Spleethe. 'You mutinous bilge-cur!' he roared.

But Mugbutt was too quick for him. As the captain lunged forwards, he raised his spear – as massive and heavy as befitted the powerful flat-head goblin – and leapt between them. The chiming sound of metal on metal filled the air as the captain and the flat-head launched themselves into deadly battle.

*Clash! Crash! Clang!* The fight continued, fast and furious. Cloud Wolf howled with rage.

'Blood and thunder!' he roared, 'I'll have the pair of you sky-fired!' He parried away the increasingly frenzied attacks from Mugbutt. 'I'll split your gizzards. I'll rip out your treacherous hearts . . .'

'Waah-waah!' the banderbear shouted out, and tore at the ropes that bound him to the helm.

The *Stormchaser* dipped and rolled. If it drifted towards the outer reaches, where the storm was raging at its wildest, the sky ship would be turned to matchwood in an instant.

'No, Hubble,' Cloud Wolf called out urgently. 'I . . . I'm all right. You must hold a steady course.'

The raised voices, the clash of metal, the pounding of feet – Twig could scarcely believe what he was hearing. Was his father fighting on his own? Where were the rest of the crew and why didn't they come to their captain's aid?

'TEM BARKWATER!' he bellowed, and beat his fists desperately against the locked door. 'STOPE BOLTJAW!'

All at once, the door burst open. Twig tumbled forwards and was immediately grasped by Slyvo Spleethe. 'I told you to keep your mouth shut,' he hissed as he wrenched Twig's arm up behind his back with one hand and pressed the knife to his neck with the other.

'Wh . . . what's happening?' Twig said.

'You'll find out soon enough,' Spleethe spat as he frog-marched Twig across the sparking deck. 'Do exactly what I say,' he instructed, 'and you won't get hurt.'

Quaking with terror, Twig was bundled round the

skirting-deck and up the narrow flight of stairs which led to the helm. The scene which greeted him filled him with sickening dread.

Cloud Wolf and Mugbutt were locked in mortal combat. Eyes blazing, jaws set, the pair of them were fighting for their lives. Their weapons clashed together with such ferocity, that spark after dazzling yellow spark jumped up out of the fizzing blue.

Twig wanted to leap forwards and fight by his father's side. He wanted to slay the wicked mutineer who dared to raise his hand against Captain Cloud Wolf.

'Easy now, Master Twig,' Spleethe hissed in his ear, and increased the pressure on the dagger at Twig's neck. 'If you value your life.'

Twig swallowed anxiously. The fight continued. He couldn't look; he couldn't turn away. Now Mugbutt seemed to be winning, now Cloud Wolf had the upper hand. And all the while, the surrounding storm gathered strength. The lightning flashed again and again, illuminating the curdled clouds and glinting on the flashing blades.

There was no grace to the fight, no finesse. Mugbutt, as the stronger of the two, was content to hack and slash away, battering the captain into submission. Twig tensed nervously as he watched Cloud Wolf being driven back towards the far wall.

Spleethe, fearing the youth was going to cry out, clamped his hand over Twig's mouth. 'Patience,' he whispered. 'It will soon be over. And then I shall take my rightful place as captain of the *Stormchaser*. *Captain*

Spleethe,' he mused. 'It has a nice ring to it.'

Oh, Father, Twig thought desperately as Cloud Wolf battled gallantly on. What have I done to you?

'Tem!' he heard him crying out above the rumble of the thunder and clashing of the heavy blades. 'Stopejaw. Spiker.'

But none of the sky pirates heard him. They were too busy keeping the increasingly unstable sky ship airborne.

'The sails are working their way loose,' Tem bellowed, as he heaved round on the sail-wrench. 'Stope, realign the spinnaker bidgets while I try to secure the mainsail. Spiker, see to that tolley-rope.'

'The flight brackets are jammed,' Spiker shouted back, as the sky ship continued to toss and turn. 'Stope, can you help me?'

'I've only got *ah* the *ah* one pair of hands,' Stope grumbled. 'And if I don't *ah* untangle this *ah* nether-fetter soon, we'll all be goners.'

At that moment, a particularly violent gust of wind struck the port bow. Stope Boltjaw cried out as the sky ship listed, and the matted mass of rope and sail was snatched from his hand. At the other end of the sky ship,

Cloud Wolf lost his balance and staggered across the deck.

'Waah!' cried the banderbear. If the other crew members could not come to his captain's aid, then surely he should do something.

'No, Hubble!' Cloud Wolf said breathlessly, as the sky ship lurched back to starboard. 'Keep hold of the helm, or we will all perish. That's an order.'

Tears welled up in Twig's eyes. Even now – as his father's arms grew weak – Cloud Wolf was more concerned with his crew than he was with himself. How valiant he was. How knightly. He, Twig, did not deserve such a father.

*Clash! Crash! Hack and slash!* Mugbutt's spear slammed down time and again, and with such force and speed, that Cloud Wolf could do nothing but defend himself. All at once, the sky lit up with a sudden flash of blinding light, the *Stormchaser* gave another awful lurch and the whole sky ship pitched forwards.

'The mast is cracking!' Spiker screamed.

'Secure the main-fetter!' Tem roared. 'Lower the sails!'

Cloud Wolf, with his face to the stern, stumbled back. Mugbutt was quick to seize the advantage. He leaped forwards and swung savagely with his spear.

Cloud Wolf ducked. The heavy blade missed him by a fraction. Mugbutt roared with fury and lunged again. Twig gasped – then sighed with relief – as Cloud Wolf knocked the flat-head's weapon away just in the nick of time and countered with a sudden attack. His sword thrust forwards at Mugbutt's chest.

Yes! Yes! Twig thought, urging the sword on.

But it was not to be – for at that moment a terrible sound of splintering wood ripped through the air as the mast snapped off, a third of the way up, and came tumbling down.

It crashed onto the deck and tipped over the side, where it remained, suspended in mid-air below the port side. The sky ship listed sharply to the left and threatened to roll right over.

'Cut the ropes,' Tem yelled, as he began slicing through the main-fetter. 'NOW.'

Stope and Spiker leaped to his side and began slicing and slicing at the tangled ropes and rigging. With half the ropes cut, the rest abruptly broke as one under the heavy weight, and the mast dropped down through the sky. The *Stormchaser* rolled back to starboard.

Twig let out a muffled cry as he and Spleethe toppled backwards, and he felt the knife nick the soft skin at his throat. His father was faring even worse. Not only had the sudden jolt thrown Mugbutt out of reach of the thrusting sword, but now Cloud Wolf was staggering towards him, off-balance, sword flailing and utterly defenceless. Twig froze as the flat-head grabbed his spear again and raised it up. Another second and his father would impale himself on the great jagged blade.

'WAAAH!' Hubble roared as he too saw what was about to happen. He tore furiously at the ropes which bound him to the wheel.

Mugbutt, startled by the noise, glanced up and realized, to his horror, how close to the tethered bander-

bear he had ended up standing. One of his mighty arms was raised. Hubble roared again and swung out savagely. Mugbutt leaped desperately to his left – fast, but not fast enough.

The blow caught the flat-head on the arm. It sent the spear spinning off across the deck, and Mugbutt himself hurtling to the floor. Cloud Wolf was on him like a shot. Without a moment's hesitation, he brought his sword down, hard and sharp, severing the goblin's head with a single blow. Then, bloodied sword raised, he turned murderously on Spleethe.

'And now you,' he stormed. 'You . . .' He fell silent. His eyes widened; his jaw dropped. 'Twig!' he muttered.

Slyvo Spleethe sniggered as he pulled the blade oh-so-gently across Twig's throat. 'Drop your weapon,' he said. 'Or your *son* gets it.'

'No,' Twig cried. 'Don't do this for me. You must not.'

Cloud Wolf tossed his sword aside and let his arms drop defencelessly. 'Release the boy,' he said. 'You have no quarrel with him.'

'Maybe I will. Maybe I won't,' Spleethe teased. He put away his dagger, but drew his own sword in a flash. 'Maybe I'll . . .'

The sky cracked and flashed, and the *Stormchaser* pitched wildly, first to one side, then to the other. The sky ship was drifting perilously close to the edge of the storm – and there was nothing Hubble could do to stop it.

Then all at once and before anyone realized what he was doing, Spleethe let go of Twig. He shoved him to the floor and raced headlong at the captain, sword raised.

'Aaaaaa!' he screamed.

The sky ship shuddered violently. Every beam, every plank, every joint creaked in protest.

'Two minutes, and counting,' Twig heard Spiker calling – then, with sudden alarm, 'Tem! Boltjaw! The captain's in trouble!'

At long last the others had noticed that something was wrong. But too late. Far too late. Already Spleethe's sword was slicing down through the air towards Cloud Wolf's exposed neck.

Below the hull, one of the port hull-weights was being shaken loose. Abruptly, it broke free and tumbled down through the sky. The *Stormchaser* keeled to starboard.

The sword landed heavily, missing its target, but burying itself deep in the top of Cloud Wolf's arm – his sword arm. Slyvo Spleethe's lip curled. 'You were lucky that time,' he said. 'You will not be so lucky again.' He raised the sword a second time. '*I* am captain now!'

'Hubble!' Twig cried out desperately. '*Do* something!'

'Wuh-wuh!' the banderbear bellowed, and gripped the wheel. The captain had told him – *ordered* him – to stay put.

For a moment, their eyes met. 'Wuh-wuh,' said Twig.

'WAAH!' Hubble roared. Mind made up, his eyes blazed and his hair bristled as he ripped the ropes from their moorings, and tore them to pieces as if they were made of paper. 'WAAAH!'

A shaggy white mountain, he stormed towards Spleethe in a flurry of flashing claws and bared teeth. He seized the scurrilous quartermaster round the waist, raised him up in the air and slammed him furiously back down onto the deck. Then, before Spleethe could so much as move a muscle, the banderbear roared again and came crashing down on the quartermaster's back.

There was a thud. There was a crack. Slyvo Spleethe was dead – his spine broken in two.

Twig climbed shakily to his feet, and desperately clung hold of the balustrade as the storm-tossed sky ship pitched and rolled, totally out of control. The mutinous usurpers might have been dealt with and his father's life spared – but the situation was grim.

With no-one now at the helm, the wheel was spinning, while the sails that remained flapped uselessly overhead. Below the hull, two more of the balance-weights shook themselves loose. The *Stormchaser* tossed and twisted, bucked and dived. Round and round it spun, threatening at any moment to tip upside down and scatter the hapless crew to certain death below.

Cloud Wolf struggled to pull himself up with his one good arm, wincing with pain as he did so. Tem Barkwater who, with the others, had finally made it to the bridge, struggled to get to him.

'Leave me!' Cloud Wolf cried fiercely.

A blinding flash tore across the sky, lighting up the *Stormchaser* and revealing the true extent of its damage. Any second now, it would break up completely. Cloud Wolf spun round to face his crew.

'ABANDON SHIP!' he bellowed.

The crew stared back at him incredulously. What madness was this? Abandon ship, when they were on the verge of reaching their destination?

At that moment, the air all round them exploded with the clamour of countless small birds as they billowed up from the bowels of the ship. Their triangular wings and whiplash tails, all frantically beating, flashed black against the dazzling background. Thousands of them,

there
were,
yet they
flew with
s i n g l e
intent. When
one turned, they
all turned.
Squawking, squeaking,
screeching, the flock
wheeled this way and that as if
to the command of some unseen
choreographer.

'Ratbirds,' Tem murmured with horror. He
knew – as did every sky pirate – that ratbirds only

abandon a sky ship that is truly doomed. He spun round. 'You heard the cap'n,' he bellowed. 'Abandon ship!'

'And alert both the Stone Pilot and the professor,' Cloud Wolf called out.

'Aye aye, cap'n,' said Tem Barkwater, and staggered off to do the captain's bidding.

Spiker was the first to go. As he threw himself from the balustrade he called back, 'We are crossing into the Twilight Woods . . . Now!'

The rest of the crew soon followed him. Despite the awful danger of remaining on the *Stormchaser* a moment too long, one by one they knelt down and kissed the deck, before climbing reluctantly up onto the side and leaping off into the purple air. Stope Boltjaw. The Stone Pilot. Tem Barkwater and the Professor of Light. As the blast of air struck them, so the spring mechanism of their parawings leapt up, the wind pockets inflated with air and they glided off and away.

Back on the bridge, Cloud Wolf was making his way to the helm, step by agonizing step, as the sky ship continued to judder and jolt.

'You too, Hubble,' he shouted at the steadfast banderbear. 'Leave your post. Go!' The great beast surveyed him dolefully. The sails fluttered and tore. 'Now!' roared Cloud Wolf. 'Before the sky ship goes down.'

'Wuh-wuh,' he cried, and lurched off to obey. As he moved away, Cloud Wolf saw that the banderbear had been shielding a second member of the crew who had not yet left the sky ship.

'Twig!' he barked. 'I told you to go.'

The swirling clouds squirmed. The *Stormchaser* shuddered and creaked.

'But I can't! I won't leave you!' Twig cried out. 'Oh, forgive me, Father. This is all my fault.'

'Your fault?' Cloud Wolf grunted as he struggled to take control of the helm. 'It is *I* who is to blame – leaving you at the mercy of that scoundrel Spleethe.'

'But . . .'

'Enough!' roared Cloud Wolf. 'Leave now!'

'Come with me!' Twig pleaded.

Cloud Wolf said nothing. There was no need. Twig knew that his father would sooner lose his own life than his ship.

'Then I'll stay with you!' he said defiantly.

'Twig! Twig!' Cloud Wolf cried, his voice barely audible above the rush and rumble of the storm. 'I may lose my ship. I may yet lose my life. And if that is my fate, then so be it. But if I lost you ... It would ...' He paused. 'Twig, my son. I love you. But you must leave. For you and for me. You understand, don't you?'

Tears welling in his eyes, Twig nodded.

'Good boy,' said Cloud Wolf. Then, lurching awkwardly from one side to the other, he hurriedly unbuckled his sword-belt, wrapped it round the scabbard and thrust out his hand. 'Take my sword,' he said.

Twig reached forwards. His fingers grazed his father's hand. 'We will see each other again, won't we?' he sniffed.

'You can depend on it,' said Cloud Wolf. 'When I regain control of the *Stormchaser* I shall be back for you all. Now go,' he said, and abruptly returned his attention to the rows of weight and sail levers.

Sadly, Twig turned to leave. When he reached the outer balustrade, Twig looked round and stole a final look at his father. 'Fare fortune!' he cried to the blasting wind, and launched himself into the air.

The next instant he screamed out in terror. He was dropping like a stone. The parawings must have been damaged when Spleethe had thrown him into the store-cupboard. Now they were jammed. They would not open.

'Father!' he screamed. 'FA-THER!'

# ·CHAPTER TWELVE·

# INTO THE TWILIGHT WOODS

Twig screwed his eyes tightly shut as he fell, faster and faster. If ever he had needed the caterbird – who, since Twig had been there at its hatching, had sworn to watch over him – then surely it was now. Yet, as he continued to tumble through the sky, the caterbird failed to appear.

The air sped past Twig, snatching his breath away. He had all but abandoned hope when, suddenly, he heard a loud click. The mechanism on the parawings sprang up, the wings flew open and – *whooopf* – the silken pockets billowed out. Caught by the wind, Twig was tossed back upwards like a leaf in a gale.

He opened his eyes, and struggled to right himself. It was the first time Twig had had to perform a real emergency leap, yet when he pushed his legs back and his arms forward, as he had been taught, he found

himself gliding effortlessly with the wind. 'Flying,' Twig cried excitedly, as the wind sent his hair streaming back behind him. 'I'm flaaaah-ying!'

All round him, the air crackled and hummed. Something was happening. Something new; something bizarre. The lightning which, up until that moment, had been confined to the surrounding wall of cloud, suddenly began darting forwards to the centre of the storm in long, wispy threads. They danced and spiralled and began weaving themselves together in a ball of electric light.

Twig gazed in wonder. 'This is it,' he whispered excitedly. 'The Great Storm must be about to discharge its single mighty lightning bolt.' His hair stood on end; his head thrilled with anticipation. 'This is what it has all been building up to. This is what we came to see – the creation of stormphrax.'

The ball of light grew larger and larger, and larger still. Twig winced. He couldn't tear his eyes away – yet neither could he look without blinking. And when he did blink, he noticed something small and dark at the centre of the pinky-green afterglow.

'The *Stormchaser*,' he gasped.

He blinked again. There was no doubt. The sky ship was in the middle of the lightning ball which was, itself, in the middle of the Great Storm. And there at the very centre of it all, was his father, Cloud Wolf: Quintinius Verginix – the finest scholar ever to have passed out from the Knights' Academy – still valiantly holding his beloved *Stormchaser* on course. Twig's heart swelled with pride.

The humming noise grew louder and higher. The light grew more intense. The charged air itself seemed to tremble with foreboding.

What was going to happen?

Behind him, Twig felt sudden turbulence that heralded the rear of the Great Storm. It buffeted at his back and set him dipping and diving. His parawings creaked and strained, and Twig could do nothing but hold on and pray that they would not be torn from his shoulders.

Above him, the dazzling streaks of lightning were gradually fading as the electrical force was drained from the clouds. Twig's hair abruptly lay flat. All the energy of the storm was now encapsulated in that single ball of lightning. It hovered in mid-air, throbbing with energy, pulsing with light, roaring with life.

Twig held his breath as he continued to glide slowly downwards. His heart was pounding, his palms were wet. 'Sky protect me,' he murmured anxiously.

Then, all at once and without any warning at all –

BOOM!!! – the lightning ball exploded with an almighty
crash and a flash of blinding light.

Shock waves rippled outwards across the sky. Twig
quaked with terror. The next instant he was thrown
backwards by the ferocious blast, and tossed into the
oncoming bank of cloud.

'Aaaaggh!' he screamed, as the roaring, swirling wind
tossed him around. He kicked out desperately and tried
to flap his arms – but in vain. The wind was too powerful. It was trying – or so it seemed to Twig – to rip him
limb from limb. All he could do was abandon himself to
the overwhelming force of the turbulent air.

Over and over he tumbled. The silken pockets of the
parawings were blown inside out, and he cried out in
alarm as he found himself spinning round and down

through the rolling purple clouds.

'NOOO!' he screamed.

Further and further he dropped, arms limp and legs akimbo, too frightened to try realigning the parawings in case the wind caught them awkwardly and snapped them in half. His neck was twisted. His back was bent double.

'No more!' Twig whimpered. 'Let it be over.'

And, at that moment, it *was* over. Finally reaching the back of the cloud, Twig was spat out of the wild and thrashing frenzy of the Great Storm like a woodsap pip. In all, the entire terrifying ordeal couldn't have lasted for more than a few seconds. To Twig, it might have been a hundred years.

'Thank Sky,' he whispered gratefully.

An eerie stillness fell. It was as if the very air had been exhausted by the passing maelstrom. Twig shifted round and, as his parawings righted themselves once more, he continued his slow gliding descent. Ahead of him, he saw the Great Storm retreating. It slipped across the clear blue sky, beautiful and majestic, and glowing like a massive purple paper-lantern.

'Is that it?' Twig murmured. 'Have I missed the bolt of stormphrax itself?'

He hung his head in disappointment and was looking down at the Twilight Woods when all at once he heard another noise. It sounded like paper tearing, like hands clapping. Twig raised his head sharply and stared ahead. Protruding from the base of the purple storm was a point of brightness.

'Here it is!' he exclaimed. 'The bolt of lightning. The stormphrax itself!'

Longer and longer the jagged shaft grew, yet impossibly slowly – as if the clouds themselves were holding it back. Twig was starting to wonder whether it would ever be released when, all of a sudden, a resounding CRACK! echoed through the air. The bolt of lightning had broken free.

Like an arrow, it sped down through the sky, scorching the air as it passed. It crackled. It sparked. It wailed and whistled. A smell like toasted almonds filled Twig's nostrils, setting them quivering.

'It's . . . it's wonderful,' he sighed.

Down, down the lightning bolt hurtled. *Zigger-zagger,*

*zigger-zagger*. Through the upper canopy of leaves – hissing and splintering as it passed – and on to the ground below. Then, with a crackle, a thud and a cloud of steam, it plunged into the soft earth. Twig stared at the shaft of lightning standing tall amongst the trees below him, and trembled with awe and wonder.

'Stormphrax,' he whispered. 'And *I* saw it being formed.'

The Great Storm was by now nothing more than a distant blur of purple, low on the horizon and speeding out of sight. Now it was gone, Twig could hardly recall what it had been like trapped inside, tossed and thrown by the violent winds.

The air was sluggish, moist, heavy. It clung like damp cloth.

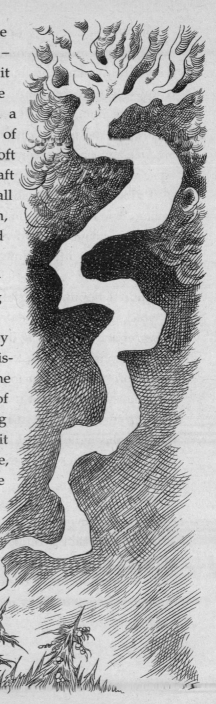

For Twig, still so high up, this was not good.

With a little breeze behind them, the parawings were wonderfully manoeuvrable. When the air was as still as it now was, however, parawinging was perilous. Steering was quite impossible. It took every ounce of skill to ensure that the silken wing-pockets remained filled with air. One awkward movement, and the wings would collapse and he would plummet to the ground below.

'It's like sailing a sky ship,' he recalled his father once saying. 'You have to maintain an even keel at all times.'

'Father!' he gasped. How could he have forgotten? he asked himself guiltily. Surely the *Stormchaser* could never have survived so great a blast. 'And yet, perhaps . . .' he murmured, hoping against hope. 'After all, I saw no sign of wreckage, no falling debris . . .'

Lower and lower Twig drifted; closer and closer came the stormphrax. Unable to dive down, he'd hoped that good fortune might bring him in to land near the precious substance. But it was not to be. Twig was still high up in the sky when he glided over the glistening bolt of solid lightning. He sighed with disappointment as it slipped back between his feet and disappeared behind him.

Too frightened to swoop, or even to look, round, Twig could do nothing but hang on, hold tight and remain as still as he possibly could. The patchwork of treetops, drenched in golden half-light, was coming nearer with every passing second. Sooner or later, he would have to land. He fingered the various talismans and amulets around his neck.

'Into the Twilight Woods,' he whispered, scarcely daring to guess what he might find there.

The further he descended, the more sluggish the air became. It grew warmer, heavier – almost suffocating. Droplets of water sparkled from every inch of his body. Faster and faster he dropped. The parawings fluttered ominously. Suddenly, and to his horror, Twig realized that he was no longer gliding at all ... He was falling.

'No,' he cried out. This couldn't be happening. Not now. Not after everything he'd been through. 'NO!'

His voice echoed forlornly as down, down, down, he went. Tumbling round in the golden light. Crashing through the upper canopy. Bouncing against the branches and ...
THUD!

He landed heavily, awkwardly, and cracked the side of his head against the roots of a tree. The soft twilight glow instantly went out. Twig found himself in absolute darkness.

How long he remained unconscious, Twig never discovered. Time has no meaning in the Twilight Woods.

'Hold steady,' he heard. 'Nearly there.'

Twig opened his eyes. He was lying on the ground beside a tall, angular tree, gnarled with age. He looked round, and everything seemed to swim before him. Rubbing his eyes made no difference. It was the air itself – thick and treacly – that was distorting his vision.

He climbed groggily to his feet, and gasped. There in front of him was a knight on a prowlgrin charger, caught up in a tangle of leather harness straps, dangling a few feet from the forest floor.

Twig's eyes travelled from the rusting figure, up the snarl of twisted ropes, to the great skeletal hulk of a wrecked sky ship, speared on a jagged treetop. Ancient winding gear poked out from the ship's side like an angry metal fist. The knight swayed in the torpid air.

'Wh . . . who are you?' asked Twig tentatively.

From deep within the knight's visor, the voice came again.

'Hold steady, Vinchix,' it said. 'Nearly there. Hold steady, now.'

The white bones of the prowlgrin protruded from its papery, mummified skin, its empty eye-sockets stared out from the metal helmet bridle on which, in gold letters, the word *Vinchix* could just be picked out. It whinnied pitifully.

Twig swallowed hard. 'Can you hear me?' he asked the knight, his voice thin and quavery.

'Hold steady, Vinchix,' came the words again.

Twig stretched out a hand and touched the visor. Flakes of red rust fell away. Gently, scarcely daring to breathe, Twig raised the knight's visor.

Twig screamed in horror and recoiled. He spun round and, driven by blind panic, sped off into the heavy, golden depths of the Twilight Woods. No matter how fast or far he ran, however, the vision of the knight – decomposing, yet not dead – remained seared into his brain. The parchment skin shrunk tight on the grinning skull; the lifeless staring eyes; and, worst of all, the thin bloodless lips of the knight, still moving. 'Nearly there, hold steady, now.'

On and on Twig went, alone and lonely, searching for the bolt of stormphrax, hoping and praying that his fellow crew-members were doing the same.

The half-light of the Twilight Woods confused his eyes. One moment it glowed a rich golden yellow, the next it shimmered in black and white. Deep shadows, pools of brightness. Charcoal and chalk. The chiaroscuro of darkness and light which confused everything it fell upon.

Ancient trees, with their gnarled trunks and twisted branches, seemed to writhe in the liquid air, taking on shapes of goblins and ogres and gruesome giants.

'They're just trees,' Twig reminded himself. 'Just trees is all they are.' The words sounded musical, and oddly reassuring as he repeated them. 'Just treesy-weesy trees. That's all, just . . .'

'Twig!' he shouted, and shook his head from side to side. He must pay attention, he must remain in control.

He continued over the soft mattress of fallen leaves, staring down at his feet. The ground was covered with tiny sparkling crystals, like a sprinkling of salt, like a skyful of stars. Twig smiled to himself. 'See how they glitter,' he whispered. 'See how they glisten. See how they glimmer. See how they gleam . . .'

'TWIG!' he bellowed once again. 'Stop it!' And he slapped his face on both sides, once, twice, three-four-five times. He slapped it until it was pink and smarting. 'Keep your mind on the task at hand,' he said firmly. 'Don't let it wander.'

But this was easier said than done for the Twilight Woods were enchanting and seductive. They whispered, they echoed – they enticed. And as Twig made his way deeper and deeper into the woods, he was terrified to discover just how simple it was for his mind to drift away . . . to wander off . . . to disappear on distant flights of fancy . . .

'You are Twig, son of Cloud Wolf the sky pirate captain,' he reminded himself sharply. 'You are in the Twilight Woods, brought here by the Great Storm. You are searching for stormphrax, for the crew of the *Stormchaser* – for a way out.'

So long as he could hold on to these truths, he would be all right. But with every step, it was becoming harder. The woods seemed to be closing in around him, impinging on his senses. They filled his eyes with their liquid distortion, his ears with their echoing whispers, his nose and mouth with lushness – and decay.

As he stumbled on, he thought he glimpsed something out of the corner of his eye. He looked furtively over his shoulder, then frowned with confusion. There was nothing there.

'But I could have sworn . . .' Twig muttered anxiously.

Time after time, it happened. Something *was* there. He was sure of it. Yet no matter how fast he spun round, he never caught sight of whatever it was.

'I don't like this,' he shuddered. 'I don't like it at all.'

Behind him he heard a faint *clip-clop* sound. It caught him unawares and, before he knew it, Twig was back in the woodtroll cabin of his childhood. Spelda

Snatchwood – the woodtroll who had raised him as her own – was busying herself around the cabin, her bark sandals clipping and clopping on the wooden floor. The

memories were so clear, so vibrant. He saw lufwood burning in the stove and smelt the pickled tripweed on Spelda's breath. 'You are my mother-mine,' he whispered. 'And you are Twig, my beautiful boy,' she whispered back.

Twig started at the sound of his name. He stared ahead, unable for a moment to make sense of the shimmering gloom. Were those eyes staring at him whenever he turned his head away? Were those claws and teeth glinting just out of sight?

'You are Twig, son of Cloud Wolf,' he told himself. 'You are in the Twilight Woods. You are searching for your crew-mates – for a way out.' He sighed. 'A way out of this nightmare.'

A soft squeaking-squealing sound filled his head. Metal on unoiled metal. Twig smiled. It was supper-time on board the *Stormchaser*, and the sky pirates were all seated round a long bench tucking into a meal of baked snowbird and earthapple mash. It was silent apart from the regular *squeak squeak squeak* of Stope Boltjaw's ironwood jaw as he chewed. 'Sounds like we've got a woodrat in our midst,' Tem Barkwater noted and laughed. 'Eh, Twig? I said, it sounds like . . .'

Twig grimaced. It had happened again. How long before the treacherous woods robbed him of his mind completely? 'You are Twig,' he said, uncertainly. 'You are in the Twilight Woods. You are searching for . . . for . . .'

Just then, from his right, there came the unmistakable sound of a prowlgrin whinnying. Twig groaned. He must have been going in a huge circle. All that walking – all that *concentrating* – only to find that he had come right back to the same spot.

He scoured the tops of the trees for any sign of the wreck of the sky ship – but found none. Puzzled and uneasy, Twig chewed at the end of his scarf. Perhaps I imagined it, he thought. Perhaps . . .

Panic rose in Twig's throat.

'St . . . stay calm,' he told himself. 'Concentrate on what's ahead. Don't look round. You'll be fine.'

'Steady, Bolnix, you'll be just fine,' wheezed an ancient voice.

Twig looked up sharply. His eyes focused – and his heart missed a beat.

# ·CHAPTER THIRTEEN·

# THE SEPIA KNIGHT

In front of him was a second knight. He was encased, from top to toe, in rusting armour, and seated upon a prowlgrin. As he moved round in the saddle, the heavy metal plates clanked and rattled; the gauges clicked, the pipes whistled softly.

'Hold steady now, Bolnix,' said the knight, his cracked voice reedy, sibilant.

Twig saw two eyes glinting from behind the helmet visor. He shivered apprehensively, and looked away. The prowlgrin, old and weak, shifted from foot to foot agitatedly.

'Steady, Bolnix,' said the knight again. 'Not too close, now.'

Wheezing with effort, the knight pulled off a gauntlet. Twig stared at the hand which was revealed. It was as gnarled as the branches of the ancient trees. Clunking and clanking, the knight raised his arm and began fumbling with the visor.

'Steady now,' he said.

Twig froze as the visor creaked rustily, and slowly swung open. He found himself staring into a pair of startlingly blue eyes, sunk, like half-excavated jewels, deep into an ancient, craggy face.

'Is that you, Garlinius? I have searched for so long.' The voice was as ancient as the face – and twice as melancholy.

'No,' said Twig, approaching the figure. 'Please sir, I've been shipwrecked. The *Stormchaser* . . .'

The knight recoiled, the pipes and gauges on his armour rattling alarmingly. The prowlgrin snorted with unease. 'You speak to me of stormchasing, Garlinius! You, who robbed me of the *Storm Queen*, and never returned. Oh, Garlinius, I searched for you so long. If you only knew.'

'Please,' said Twig, taking a step closer. 'I am not Garlinius. I'm Twig, and I . . .'

'Garlinius!' cried the knight, his mood suddenly improved. Returning the gauntlet to his hand, he leaped from the prowlgrin and grabbed Twig by the shoulder. 'It's so good to see you!' he said. 'We parted on bad terms. We knights should never do that. Oh, but Garlinius, I have suffered since I've wandered these woods, searching and searching.'

The knight was staring into Twig's face, his eyes burning an iridescent blue. The metal gauntlet tightened its grip.

Twig winced, and tried to pull away. 'But I'm not Garlinius,' he insisted. 'I'm Twig. I am searching for my crew-mates, my . . .'

'Lost and searching,' the knight howled. 'I too. I too. But it matters, now, not a jot. For we are reunited once more. You and me, Garlinius,' he said, gripping Twig's shoulder still more tightly. 'Me and you.'

'Look at me!' Twig cried desperately. 'Listen to what I am telling you. I am *not* Garlinius.'

'If you only knew how long I searched,' the knight sighed. 'Searching, always searching.'

'Leave me alone!' Twig shouted. 'Let me go!'

But the knight would not let go. And no matter how much Twig squirmed or wriggled, he could not break free from the pincer grip of the heavy gauntlet.

Instead, and to his intense horror, he found himself being drawn closer and closer to the knight until he could feel the ancient creature's warm, fetid breath in his face. The knight raised his other hand, and Twig shivered with revulsion as he felt the bony, crepey fingers exploring every inch of his head.

'Garlinius,' said the knight. 'The aquiline nose. The high forehead. How well we are re-met.'

Up so close, Twig saw that the knight's armour was coated in a fine layer of sepia dust. It moved over the metal breastplate almost like a liquid. Now he could see his reflection in the metal underneath; now his face was gone again.

'If you only knew how lonely I've been, Garlinius,' the knight cried out. 'How long I've searched.'

Twig was beginning to panic. 'I must break free,' he muttered through gritted teeth. 'I must get away.'

He reached up, grabbed the gauntleted hand that gripped his shoulder and pulled with all his might.

'Garlinius!' protested the knight pitifully.

Twig brought his knee up hard, and connected with the knight's breastplate with a loud clang. The knight fell back and landed heavily with an echoing clatter on the crystal-covered ground. A cloud of sepia dust flew up into the air. Twig fell to his knees coughing violently.

'Garlinius!'

The knight was back on his feet. In his hand he held a long saw-toothed sword, vicious-looking despite the rust that cloaked it.

'Garlinius,' he said again, his voice suddenly thin and menacing. His blue eyes looked straight into Twig's, their clear intensity mesmerizing him for an instant. The knight raised the sword.

Twig stopped breathing.

The knight's wizened face creased with confusion. 'Garlinius?' he called out. 'Where are you?'

His eyes bore into Twig's.

'Come back, Garlinius,' he implored. 'We can be friends again. If you only knew how long I've searched. Garlinius! Please . . .'

Twig shuddered with pity. The knight was quite blind. The Twilight Woods had robbed him of his senses, every one; of his wits, of his reason – yet left him with his life. He would never rest. He would never find peace. Instead, he was doomed to continue his never-ending search for ever and ever. Nothing in the Deepwoods was as cruel as this place, thought Twig. I must get out! I won't let the evil Twilight Woods have *my* wits, *my* sight . . . I will escape.

The knight, hearing no reply, turned regretfully away. 'So near,' he whispered. 'Always so near, and yet . . .'

He whistled softly through his rotten teeth and the prowlgrin padded obediently to his side. Wheezing and panting, the knight clambered back into the saddle.

'I will find you, Garlinius,' he cried in his frail, cracked voice. 'A quest is a quest for ever. Wherever Vinchix takes you, Bolnix and I will follow.'

Twig held his breath and remained absolutely still as the knight shook his fist in the air, tugged on the reins and rode off into the depths of the Twilight Woods. The golden light gleamed on the back of his armour as he faded into the confusing patchwork of light and shade. The creaking grew softer, the clip-clop footfalls fading away to nothing.

Finally, Twig let out his breath, and gasped for air. As he did so, he felt a sharp pinch at his shoulder. The sepia knight's gauntlet still held its grip.

# ·CHAPTER FOURTEEN·

# LOUDER CRIES,
# SOFTER WHISPERS

### i
### In the Mire

Screed Toe-taker patted his stomach. The oozefish had tasted as vile as ever – bitter, bony and oily – but they had taken the edge off his hunger. He leaned forwards and dropped the bones into the fire where they crackled and burst into flames; the heads and tails, he tossed to the scavenging white ravens which had been hopping round the wrecked ship expectantly ever since the first wisps of fishy smoke had risen into the air.

'There you are, my lovelies,' he rasped.

The birds squabbled noisily over the scraps of food – pecking, scratching, drawing blood – until, one by one, they each seized a piece that suited them, leaped up into the air and flapped away to eat it in peace.

'Oozefish,' Screed snorted, and spat into the fire.

It was years since Screed had first set up home in the bleached wasteland, yet he had never got used to the taste of the food the Mire had to offer. Occasionally, of course, he would pilfer the provisions brought by the hapless goblins, trolls and the like, whom he would lead to their deaths. But their supplies of stale bread and dried meat were scarcely any better. No. What Screed Toe-taker craved was the food he had once eaten every day – hammelhorn steaks, tildermeat sausages, baked snowbird . . . His mouth watered; his stomach groaned.

'One day, perhaps,' he sighed. 'One day.'

He picked up a long stick and poked thoughtfully at the embers of the fire. The weather was calm this morning, with little wind and no clouds – unlike the previous day, when the sky had churned and rumbled with the passing storm. It had looked like a Great Storm. And he remembered the sky ship he'd seen speeding towards it like a flying arrow.

'Stormchasing,' Screed muttered, and sneered. 'If they only knew!' He cackled with laughter. 'But then, of course, by now they *will* know. The poor fools!' he said, and cackled all the louder.

The sun rose higher in the sky. It beat down fiercely, causing a swirling mist to coil up out of the swampy mud.

'Come on then,' Screed said, as he wiped his mouth on his sleeve. 'Can't sit round here all day.'

He heaved himself to his feet, kicked wet mud over the smouldering embers and ashes and surveyed the horizon. A broad smile spread across his face as he stared across the hazy Mire to the Twilight Woods beyond.

Who would arrive next, desperate for a guide to lead them across the Mire? he wondered, and sniggered unpleasantly. 'Looty-booty,' he whispered, 'here I come!'

## ii
## In the Palace of the Most High Academe

Vilnix Pompolnius yelped with pain and sat bolt upright. 'Imbecile!' he shouted.

'A thousand, nay, a million apologies,' Minulis cried out. 'I slipped.'

Vilnix inspected the injured finger and licked away a drop of blood. 'It's not too serious,' he said, and smiled. 'Anyway, a little bit of pain never did anyone any harm.'

'No, sire,' Minulis agreed eagerly.

Vilnix settled himself back on the ottoman and closed his eyes. 'You may continue,' he said.

'Yes, sire. Thank you, sire. At once, sire,' Minulis babbled. 'And you may be sure, it won't happen again, sire.'

'It'd better not,' Vilnix snarled. 'There are many who would leap at the opportunity of becoming personal manservant to the Most High Academe of Sanctaphrax – should the post suddenly become free. Do I make myself clear?'

'*Crystal* clear, if I might make so bold,' said Minulis ingratiatingly.

With the utmost care, he lifted the bony hand once more and resumed the manicure. The Most High

Academe liked his nails filed to needle-points. They enabled him to scratch his back most satisfyingly.

'Minulis,' said Vilnix Pompolnius at length, his eyes still closed. 'Do you dream?'

'Only when I sleep, sire,' he replied.

'A good answer,' Vilnix replied. 'And one that illustrates the difference between you and me.'

Minulis went on with his filing in silence. The Most High Academe did not like to be interrupted.

'The only times *I* dream is when I am awake.' He opened his eyes. 'I dreamed of all this,' he said, sweeping his free hand round the sumptuous Inner Sanctum in a wide arc. 'And lo and behold, my dreams all came true.'

Minulis nodded. 'The Council of Sanctaphrax is lucky indeed to have so wise and venerable a scholar as its Most High Academe.'

'Quite so,' said Vilnix dismissively. 'And yet, since reaching the pinnacle of success, I have missed my dreams.'

Minulis tutted sympathetically.

Abruptly, Vilnix sat up and leaned forwards conspiratorially. 'I'll let you into a little secret, shall I?' he whispered. 'Following my supper with the Leaguesmaster and my little chat with that nightwaif creature, I have started dreaming again. Wonderful dreams,' he said softly. 'Dreams more vivid than any I have ever had before.'

# iii
## In the Backstreets of Undertown

Deaf, destitute and on the street, Forficule had sunk just about as low as it was possible to sink. No use to anyone, least of all Mother Horsefeather – who he knew wouldn't now give him so much as a second glance – he sat cross-legged on a threadbare blanket, his head swathed in bloody bandages, watching the good citizens of Undertown scurry past him without a second look.

'Spare a little change?' he cried out at intervals, and rattled his tin cup. 'Help save a poor soul less fortunate than yourselves.'

His words, however, fell on ears as deaf as his own. After eight hours of begging, the cup still contained no more than the brass button that he himself had placed there that morning. By sundown, Forficule was about to leave when somebody did finally pause beside him.

'Spare a little change,' he said.

'A little change?' the newcomer said softly. 'Come with me and I'll make you rich beyond compare.'

Forficule made no reply. He hadn't heard a single word. Slitch – reluctant to repeat his offer any louder – crouched before him and rubbed his thumb and middle-finger together. Forficule looked up and concentrated on the gnokgoblin's lips.

'Money,' Slitch mouthed. 'Wealth. Riches. Come with me.'

If Forficule had been able to hear Slitch's thoughts – or

even his voice – he would have recognized him at once as the unscrupulous goblin who had caused the death of the unfortunate slaughterer, Tendon. But Forficule could hear neither. Like a baby, he had to take the smiling goblin's words at face value. He climbed to his feet, tucked the grimy bundle of rags under his arm, and let himself be led away.

Perhaps it was his desperation that left Forficule as blind as he was deaf. Or perhaps he didn't want to remember what he had seen before. At any rate, he did not remember the familiar scene in the hut, of mortar, pestle and crystal.

'Stormphrax,' Slitch mouthed, and smiled as he handed the nightwaif the pestle.

Forficule nodded.

'But hang on a moment,' Slitch went on. He turned and removed a phial of deep yellow liquid from the shelf. 'Dampseed oil,' he explained, and removed the cork stopper. 'If we pour a little into the bowl with the crystal, then . . .' He stopped. 'What are you doing? NO!' he screamed and lunged at the nightwaif.

But it was too late. With his eyes fixed on the glistening, sparking shard of stormphrax, Forficule had heard nothing of Slitch's explanation. He gripped the pestle firmly in both hands. 'Here we go,' he whispered, and brought it sharply down.

BOOM!

CRASH!

The crystal of stormphrax exploded with terrifying force, taking the hut with it. The roof flew off, the walls flew out and the floor became a massive crater. As the dust settled, two bodies could be seen, locked together in a fatal embrace.

# iv
## Outside the Bloodoak Tavern

'What in Sky's name was that?' the Professor of Darkness exclaimed.

Mother Horsefeather shook her head. 'You academics,' she chided. 'Heads in the clouds in your castles in the air. You've got no idea, have you?'

The pair of them were taking an early evening stroll together. They had urgent business to discuss and, since the Bloodoak tavern had proved to be so open to eaves-dropping, had taken their conversation outside.

'So, tell me,' he said. 'What was that noise? It sounded like an explosion.'

'It *was* an explosion,' she said, her ruff of neck feathers bristling. 'Every time some poor fool tries to turn storm-phrax into phraxdust there is an explosion.'

The Professor of Darkness started with surprise. 'But where do they get this stormphrax?' he asked.

Mother Horsefeather clacked her beak impatiently. 'The black-market is flooded with the stuff,' she said. 'Word has it the Most High Academe himself is author-izing it in the hope that someone, somewhere, will unlock the elusive secret to safe phraxdust production, though . . .'

'But . . . but this is outrageous!' the Professor of Darkness spluttered. 'I had no idea . . . No wonder the treasury is so depleted.' He shook his head. 'I curse the day I first laid eyes on that traitorous usurper, Vilnix Pompolnius.'

'Yesterday is over,' said Mother Horsefeather curtly. 'Tomorrow is still to come.'

'I know, I know,' said the professor, 'but what can we do? I've already told you that both Vilnix *and* the Leaguesmaster now know that Cloud Wolf has set off in search of stormphrax. Both await his return. Both have the means to confiscate his cargo – and if one fails, then the other will surely succeed.'

'On the contrary,' said Mother Horsefeather, her eyes twinkling. 'Both will fail, you mark my words. I know Cloud Wolf for the wily old skycur that he is. While his two enemies are battling it out, he will slip between them and bring the cargo of stormphrax to me, just as we agreed.' Suddenly, her eyes narrowed. She spun round. 'Anyway, how do *you* know so much, eh?' she said. 'Are you now privy to the Most High Academe's thoughts?'

'No, I . . .' the professor began. 'I see your ignorance of Sanctaphrax equals my own of Undertown. Intrigue, whispers, gossip – the black-market of our noble floating city is flooded with the stuff!' he said, and smiled.

'Forficule,' said Mother Horsefeather, 'was it . . .?'

'Forficule told Vilnix everything,' the professor said.

Mother Horsefeather hawked noisily and spat on the ground. 'No wonder the little squit was too ashamed to show his face,' she squawked.

'Tortured, he was, until he did,' the professor explained. 'He had no choice. But no, I didn't learn of the Most High Academe's plans from Forficule.'

'Then who?' Mother Horsefeather demanded to know.

'From someone who has sworn allegiance to the position of power, rather than the individual who holds it,' the professor explained. 'His name is Minulis,' he said. 'He is personal manservant to Vilnix Pompolnius – and he senses that changes are coming.'

Mother Horsefeather cackled with delight. 'Then it's up to us to ensure that he senses right!'

# ·CHAPTER FIFTEEN·

# DEAD OR ALIVE

Twig stopped mid-stride and peered up into the golden sky. Had he noticed something moving, something flying overhead? Or was it just another illusion, another cruel trick of the watery light?

'Father,' he cried out. 'Is that you?'

'You . . . you . . . you . . .' the woods cried back.

Twig shuddered miserably. There was nobody there – there was *never* anybody there. The mocking faces that he saw, sneering and jeering at him out of the corners of his eyes, vanished each time he turned to confront them. Nothing remained but wraith-like twists of mist. He was alone. Quite alone.

And yet, as he turned back and continued on his solitary journey, the feeling of being watched persisted. It gnawed at his mind relentlessly.

'Over here,' someone or something whispered. 'Here!

Here!' Or was it just the sound of the rising breeze, warm and oily, lapping at the ancient trees?

Twig felt dizzy, disorientated, unable to trust what his ears or his eyes were telling him. The trees swayed and the branches reached out towards him, their long woody fingers plucking at his clothes, pulling his hair.

'Leave me alone!' Twig howled.

'Alone . . . alone . . .' the woods called back.

'I won't stay here for ever!' he screamed.

'For ever . . .'

Twig thrust his hand into the knight's gauntlet, reached round and pulled his father's sword from its scabbard. Grasping the hilt helped him to hold on to who he was – Twig, son of Cloud Wolf. In the Twilight Woods, he needed all the help he could get to remember even that. Yet the sword brought with it guilty memories, shameful memories.

Cloud Wolf had blamed Slyvo Spleethe for kidnapping him and dragging him reluctantly on board the *Stormchaser*. Twig knew that wasn't what happened. He had gone willingly. More than that, it was he who had revealed to the treacherous quartermaster that Cloud Wolf was his father. In so doing, he had betrayed the captain's greatest weakness. He might as well have stabbed him in the back.

'I didn't mean to,' he mumbled. 'Really, I didn't. Oh, Father, forgive me for my wilful ignorance, for my utter stupidity, for my lack of thought . . .'

The gleaming eyes and glinting teeth emerged from the shadows and hovered at the edge of his field of

vision once more. Twig raised his
gauntleted hand and rapped it
sharply against his head. It didn't
pay to dwell on *lack of thought* in
the Twilight Woods.

As he lowered his arm, he
watched the coating of fine
dust slip around on the polished surface of the gauntlet, and
fall from the metal fingers like droplets of liquid. It was
only by this piece of armour which had been left behind,
that he knew his encounter with the sepia knight had
been more than a mere figment of his imagination.

'You are searching for stormphrax,' Twig told himself
as he set off once more. 'You are searching for the crew
of the *Stormchaser* – you are searching for a way out.'

On and on he stumbled. On and on and on. So far as
Twig was concerned, time might as well have stopped
completely. He didn't feel hungry. He didn't feel thirsty.
He didn't feel tired. And yet, as he continued on through
the bright and shadowy depths, in the grip of the
enchanting torpor, Twig's apprehension grew.

'Twilight Woods,' he snorted. '*Nightmare* Woods, more
like it.'

The wind rose higher, rustling the leaves and sending
their coating of glistening crystals showering down to
the glittering ground below. Twig stared, mesmerized by
the scintillating display. And as they fell, he became
aware of a sound – light and delicate – like the soft
tinkling of wind-chimes.

As it grew louder, Twig stopped and cocked his head to one side. What could be making such sweet and melodious music? It seemed to be coming from his left.

'I am Twig,' he reminded himself as he raised his sword in his gauntleted hand. 'I must leave this place. I will not become like the sepia knight.'

'. . . like the sepia knight . . .' the woods whispered back.

Twig followed the unearthly music, picking his way through the trees and undergrowth, trying his best to ignore the cries of disbelief that echoed just out of earshot. Up ahead, a bright, silvery light gleamed from the shadows. Twig broke into a run. He slashed impatiently at the undergrowth with his sword. He held back the razor-sharp creepers with the gauntlet. Closer and closer he got. A sweet almond-like perfume wafted around him. The light intensified, the jangled music grew louder.

And then he saw it . . .

There, with one end buried deep in the ground and the other rising zig-zag high up into the air, was a tall and magnificent crystal. It was the bolt of lightning, now solid, which Twig had watched being discharged from the Great Storm.

Twig gasped. 'Stormphrax,' he whispered.

Close to, the lightning bolt was even more remarkable than he had imagined. Flawless, unblemished and as smooth as glass, it pulsed with a pure white glow. The noise, he realized, was coming from the top of the jagged bolt, far above his head.

'It's cracking,' he murmured in alarm. 'It's . . . breaking up!'

At that moment, there came a loud sound, like bells
tolling, and a huge chunk of the crystal hurtled down
through the air towards him in a shower of tiny glittering particles. Twig leapt back, fell to the ground and
stared in horror as it landed, with a heavy thud and a
puff of sepia dust, exactly where he had been standing.

The bell-like ringing sounded again and two more, even larger pieces of stormphrax landed beside the first. They too embedded themselves in the ground, and all three promptly disappeared.

'They're burying themselves,' Twig realized.

He remembered, of course, that in absolute darkness a thimbleful of stormphrax was as heavy as a thousand ironwood trees – now he could see what this meant in practice. The dark and immeasurably heavy underside of each of the giant pieces of crystal was dragging the rest down.

*Thud, thud, thud. Thud. Thud-thud.* Several more blocks fell. Twig scuttered backwards on his hands and feet, terrified that one of them would land on him. Some were small. Some were very large. All of them buried themselves where they landed, deep down in the absolute darkness below.

Then, in a grinding symphony of noise, the lightning bolt gave a lurch, and Twig saw that it, too, was sinking beneath the surface. It was this downward movement which was causing the top to splinter and crack – and the more crystal that disappeared into the darkness, the stronger the pull became.

Twig shook his head in dismay. Even if the *Stormchaser* had been anchored right there above the clearing, how difficult it would have been to retrieve the pieces of stormphrax. Suddenly, with a final *shwooohk-POP!* the final section of stormphrax sank down out of sight.

'Gone,' he whispered.

He stood up and looked around the clearing. Apart

from the burnt and broken branches, there was no sign that the bolt of stormphrax had ever been there. Distant laughter echoed.

'Gone,' he said again, hardly able to believe his eyes.

All those years of waiting for a Great Storm. And all the dangers that chasing the storm had involved. The broken mast. The abandoning of the sky ship. The loss of his father. And for what? For a bolt of lightning which had disappeared within hours of reaching its destination – and almost killed him in the process!

Except, thought Twig with a shudder, it wouldn't have killed me, would it? A piece could have broken my back or stoved in my skull – but I wouldn't have died. Icy fingers strummed up and down Twig's back at the macabre thought of what *might* have happened.

'And now, all that's left is this,' he said, kicking angrily at the sprinkling of crystals, too small to sink with the rest, which rested on every surface like frost. A cloud of glittering dust flew up into the glinting air. Twig felt sick. He wanted to cry. He wanted to scream. 'Stormchasing!' he cursed bitterly. 'A fool's errand, more like.'

'Yet oddly appealing for all that,' came a cracked, reedy voice from behind him.

Twig started, then raised his eyes impatiently to the sky. The sepia knight was the last person he wanted to meet again.

'Twig,' came the voice again. 'It is Twig, isn't it?'

'Yes,' Twig snapped as he spun around. 'It's . . .' He stopped short. It was not the sepia knight; neither was it a phantom, a ghoul, a trick of the light. 'YOU!' he exclaimed.

'Indeed it is,' the Professor of Light said as he peered up at him awkwardly. 'Though slightly the worse for wear, I fear. I couldn't quite get the hang of those parawings,' he explained. 'Had quite a tumble.'

Twig stared back at him in open-mouthed horror.

'Do I really look that bad?' he said, and sighed wearily. 'I do, don't I?'

Twig felt a lump coming into his throat. 'Your neck,' he whispered. 'It's . . .'

'Broken,' said the professor. 'I know.' He raised his hands, clamped them to either side of his head and pulled it up until his eyes met Twig's. 'Is that better?' he asked, and smiled weakly.

Twig nodded. The next moment, however, the professor sneezed on the dust, and the whole lot flopped forward again. Twig tried hard to swallow away the rising feeling of nausea.

'We need to fix it in place, somehow,' he said, and turned round – ostensibly to look for something that he might use, but actually to avoid eye-contact with the terrifying sight of the professor's lolling head. 'A stick,' he muttered busily. 'Hang on,' and he dashed off into the trees.

The next minute he was back, carrying a long and – for the ancient trees of the Twilight Woods – straight branch, which he had broken off a nearby tree.

'This ought to do the trick. If I place it against your back, like so. And bind it tightly with my rope like . . . so. That's it.'

He stepped back to check his handiwork. From the back, it looked as though the professor had a young sapling growing out of his spine.

'Now, for the head itself,' he chattered on, as he pulled a length of bandage from a pocket. 'That ought to be enough. Let's just see.'

The professor, whose chin was resting against his chest, glanced up as far as he could. 'What are you going to do?' he asked.

'I'll show you,' said Twig. 'If you raise your head again then I'll secure it to the branch at the back. To stop it falling forwards again.'

'Excellent idea,' said the professor enthusiastically. He lifted his head up for a second time, and rested it gently against the branch.

Twig wound the bandage round and round the professor's forehead and the makeshift support, clamping the two together. When the bandage was all but used up, he tore the end in two and tied a double knot. 'There,' he said at last.

The professor removed his hands. His head remained upright. Twig breathed a deep sigh of relief.

'Outstanding piece of improvisation,' the Professor of Light exclaimed. 'I must say, that Tem Barkwater was right. You are indeed an ingenious young fellow.'

Twig started with surprise and delight. 'Tem?' he said. 'Is Tem here or . . .?' The spectral air flickered gleefully and chimed with unpleasant laughter. Twig's stomach sank as he realized his likely mistake. 'Or were you talking to him on the *Stormchaser*?' he said.

'No, no,' replied the professor. 'We hardly exchanged a word on board ship. No, he is here, in the Twilight Woods . . .' A look of bewilderment passed over his face. 'We were together, only a moment ago. We . . . I was looking at . . .' He turned round awkwardly and stared at Twig. 'I can't remember what I was looking at.'

Twig nodded, and glanced round uneasily at the shifting shadows. 'This is a treacherous place,' he said softly. 'There's something here . . . Or someone – or maybe, many. I don't know. But I see faces I can't focus on, hear voices that fade away when I try to listen.'

'That's it,' the professor said dreamily. 'Questions searching for answers. Theorems looking for proof . . .'

'Why,' Twig went on, and raised the sword high in his gauntleted hand, 'if it weren't for these . . . The sword reminds me of where I came from and who I am. The gauntlet, of what I must never become. Without them, I fear I would lose myself completely. Oh, Professor, we have to leave these woods as soon as we can.'

The professor sighed, but did not move. 'Twig,' he said softly. 'My neck was broken in the fall. It was only because I landed in this place that I am still alive. I cannot leave the immortality of the Twilight Woods,' he said. 'I would die in an instant if I did.'

Twig shook his head miserably. The professor was right, of course.

'But it's not so bad. Now I can study stormphrax for ever.' He smiled. 'And what more could a Professor of Light ask for?'

Twig smiled back, but his heart chilled at the words. If the professor could not go, then where did that leave him? Alone again? Abandoned? The thought was more than he could bear.

'Professor,' he said tentatively. 'You will help me find the others, won't you?'

The professor turned and surveyed him gravely.

'What type of a person do you take me for?' he said. 'We academics of Sanctaphrax are not all as rotten as that traitorous foulpox; that upstart knife-grinder, Vilnix Pompolnius – no matter what you may have heard to the contrary.'

'Sorry, I didn't mean . . .' said Twig. 'It's just . . . I couldn't . . . I can't . . .'

'Hush now, Twig,' said the professor.

'I've got to leave!' Twig cried out. 'I've got to. Before it's too late.'

'. . . too late . . . too late . . .' the woods taunted.

The professor wrapped his arm awkwardly round Twig's shoulder. 'I give you my word,' he said. 'I shall not abandon you. After all,' he said, nodding back at the branch which was supporting his head, 'one good turn deserves another.'

'Thank you,' Twig sniffed, and looked up. 'I . . .'

The professor was staring into mid-air, a smile playing over his lips. Once again, his mind had been lured away by the treacherous spectres and phantasms that haunted the darkest corners of the woods. The crystals sparkled. 'Light incarnate,' he whispered dreamily. 'Light made whole.'

'Professor,' Twig shouted, anxiously. 'Professor! You gave me your word!'

# ·CHAPTER SIXTEEN·

# CAPTAIN TWIG

'Professor!' Twig screamed into his companion's ear. 'It's me, Twig. You must help me.'

But the professor merely turned away, raised his arm and began scrutinizing the back of his hand. 'See how the crystals cling to each individual hair,' he marvelled. 'And how the light illuminates its entire length, from follicle to split end.'

Twig nodded. The hairs were indeed shining. But, so what? 'Professor,' he tried again, 'listen to me.'

'You're right, my old and trusty friend and rival,' the professor said. 'It does seem to soak up the light. Trust you to notice the particles of sepia dust in-between. Such a substance must indeed have purifying qualities . . .'

Shaking his head, Twig turned away. Just as the sepia knight had mistaken him for his old compatriot, Garlinius, so the professor was now seeing and hearing him as the Professor of Darkness. It was hopeless. Utterly hopeless.

Twig fought back his tears. 'You come with me,' he said, as he took the professor gently by the wrist and led him away. 'Come on. Two heads are better than one – even if one of them *is* broken and empty.'

They hadn't gone more than a dozen paces when the Professor of Light stopped and turned on Twig. 'What exactly do you mean by "broken and empty"?' he demanded.

Twig burst out laughing. 'Professor!' he exclaimed. 'Welcome back!'

'Oh, Twig,' the Professor of Light said softly. 'What a remarkable place this is.'

Twig smiled uncertainly and, as the unlikely pair continued their search for the rest of the crew of the *Stormchaser*, he kept quiet as the professor rambled on and on about the stormphrax crystals.

'Light in physical form,' he enthused. 'Solid energy. Can you imagine such a thing, Twig? Volatile in bright light, stable in the twilight glow, yet heavy beyond reason when cloaked in darkness. Stormphrax is a wondrous substance and no mistake.'

Twig nodded. That much, at least, he knew to be true.

'But then weight, as Ferumix demonstrated so well, is relative,' the professor went on. 'x equals y + z over pi, where x represents weight, y, the surface area of the crystal and z, its translucency.' He frowned. 'Or do I mean radiance?'

Twig stared at him uneasily. Did the professor's

calculations prove that he still had his wits about him –
or was he simply uttering meaningless gibberish.
'There's certainly a lot of the stuff,' he commented, as he
glanced about him.

'Indeed!' the professor exclaimed. He turned stiffly
round to look at Twig. His eyes glinted wildly. 'And I
intend to count it all – every last particle – thereby allowing me to establish just how many Great Storms it has
taken to produce this number of crystals, and how long.
Epochs. Millennia,' he whispered reverently. 'Aeons.'

Twig shook his head. All this talk of time spinning
away endlessly troubled him. The air rippled, and voices
whispered to him from the harlequin shadows. Gentle,
soothing voices. Enticing voices.

'You are Twig,' they murmured. 'You are sixteen years
old. How much you have seen and done in that short
space of time . . .'

And, as Twig continued to stare into the flashing
diamonds of light and shade, he saw scenes he
recognized, places and people he knew. Taghair,
the oakelf, who had shown him his name.
Hoddergruff, a woodtroll neighbour. On board the
*Stormchaser* with the sky pirates. In the back room of the
Bloodoak tavern. Mother Horsefeather, Forficule –
Cloud Wolf.

'How much more has the eternity of the Twilight
Woods to offer,' the voices lulled.

Twig stared at the face before him. 'Father?' he murmured, and took a step forwards.

Cloud Wolf's spectral form slipped back and hovered

just out of reach. 'Farther than you think,' he replied, his voice low and resounding. 'But stay awhile,' he said. 'Search and you will find me. One day, Twig. Just keep on searching, and one day . . .'

'NO!' screamed Twig. 'You're not my father. Not my *real* father.' He gripped the gauntlet round the hilt of the sword and pulled it from its scabbard. 'Leave me, whatever you are!' he shouted, and began slashing frantically all round him.

The air crackled and curdled. The faces retreated. They jeered and gesticulated and poked out their tongues.

'Stay awhile? I will not stay here!' he cried out.

'. . . stay here . . .'

'Be gone, I say,' roared Twig. 'Be gone!'

'. . . gone . . .'

And they were. Twig found himself staring into the troubled eyes of the Professor of Light. His gnarled fingers gripped him firmly by the shoulders.

'Can you hear me, lad?' he shouted. 'Twig!'

'Yes,' he said. 'I can hear you . . . Oh, Professor,' he whimpered, 'if I don't leave the Twilight Woods soon, then I must surely stay here for ever.' He tightened his gauntleted grip on the sword and brandished it in the air. 'TEM!' he bellowed. 'SPIKER! STOPE! HUBBLE! WHERE ARE YOU?'

His words echoed and faded away to nothing. Twig hung his head. It was hopeless. It was . . . but wait. He cocked his head to one side.

'What is it?' asked the professor.

'Sssshh!' Twig hissed, and closed his eyes to concentrate all the harder. And there it was again. Low and plaintive – the faint but unmistakable sound of a banderbear yodelling its greetings.

As a child, Twig had often lain in bed listening to the massive solitary creatures calling to one another across the vast distances of the Deepwoods. So far as he knew, there were no banderbears in the Twilight Woods – save one.

'HUBBLE!' he cried, and yodelled back as best he could. 'Wa-ah-ah-ah!'

'Wa-ah-ah-ah-ah!' came the reply, closer now.

Gripping his sword – just in case – Twig broke into a run.

'Wuh-wuh!' he called excitedly.

'Wuh-wuh!' The voice was closer than ever. The next moment there came the sound of cracking and splintering wood, and Hubble himself – the giant albino banderbear – came crashing out of the shadowy trees towards him.

'Hubble!' Twig exclaimed.

'T-wuh-g!' roared the banderbear, and the pair of them fell into each other's arms and hugged warmly.

'I feared I would never see you again,' said Twig at length, as he pulled himself away. As he did so, he realized they were not alone. Just as the Professor of Light had followed him, so the rest of the crew had followed Hubble. Twig wiped his tears away, and smiled round at the circle of grinning faces.

'Tem,' he said. 'Spiker. Stope, Stone Pilot – it is *so* good to see you all.'

'And it warms my heart to discover that you, too, are safe, Master Twig,' said Tem Barkwater. He paused. 'I . . . that is, we hoped the captain might be with you.'

Twig shook his head. 'Cloud Wolf refused to abandon the *Stormchaser*,' he said. 'The last I saw of him, he had regained control of the sky ship and had steered it to the very centre of the Great Storm.'

'Good old cap'n Cloud Wolf,' said Tem Barkwater. 'The bravest sky pirate I ever met, and that's a fact. He'll be back to find us soon enough, you see if he isn't.'

Twig nodded, but said nothing. Now was not the time to mention the ball of lightning he had seen surrounding the sky ship, nor the explosion that followed. There was no point in crushing the sky pirates' hopes. On the other hand, waiting around for Cloud Wolf to return could prove fatal. In the event, it was the Professor of Light who came to his aid.

'You must all leave here as soon as you can,' he said.

The sky pirates turned to look at him. 'Without the cap'n?' said Tem, horrified.

'We have no way of knowing where the captain is,' said the professor. 'And in his absence, I recommend we elect a new captain. Someone to whom we all pledge our allegiance, someone who will lead us to the edge of the Twilight Woods.'

Tem shuffled about awkwardly. 'Who then?' he said gruffly.

'Why, Twig, of course,' said the professor. 'Who else? As the erstwhile captain's son and heir . . .'

The sky pirates gasped as one. Tem Barkwater shook his head in disbelief. 'Son and heir?' he exclaimed. 'What, young Twig? But, he can't be.'

'Are you doubting my word?' the Professor of Light demanded stiffly.

'No . . . Yes . . . I mean . . .' Tem bumbled.

'Quintinius . . . that is, Cloud Wolf told me himself,' the professor said. 'That is why he intended leaving the lad back in Undertown. For his own safety.'

Tem whistled through his teeth. 'I remember the cap'n once telling us about a child born to him and the lady Maris,' he said. 'They had no choice but to abandon him to his fate in the Deepwoods . . .' He turned to Twig, who nodded.

'I was that child,' he said.

Tem stared for a moment, nonplussed. Then, abruptly, he drew his sword, raised it high and fell to his knees. 'To you, Captain Twig, son of Cloud Wolf, I pledge my life.'

Seeing his example, Spiker, Stope Boltjaw and the Stone Pilot followed suit. Twig reddened. It was all happening so quickly. Sky pirate captain – and he didn't even have a sky ship! Nevertheless, as custom required, he drew his own sword and crossed it with the raised swords of the sky pirates, one after the other.

'And I to you,' he said. 'And I to you.'

The sky pirates replaced their swords, raised their heads and cried out, 'Captain Twig, we await your word.'

'Yes, well, I . . .' Twig faltered. His face turned redder still.

'There is a star,' the Professor of Light interjected. 'The East Star. Not only is its light a constant amidst the shifting passage of the constellations, but it is also bright enough to be seen by twilight.' He bent his knees and looked up awkwardly into the sky. 'There,' he said, pointing. 'There it is.'

The sky pirates all turned and looked. One after the other, they too saw the East Star, twinkling softly in the golden glow. Twig nodded. It was time for him to assume the control he had been given.

'If we keep the star in front of us,' he said, 'it will ensure that we are walking in a straight line. Sooner or later, we are bound to reach the edge of the Twilight Woods. Are you with me?'

'Aye aye, cap'n,' they replied. 'We are with you.'

'Then let us go,' Twig said. 'Professor, you walk with me. Hubble, you bring up the rear. Make sure no-one straggles or strays.'

'Wuh-wuh,' the banderbear replied.

They set off once more, with Twig feeling more confident than at any other time since his arrival in the Twilight Woods. He had a purpose now: an aim, a destination. What was more, he had responsibilities beyond himself. He glanced back at the crew as they waded after him through the thick, liquid air.

They had all suffered injuries during their emergency escape. Spiker's arms and face were badly bruised, Tem Barkwater's nose looked broken, the Stone Pilot was limping awkwardly, while Stope Boltjaw had lost his makeshift lower jaw, leaving his head gaping open in a permanent, empty grin. Worst of all, however, was Hubble.

At their initial reunion, Twig had been too overjoyed to notice. But now, as he looked at the banderbear, he saw that he was in a sorry state. The white fur down his front was stained and matted with blood, and he wheezed noisily with every step he took. Twig could only pray that his old friend's injuries were not as bad as they appeared.

Twig turned back, and checked they were still heading towards the star. 'It was good of you to accompany us,'

he said to the professor.

'Ah, well,' he said. 'My motives were not altogether selfless, for I too need to find the edge of the Twilight Woods.'

Twig was surprised. 'But I thought you intended staying here,' he said.

'Indeed I do,' said the professor. 'But if I am to calculate the number of Great Storms I must first establish the total area of the Twilight Woods. And I can't do that by remaining somewhere in the middle.'

'No,' said Twig absent-mindedly. 'I suppose you can't.'

Something had occurred to him – something worrying. Assuming they did make it to the edge of the Twilight Woods, what then? The Mire was notoriously dangerous even to fly over; how much more dangerous

it would be to cross on foot. What was more, as captain, he would be responsible for his crew's well-being. Shivering with anticipation, Twig turned back to the professor for advice.

'What the . . .!' he exclaimed. The professor was not there. He spun around in a panic, and saw him several paces back, crouched down stiffly on a bank beside a tree.

'To see a world in a grain of stormphrax,' he was saying. 'To hold infinity in the palm of one's hand . . .'

'Professor!' Twig shouted, and shook him firmly by the shoulder.

The Professor of Light turned and stared into Twig's eyes. Slowly, slowly, there was recognition. 'Twig,' he said. 'I . . . I am so sorry,' he said. 'Let us continue,' he said.

'Thank you, Professor,' said Twig. 'I . . .' He paused and turned to the others. 'This is too hazardous,' he said. 'We must make sure that none of us wanders off – even if his mind does.'

'A rope,' said Spiker.

'Of course!' said Tem Barkwater enthusiastically, as he swung his own coil of rope down from his shoulder. 'We must all tie ourselves together in a line.'

Twig nodded and supervised the operation. He kept Hubble at the back, tying the rope right round his immense waist. Next, at regular intervals, he made slip-knots, got the sky pirates to put their left hands through the loops and tightened them around their wrists, one after the other. Tem Barkwater, Spiker, Stope Boltjaw, the

Professor of Light. Lastly, he tied the remaining length of rope around his own waist.

'Right,' he announced. 'Onwards!'

Bound together, the ramshackle crew continued through the Twilight Woods, on towards the distant star twinkling far, far in front of them. Twig shuddered. 'I hope the end is not too far,' he whispered.

'. . . too far . . .' the air whispered back.

Just then, a sudden commotion erupted behind him. Twig spun round and looked down the line of sky pirates. Someone was missing.

'Where's Stope Boltjaw?' he demanded, as he strode angrily towards the empty slip-knot.

'Gone,' said Spiker.

'Gone?' said Twig.

'Kept muttering about how he couldn't, how he *wouldn't* leave his precious jaw behind. The next thing I know, he's trotting off into the undergrowth.' He pointed. 'Over that way.'

Twig shook his head and turned on the others furiously. 'How could you have let this happen?'

'Wuh-wuh, wuh,' the banderbear explained.

It was then that Twig realized Hubble was not merely standing beside Tem Barkwater, but was holding him tightly. He, like Stope Boltjaw, had broken away from the rope.

'What is it? What happened?' he said. 'Tem? What's the matter?'

But Tem would not return his gaze. 'Leave me be!' he snarled. 'Let me go.' His eyes suddenly focused on something to his left. 'Cal!' he shouted out. 'Don't go without me.'

Twig turned, but there was no-one there – at least, no-one visible to him.

'Cal!' Tem shouted. 'Wait for me. Oh, my poor, wonderful brother – it has been so long.' He thrashed violently in Hubble's arms. 'LET ME GO!' he roared. 'NOW!'

Twig stared at the huge, red-faced sky pirate struggling in Hubble's arms like a toddler in the middle of a tantrum, and shook his head in dismay. The Twilight Woods were taking their toll on the crew's sanity far more quickly than he had thought possible.

'My brother,' Tem was ranting. 'I have searched so long . . .'

'It's an illusion, Tem,' Twig said. 'A trick. There's no-one there.'

'Cal!' he cried out. 'Cal, answer me,' and he began struggling all the more violently. 'LET ME GO!' he boomed.

Twig bit into his lower lip. Ever since he had first met up with the sky pirates, Tem Barkwater had always been so good to him – how could he now abandon him to the Twilight Woods? Yet, in his present state, he was a danger to them all. Certainly Hubble, injured as he was, would not be able to hold him for much longer. He turned to the banderbear sadly.

'Let him go, Hubble,' he said.

The moment Hubble released his grip, Tem calmed down. He looked round about him blindly for a moment – then smiled. 'Cal,' he cried, and trundled back the way they'd come. 'Cal, wait for me.'

As Twig watched him lumbering away, tears welled up in his eyes. Big old dependable old Tem Barkwater was going. 'Bye bye, my friend,' he called. 'And may you find who you are looking for.'

He felt a soft but heavy hand on his shoulders. It was Hubble. 'Wuh-wuh,' the giant creature said softly.

'I know,' said Twig. 'We'll *all* miss him.'

Down in number, and in spirit, the party continued in the direction of the East Star – Spiker, the Stone Pilot and Hubble, with the Professor of Light and Twig up at the front. They walked in silence. They walked alone. The abandoned rope lay on the ground far behind them, already gathering dust. Twig gripped his sword and gritted his teeth.

How did such a fearful place ever come to exist? Twig wondered miserably. He turned to the others. 'Come on,' he urged. 'Keep up. It can't be far now.'

'Right behind you, cap'n,' said Spiker, breaking into a trot.

'Wuh-wuh,' added Hubble and lumbered wheezily after him.

The Stone Pilot, on the other hand, must have mis-understood what Twig had said. He stopped and began waving his arms and stomping his feet as much as the heavy overcoat and heavier boots would allow. Sepia dust rose up in clouds. The glass eye-panels set into his hood gleamed dazzling gold.

'Oh, no,' Twig sighed. 'Not you, too.'

The Stone Pilot – the most practical and loyal of all the sky pirates – had also ended up succumbing to the immortal madness of the Twilight Woods.

'Wuh-wuh?' said Hubble.

'I don't know,' said Twig. He approached cautiously. With the Stone Pilot's head completely hidden beneath his long heavy hood, it was difficult to guess what might be going on in his mind. 'Can you hear me?' he bellowed. 'Are you all right?'

A gruff and muffled grunt emerged from the hood, and the Stone Pilot pushed Twig roughly aside and pointed.

'I know,' said Twig. 'I have also seen . . .'

'GRURRGH!' the Stone Pilot grunted impatiently. He spun Twig round and grasped him by the head.

'What the . . !' Twig exclaimed. 'Have you gone mad? Hubble! Help!'

The Stone Pilot grunted again, and twisted Twig's head around, forcing him to look where he'd been point-ing. Hubble came trundling headlong towards them. 'WUH!' he roared.

'Gruuh grunh!' the Stone Pilot's muffled voice insisted.

'Oh!' gasped Twig as he finally realized what the Stone Pilot had seen.

Hubble lunged awkwardly at the Stone Pilot.

'It's OK!' Twig screamed. 'Look!'

All of them turned and stared ahead. And there, between a gap in the trees directly beneath the East Star, shone a patch of bleached brightness.

'It's the Mire,' Twig whispered. He turned to the others excitedly. 'We've made it! We've reached the edge of the Twilight Woods and . . .' He paused. Were his eyes deceiving him once again, or was there someone there? He peered more closely. Yes. There was no doubt. A gaunt, angular figure, hands on hips and legs astride, was standing silhouetted against the brightness beyond.

Hubble sniffed the air and growled uneasily, his wispy ears fluttering with suspicion. Unaware of the bander-bear's misgivings, Twig strode ahead with the Professor of Light.

'I'm leaving!' he called into the dancing patterns of light and shade. 'And I won't ever come back.'

'. . . come back . . . come back . . .' the woods called back, coaxing, cajoling.

Twig fixed his gaze giddily on the stooped figure up ahead. The air whispered and shimmered as, all round, the squirming, swirling mist of ghostly creatures struggled to steal him away once and for all.

'. . . come back . . . come back . . .' they echoed.

'Never,' Twig cried, and fumbled for his sword. 'Never!'

'. . . ever . . . ever . . . ever . . .' the woods replied.

# ·CHAPTER SEVENTEEN·

# THE MIRE TAKES ITS TOLL

Screed Toe-taker watched the approaching party from under hooded eyes. A mixture of amusement and disdain played on his thin, white lips.

'Well, well, well,' he rasped. 'What *have* we here?'

As a rule, the travellers who passed his way journeyed in groups of their own kind. A gang of darkridge goblins, a gaggle of barkelves, a family of woodtrolls – or, he remembered with a smirk – gnokgoblins.

But this shower!

He stooped and squinted. There was a youth. And an elderly character – perhaps his grandfather – who looked as if some tree or other had taken root in the back of his white robes. Then a small creature – an oakelf, by the look of him. And someone or something in heavy hooded clothing. And ... Screed groaned. 'A bander-bear,' he muttered huskily.

Screed Toe-taker was wary of banderbears, and with good reason. Not only were the creatures prodigiously strong, but they were also oddly intuitive. Only once before had he tried to take a banderbear's toes – it had almost cost him his life.

Screed smirked. 'Almost!' he whispered for, as always, the element of night-time surprise had proved too much for his victim. 'Mind you,' he said, 'he wasn't nearly as big and mean-looking as this character. I'm going to have to watch my step.'

Those last few steps were proving the most challenging of all for Twig. As he stumbled onwards the spectres, wraiths and ghouls taunted him wickedly. 'Your father, Cloud Wolf,' they whispered. 'Will you leave him here? Alone? Without his only son?'

'I have no choice,' Twig muttered tearfully.

'Come on,' he heard the professor saying. 'Put on your gauntlet and raise high your sword. You can make it, Twig. You can break free of the Twilight Woods.'

'Yes . . .' Twig said uncertainly. He did what the professor had told him. 'Yes, I can – I *will* make it.' He paused. 'Are the others with us?'

'We're all still here,' Spiker confirmed.

Twig looked up ahead. At the end of the long swirling tunnel of his vision hung the star. Below it stood the pale, angular figure. Step followed faltering step as Twig kept on towards them both.

'Not far now,' the professor said encouragingly. 'Soon be there.'

Twig spun round to face him and grasped him by the arm. 'Then you must stop,' he said. 'If you go too far you will die.'

From his position at the edge between the Mire and the Twilight Wood, Screed Toe-taker was growing impatient. 'Oh, for Sky's sake, what's going on now?' he grumbled angrily. 'If it isn't one of them, it's the other.' Then, noticing how the bander-bear's ears were fluttering, he changed tack.

'Come on!' he yelled. 'I only want to help you – before it's too late.'

As the words from outside the Twilight Woods echoed round Twig's head, the spectral voices and visions finally released their hold over him. His ears cleared. His eyes unmisted. He recognized the woods for what they were – a tawdry place, glittering yet gloomy, heavy with torpor and the reek of decay.

The Professor of Light looked up at Twig. 'I'm all right to go a little further,' he said.

'Are you certain,' said Twig.

The professor nodded. 'Quite certain,' he said, and turned away. 'Come on.'

Remembering that he was captain, Twig straightened

up and called back as Cloud Wolf would have done. 'Greetings!' he said. 'I am Twig, sky pirate captain. State your name and business.'

Screed sniggered unpleasantly. 'A whelp with the words of a woodwolf,' he muttered under his breath. He raised his head. 'My name is Screed,' he replied. 'And my business is to guide travellers across the treacherous Mire.'

The banderbear snarled ominously.

'Though perhaps you have no interest in my services,' Screed continued, his eyes skittering back and forth under lowered lids. 'Perhaps you already know all about the Mire, with its sinking-mud and poisonous blow-holes, its muglumps, oozefish, white ravens . . .'

'No, no,' said Twig. 'I might well be interested.'

He walked the last few yards of the Twilight Woods and halted at the very edge. Screed – one step away – was standing in the Mire. Between them lay an invisible line separating the two places. For a moment, they stared at one another in silence. From far away over the bleached wasteland came the sound of raucous cawing.

'White ravens,' said Screed. 'Fighting over a carcass – the smell of blood drives them to a frenzy.'

Behind him Twig was aware of the others' unease.

Screed smiled craftily. 'Sometimes they don't wait until you're dead to attack,' he rasped.

Twig winced. The Mire was – as he well knew – a harsh and perilous place, yet he did not trust this Screed character with his deathly pallor and sly bloodshot eyes.

Oh, Sky above – some sky pirate captain I am! thought

Twig miserably. And he found himself wishing once again that his father was here with him. *He'd* know what to do.

For the third time since Twig had been elected captain, it was the Professor of Light who came to his aid. Stepping forwards, he stood next to Twig.

'So how much do you charge, per individual?' he said.

*Charge!* thought Twig in alarm. The thought of paying for the guide's services hadn't even occurred to him, yet of course the curious bleached creature would want rewarding. Twig, however, didn't have a bean to his name. None of the crew did.

'Tell you what,' Screed said, rubbing his chin thoughtfully. 'Special offer for sky pirates.' He looked at them askance. 'Two hundred each.'

Twig trembled. With four of them planning to cross the Mire, that was eight hundred – eight hundred he hadn't got.

The professor, however, seemed unconcerned. 'A thousand in all,' he said. 'I can cover that.'

Now Twig was really confused. 'But . . .' he began. 'I thought . . .'

The Professor of Light turned towards him. 'After much consideration, I have decided to go with you,' he announced. 'If you'll have me, that is.'

'Yes, yes, of course,' said Twig uncertainly. 'But you said . . .'

'I will take my chances,' the professor said. 'Who knows, perhaps my neck will mend . . .' He paused. 'At any rate, I cannot stay here.'

'But you were so sure,' said Twig. 'You said . . .'

'I know what I said,' the professor interrupted. 'I thought I'd be able to research stormphrax if I remained. But I was wrong. Although the Twilight Woods would indeed give me the time to study, they would also rob me of the ability to do so.'

Screed Toe-taker tutted impatiently.

Ignoring him, the professor went on. 'I am an academic, Twig,' he said. 'Why, in Sanctaphrax I am known for the sharpness of my intellect. I can recite Dilnix's ancient *Treatise on the Properties of Light*, I know *The Thousand Luminescent Aphorisms of Archemax* by heart . . . Yet here, in this terrible mind-numbing place, I can barely remember who I am.'

'So, you mean . . .'

'I mean, I would rather die a dignified death than suffer the ignominy of an eternity of ignorance.' He pulled a leather pouch from the folds of his gown and handed it to Twig. 'There's five hundred in there,' he said. 'He can have the rest when we arrive.'

Twig turned to Screed, and shuddered as he caught the gangly individual staring down at the professor's feet, licking his lips. 'If you agree to the terms,' he said, offering the leather pouch, 'we have a deal.'

Screed looked up and smirked. 'Very glad to hear it,' he said. He took the pouch in one hand, slipped it down the front of his jerkin and reached out again to shake Twig's hand.

Twig shuddered at the touch of the dry, bony fingers. 'Come then,' said Screed, and he pulled him gently but firmly across the invisible line, out of the Twilight Woods – and into the Mire.

Twig stopped and turned back. The Professor of Light hadn't moved. Despite his resolve, it was a hard step to take – after all, it might be his last.

'Come on,' said Screed irritably. 'We haven't got all day.'

'You take as long as you like, Professor,' said Twig.

Screed snorted, and turned away in disgust. Twig put out his arm for the professor to steady himself upon.

'Thank you, Twig,' said the professor. 'Whatever may happen, my boy, it has been an honour and a pleasure getting to know you. One day you will be a fine sky pirate captain. With your own ship. I know you will.'

And, so saying, the professor took that all-important step forwards. Twig, who was expecting him to collapse at any moment, moved to support him. But the professor did not collapse. He winced with pain as he crossed into the Mire. He cried out. He stumbled a little. But he remained standing.

From behind him, Spiker, Hubble and the Stone Pilot cheered with delight. 'Well done, Professor,' they said.

'Yes, well done!' Twig beamed. 'You'll be as right as rain once we get you back to Sanctaphrax.' The professor smiled weakly. His face had turned a deathly shade of grey. Twig's face clouded with concern. 'H . . . how *are* you feeling?' he asked him anxiously.

'Alive,' the professor groaned. 'Just about. But I'm afraid I'm going to be rather slow. Perhaps it would be better if . . .'

'No,' said Twig resolutely. 'You're coming with us. We'll all take it in turns to help you.' He turned to the others. 'Come on, then, you lot. Let's go.'

'And not before time, either,' said Screed waspishly.

As the
remaining crew-
members shambled
forwards, Screed turned and
strode off. Twig followed after, with
his arm around the professor's back.

'Look lively!' Screed called back. 'And
remember, keep together, walk where I walk – and
don't look back.'

Twig's heart sank as he looked ahead and saw just
how far they had to go. The Mire seemed to stretch on
for ever. If he had been on his own, the journey would
have been daunting. With the professor leaning heavily
against him . . .

'One step at a time,' the professor wheezed, as if reading his mind. Twig nodded, and looked down at the white mud as it oozed around his feet. The professor was right. They were out of the Twilight Woods, and *that* was what mattered, for although the Mire was as perilous as it was vast, it too had boundaries. And, thanks to their fortuitous encounter with a guide . . .

'Cap'n! Cap'n!' he heard Spiker shrieking with alarm. For an instant Twig forgot that the oakelf was addressing *him*. He looked round automatically for Cloud Wolf. 'Cap'n Twig!' Spiker screamed. 'You must come quick. It's Hubble!'

Twig glanced ahead. The albino banderbear was lying in a heap on the soft ground.

'You go,' said the professor. 'I can stand unaided.'

Twig didn't need telling twice. He raced through the thick, sucking mud and fell to his knees beside his friend. 'What is it?' he said. 'Hubble, what's wrong?'

'Wuh . . . wuh-wuh,' the banderbear groaned. He clutched at his chest, and turned his massive head away.

'Hubble!' Twig cried, his eyes filling with tears. 'Hubble, speak to me. Tell me what to do.'

'Wu-uuh,' the banderbear moaned softly, and was suddenly racked with a fearful gurgling cough that sent spasms of pain shooting through his body.

Twig struggled to hold back his tears. The injuries Hubble had sustained during his descent from the *Stormchaser* were internal – and far more serious than Twig had realized. His breath came in short wheezing pants. Twig stroked the creature's neck, whispering all

the time that everything would all be all right, everything would be fine. The banderbear smiled weakly and
closed his eyes.

'T-wuh-g. Wuh-wuh. Fr-uh-nz . . .'

Suddenly, a trickle of blood – dazzling red against the
thick white fur – welled in
the corner of his mouth,
over-flowed and ran down
his cheek. Hubble coughed
again, trembled, spluttered –
and fell still.

'NO!' Twig wailed, and
threw himself round
Hubble's neck. 'Not you.
Not now. You can't be dead!' he howled. 'You seemed so
. . . so well . . .'

'It happens to the best of them,' came a mocking voice
from behind him. Twig froze. 'One minute they're fine,'
he continued. 'The next, dead as . . .'

'Screed!' Twig roared, as he leaped to his feet and
drew his sword. 'One more word and, so help me, I shall
slice you in two.'

Screed sneered. 'And condemn your crew to certain
death?' he said. 'I don't think so.' He turned away, leaving Twig quivering with impotent rage.

'Come, Twig,' said the Professor of Light. 'You can do
no more for your friend.'

'I know,' said Twig. He sniffed. 'But . . .'

'Come,' the professor repeated. 'Before that scoundrel,
Screed, gets too far away.'

## ·CHAPTER EIGHTEEN·

# TOE-TAKING

Screed Toe-taker could hardly believe his luck. When the banderbear had collapsed, it was all he could do not to leap about with delight. Struck down the moment it had left the immortality of the Twilight Woods, the most dangerous member of the group was a danger no longer.

'And the others will be easy pickings,' he whispered to himself, and wheezed with wicked laughter. 'The old fellow will slow them down nicely.' He paused, and rubbed his jaw thoughtfully. 'Still,' he added, 'it does seem a shame to let good toes go to waste. Particularly such large and hairy ones.'

He looked round to see where the rest of the group had got to, and was pleased to discover that – despite his advice – they were already strung out in a long line. Far away at the back was the oakelf. He was clearly in trouble.

'Not long now, little one,' Screed whispered menacingly. 'And not much longer for you either,' he said, turning his attention to the heavily-clothed figure limping along in the middle of the line. 'And as for you two,' he said, as he focused in on the youth and the old person on his arm, 'you, my twinkly-toed friends, will be the glitter on the icing!'

He raised his arms and cupped his bony, parchment fingers to his mouth. 'Hey!' His cracked voice echoed round the bleached landscape like the cawing of the white ravens. Neither of them paid it any attention.

'Hey, you!' Screed bellowed. 'Captain Twig!'

This time the youth looked up.

'What is it?' he called back, his voice fluttering on the wind.

'We're nearly half-way,' Screed shouted. Then he pointed behind him. 'You see that jagged bit on the horizon. It's the mast of a wrecked ship. That's where we're headed. When we get there, we can all rest up a bit.'

'We must rest now!' Twig shouted back.

Screed smiled to himself. 'Out of the question, I'm afraid. This whole area is infested with the worst type of oozefish. Eat you alive as soon as look at you.'

There was a pause.

'Well, can you at least go a little slower?' Twig called.

'Course I can, Captain,' Screed called back amiably. 'But I shan't!' he added under his breath. He raised his hands to his mouth again. 'Now, you just keep right on till you get to that shipwreck,' he said. 'You'll be all right so long as you keep going in a straight line. But watch out. There are poisonous blow-holes on both sides, and the sinking-mud is treacherous. So, don't stray from the path.'

'We won't,' he heard Twig calling back.

'Oh, and one last thing,' Screed shouted. 'Although it looks flat, the Mire is quite bumpy. Don't panic if you can't see me or the ship for a couple of minutes. Just keep going.'

'OK!' shouted Twig.

Screed chuckled to himself. What an obliging young fellow this Captain Twig was proving to be. He turned away contentedly and continued across the fetid waste-land. The white sun glinted on the distant shipwreck. Screed knew that although it was nearer than it looked, it was also farther than any of the guileless party of sky pirates would ever get.

'Muglumps, oozefish and white ravens,' he snorted. 'They are as nothing compared with me. For I, Screed Toe-taker, am the most dangerous creature in all this great white wilderness – as you will discover to your cost, *Captain* Twig,' he sneered.

Screed's words echoed round and round Twig's head. *Don't stray from the path*. It was what Spelda and Tuntum, the woodtrolls who had brought him up as their own, were always telling him. Yet if he hadn't strayed from the path then, he would still be living in the Deepwoods to this day. This time, however, Twig knew that the advice was sound, for if the professor slipped or stumbled, it could prove fatal.

With his head fixed to the branch at his back, the injured professor could not look down, and so it was left to Twig to keep an eye on where they were stepping – and that meant looking away from their destination. Each time he glanced up again, he found they had drifted to one side or the other.

'Must I do everything?' Twig complained irritably. 'Why don't you tell me when we're wandering off course?'

'I can't,' said the professor. 'My eyes are closed.'

'Well open them!' Twig snapped impatiently.

'I can't,' he repeated wearily. 'With my head fixed at this angle, my eyes are set towards the sun. If I stare at it too long, I'll go blind.' He snorted miserably. 'And what use is a Professor of Light who cannot see? I'd end up begging on the streets of Undertown.'

Twig turned away guiltily. 'I'm sorry,' he said. 'I . . .'

'Oh, my dear boy,' said the professor, 'you are the last person under Sky who should apologize. You stuck by me in the Twilight Woods; you are sticking by me now. I am, and shall remain, eternally grateful to you.' He paused. 'It's that Screed character I'd like to tear off a strip. He *said* he'd slow down.'

Twig nodded, but said nothing. Perhaps the guide *had* slowed down. He and the professor were making such painfully slow progress that it was difficult to tell.

The journey was taking on the never-ending quality of a nightmare. Every yard was like a mile, every second seemed to take an hour.

'Sky above!' the professor moaned. 'How much further to go? I don't think I can take much more of this.'

'You're going to be fine,' Twig assured him as he glanced over his shoulder to check that Spiker and the Stone Pilot were still following them. 'It can't be that far now.' He turned back and looked up ahead – and gasped with horror.

'What is it?' said the professor, his eyes snapping open.

'Screed,' said Twig, as he unhooked his telescope with one hand and frantically scoured the horizon. 'He's not there!'

The Professor of Light squinted into the distance. 'He warned us this might happen,' he said.

'I know, but . . .'

'Come now,' said the professor. 'I am old and in pain. I am allowed to be disheartened. But not you, Twig. You have your whole future in front of you.'

Twig stared ahead glumly. 'Mud,' he muttered, 'that's all I can see in front of *me*. Oh, Professor. If only I hadn't disobeyed my father, none of this would have happened. But no. I wouldn't do as I was told. Stubborn and stupid, I had to sneak back on board the *Stormchaser*. This is *all* my fault.'

'Twig, my boy,' said the professor gently. 'What's done is done. I am not about to apportion blame. The important thing now is how you deal with the consequences of your actions. If you ... WAAAAAH!' he screamed, as at that moment and without any warning, a scalding blow-hole erupted between the two of them.

'Professor!' Twig cried, as he was torn from his side.

He stared up in horror at the thick column of seething mud which shot up into the air like the trunk of a great white tree. Higher and higher it rose, loudly roaring, before folding over on itself and tumbling back to earth in a shower of thick, sticky globules.

'Professor!' Twig cried again. 'Where are you?'

'Over here,' came a quavering voice from the far side of the column of mud. 'I'm stuck.'

'Just hold on,' Twig called back. 'I'm coming to get you.'

As the mud spewed forth from the hole, clouds of noxious steam billowed up all round Twig. Coughing and spluttering, eyes streaming, he staggered forwards. The heat shimmered. The mud gushed. Twig raised his arm to his face, but nothing could keep out the breath-snatching stench.

'Can't ... find ... you ...' he gasped.

'Here,' the professor's frail voice replied. It sounded close. Twig stopped, wiped his eyes and peered through the dense mist. And there, staring back at him, was the professor, not three strides ahead.

'Stop!' he was shouting. 'Not a step further.'

For a moment, Twig could make no sense of what he saw. Clearly, the professor had not landed on his back for, although his head was most definitely at ground level, it was staring ahead, not up at the sky. And then he understood. The Professor of Light had fallen into a patch of quickmud. It was already up to his armpits.

Twig pulled his scarf from around his neck and tied it over his mouth and nose as a makeshift mask. Then, he removed his sky pirate's coat, knelt down at the edge of the sinking-mud and, with the collar and shoulders gripped tightly in his hands, tossed the other end towards the professor.

'Grab hold of it,' he gasped. 'I'll pull you out.'

The professor clung on. Twig braced his legs, leaned backwards – and pulled as he had never pulled before.

'Heave! Heave! Heave!' he grunted desperately.

Slowly, slowly, the professor began to emerge from the ground. First his chest appeared, then his stomach . . .

'Oh, my neck,' the professor whimpered. 'My poor, poor neck.'

'Nearly there,' Twig gasped. 'Just . . .'

*Squellssh . . . POP!*

The sucking mud had released its grip on the professor's legs. He lay on his front, head down.

'Professor,' said Twig urgently, as he rolled him onto his back and wiped the claggy mud from his face. 'Professor, can you hear me?'

The professor's thin, cracked lips parted. 'Yes,' he croaked faintly. 'I can hear you . . . You saved my life.'

'Not yet I haven't,' said Twig. 'But I shall. Climb on my back.'

'Oh, Twig,' the professor protested. 'I couldn't . . . *You* couldn't . . .'

'We won't know until we try,' said Twig. He slipped his coat back on, turned and hunkered down. 'Put your arms around my neck,' he instructed. 'That's it.'

Then, with a grunt of effort, he straightened up, grasped the back of the professor's bony legs with his hands and set off. Away from the quickmud, he trudged. Away from the blow-hole with its poisonous mist and fountain of scalding mud. On and on through the bleached and boggy landscape. The temperature dropped. The air cleared.

'Still no sign of Screed,' the professor muttered at
length. 'A deceitful individual if ever there was one.
Takes our money, he does, and then abandons us to our
fate. Probably sat in that shipwreck right now, with his
feet up.'

Twig raised his head and stared out across the Mire.
The shipwreck was, at last, looking nearer.

'To Open Sky with that scurvy cur,' Twig cursed, and
spat on the ground. 'With or without Screed's help,
Spiker, the Stone Pilot, you and I are going to survive
this ordeal. As captain of this crew, I give you my word.'

Screed was not in his wrecked sky ship home. The
moment he was sure that no-one would notice, he had
ducked down out of sight behind a rock and rolled in
the mud until he was covered from head to foot in the
bleached sludge.

'Make myself disappear, I shall,' he said, and chuckled
throatily.

Then, satisfied that he was perfectly camouflaged,
Screed climbed to his feet and doubled back across
the Mire as fast as he could, keeping parallel to the
path the sky pirates were taking. Although he could

see them, they couldn't see him.

'Keep to the path, you addleskulls,' he hissed as he passed Twig and the old fellow. 'Don't want you getting swallowed up by the Mire, do we? At least, not yet.'

On and on he loped. Past the curious figure in the heavy clothes; past the oakelf – now down on his hands and knees – and on towards the body of the bander-bear. As he drew close, he saw that he was not the first on the scene. The white ravens were already tearing into the carcass with their beaks and claws.

'Be gone, you bleached devils!' Screed roared as he raced towards them, arms flapping wildly.

The white ravens bounced back on their springy legs, furiously cawing – but did not fly away. Screed crouched down. Although much of the body had already been consumed by the scavengers, the feet – huge, hairy and rapier clawed – were still intact. As he tilted his head to one side, the sun glinted on the countless minute crystals trapped in the fur between the toes.

'Such beea-oootiful looty-booty,' Screed smirked.

He drew his knife from his belt and, with the detached precision of a surgeon, sliced off the toes and slipped them into his leather bag. The white ravens screeched and squawked in a frenzy of frustration.

'There,' he told them. 'All yours now.' And with that, he swung the bag onto his shoulder and loped off again. 'One down,' he chuckled. 'Four to go.'

Spiker was the first he came to. The oakelf was still down on his hands and knees – yet no longer able to crawl. His breath came fast and wheezing. Screed stood, hands on his hips, looking down at the pitiful creature. The next moment he wrapped his arm around the oakelf's shoulders and pulled backwards. The blade of his knife glinted for an instant. The oakelf gurgled, clutched at his throat – and collapsed.

'Did him a favour, really,' Screed muttered to himself as he set to work on the toes. 'Putting him out of his misery like that.' He stood up and looked ahead at the figure with the hood, still struggling painfully on.

'Ready or not,' he muttered. 'Here I come!'

The exhausting trek was taking its toll on Twig. Although little more than skin and bones wrapped up in a gown, the Professor of Light's weight seemed to be increasing as Twig lugged him, without a break, across the squelching, stagnant mud.

'Almost there,' the professor said. 'Just a few steps more.'

Suddenly, Twig found himself crossing into shadow. The air was instantly cooler. He looked up. The wreck of the great ship towered high above him.

'Thank Sky!' he gasped.

'Thank *you*,' said the professor.

Twig released the professor's legs and gently eased him off his back. 'Aaah!' he sighed, and his arms floated upwards as if by themselves. 'I feel as if I could fly!'

The professor tutted sympathetically. 'Was I really such a burden?'

'For a while back there, I thought we weren't going to make it,' Twig admitted. 'But we're here now.' He looked round. 'Screed!' he shouted.

'Screed ... Screed ... Screed ...' the name echoed unanswered into the distance.

Twig shook his head. 'Where is he? What's he playing at?'

The professor snorted. 'I wouldn't put anything past that scoundrel,' he said.

Twig started with sudden alarm. Spiker and the Stone Pilot! He'd been so intent on rescuing the professor that he'd forgotten all about the rest of his crew.

He scampered over the overturned hull of the ship, leaped across to the mast and began shinning up. Even though the boat was resting at a perilous angle on the white mud, the caternest was still by far the highest landmark in the Mire. He looked back the way he had come.

Far away in the distance, he saw something. Brown on white. Motionless. Trembling with fearful anticipation, Twig unhooked his telescope from the front of his coat and put it to his eye.

'Spiker,' he gasped, as the terrible scene came into focus.

'What's happened?' he heard the professor calling up to him.

'It's ... it's Spiker,' he called back. 'He's dead. Murdered.'

'And the Stone Pilot?' the professor asked.

Twig swung the telescope round, sweeping the glistening white plains for any sign. 'I ... I'm just trying to find him,' he blustered. Suddenly, a dark blurred shape filled the centre of the glass as it emerged from behind a bleached rock. His sweaty hands, shaking uncontrollably, slipped as he tried to adjust the focus. 'Yes!' he cried. 'It's him. And he's quite near.'

'Alive?'

Twig nodded. 'Just,' he said. 'But he's dragging his right leg badly. He can barely walk. I ...' He gasped.

'What was *that*?'

Some way behind the Stone Pilot, he had seen movement. White on white, yet visible for all that – as if the Mire itself had grown a body and a head. Someone or something was moving towards the Stone Pilot.

'What is it?' Twig trembled. 'A mud-demon? A mire-monster? The terrible muglump?'

He re-focused the telescope. The creature came into sharp relief – the gangly arms and legs, the stooping back, the skull-like head with its tight skin that plucked at the mouth and eyebrows. Twig quivered with rage. This was no mud-demon or mire-monster.

'Screed,' he hissed. 'I might have known.'

The Stone Pilot stopped. Turned. And Twig heard a muffled cry of anguish as the Stone Pilot screamed and staggered backwards. A dazzling flash of light slashed across Twig's eyes.

'And he's got a knife!'

Twig snapped the telescope shut, scrambled down the mast, over the hull and ran back into the Mire.

'Where are you going?' called the professor.

'To help the Stone Pilot,' he called back. 'Before it's too late.'

With sweat pouring and his body aching, Twig stumbled on as fast as he could. Screed and the Stone Pilot were rolling about in the mud. Closer he got. The knife glinted. Closer and closer. Now the Stone Pilot had the upper hand; now Screed was on top. If he could just . . . All at once, the Stone Pilot's head fell back, struck by a savage blow. The knife glinted again.

'SCREED!' Twig screamed.

The bony white figure instantly leapt away from his prey, and turned on the youth like a cornered animal. His yellow teeth gleamed. 'Well, well,' he rasped, as he drew a long evil-looking sickle from his belt. 'Saved me the bother of coming to you, have you? *Most* considerate.' He bounced the sickle up and down in his bony hand. The blade gleamed along its razor edge.

The colour drained from Twig's cheeks. He had so little first-hand experience of one-armed combat.

'Come on then, *Captain* Twig,' Screed taunted, and beckoned with his free hand. 'Let's see what you're made of.' He scuttled closer like a mud-crab. 'Or perhaps you'd prefer to turn and run – I'll give you a head start,' he added and cackled mirthlessly.

Twig drew his sword and stared defiantly into Screed's bloodshot eyes.

'I will stay and fight you, Screed,' he announced, praying that the wicked creature would not notice how his voice trembled, how his arm shook. 'What's more,' he said boldly, 'I will defeat you.'

Screed stared back, but made no reply. He stooped lower and began swaying from side to side. Back and forwards flashed the sickle as he tossed it from hand to hand. And all the while he kept his unblinking gaze fixed on Twig's eyes. Then he jumped.

'Waah!' cried Twig, and leaped back. The curved blade sliced through the air, low and deadly. If he hadn't moved when he did, the sickle would have ripped his stomach wide open. Again the blade came at him.

He's toying with me, Twig told himself. Driving me back towards the sinking mud. Fight back! Fight back – or die!

He braced himself. Suddenly the sickle swooshed down towards him – fast, low and wickedly glinting – Twig held his breath, gripped his sword fiercely and brought it up to meet the sweeping blade.

'Unnh!' he grunted, as the crashing blow juddered up his arm and jarred his whole body.

'Come, come, captain,' Screed leered, as he bobbed and weaved around in front of him. 'Is that the best you can do?'

Suddenly, the air was whirling with the terrifying dance of the curved sickle. It spun, it plunged, it darted and dived. Heart in his mouth, Twig thrust his sword out. It clashed against the sickle again. And again and again . . .

I will defeat you! Twig's voice screamed in his head. For Spiker. For the Stone Pilot . . . For myself.

Screed darted abruptly to the left, and lunged forwards. Twig was too fast for him. He side-stepped out of danger, deflected the sickle harmlessly away and thrust his sword at Screed's scraggy neck.

'Now!' he roared as he blundered forwards. 'You . . .' His foot slipped down the side of a concealed pothole. 'Aaaaaiii!' he squealed as his ankle went over.

As Twig crashed heavily to the muddy ground, the sword slipped from his grip and landed in the soft mud – just out of reach. Screed was on him in an instant. He pinned down Twig's gauntleted arm with his foot and tickled him under the chin with the point of the merciless blade.

'Fancied your chances with Screed Toe-taker, did you, *Captain* Twig?' he said, his face twisted with contempt.

He lifted the sickle high above his head. It was silhouetted against the sky like a black moon. The blade glinted.

'SCREEDIUS TOLLINIX!' The professor's thin, reedy voice echoed across the Mire. 'What has that creature done to you?'

Screed froze, and turned his head. 'What the . . . ?' he murmured.

Without a second thought, Twig wrenched his trapped arm free, rolled over, seized his sword and struck Screed a savage and penetrating blow in the centre of his bony chest. Thick red blood poured down the sword. It met Twig's gauntlet and turned to clear, sparkling water which splashed down his arm.

The sickle dropped to the ground with a soft *plattsh*. Screed looked down. He seemed almost surprised to see the sword protruding from his chest. His puzzled gaze met Twig's.

Twig gasped. The expression on Screed's face was changing before his eyes. Away went the evil leer; away the sneering lips and wild eyes. From the barbaric blood-thirsty maniac who, only seconds before, had been intent on tearing him to pieces, Twig watched Screed transform into someone quite different; someone calm, thoughtful – noble, even. His eyes sparkled with a faraway look and a smile

played around his mouth. The lips parted, and a single word slipped out from between them.

'Sanctaphrax.'

The next moment, he fell to the ground, dead.

Twig climbed shakily to his feet. He stared at the motionless body. 'I've killed somebody,' he murmured as he closed Screed's eyes with his trembling finger-tips.

He looked at peace now and, as in those last moments of life, oddly majestic. A lump rose in Twig's throat. What had happened to turn him into so loathsome a creature? His gaze fell on the bag strung around the dead guide's shoulders. Might his personal belongings offer a clue? Twig leaned forwards, loosened the draw-strings and looked inside.

'Whoooaargh!' He retched emptily. Tears filled his eyes, but the sight of the cluster of toes lingered. He tossed the bag away, bent over double and took long deep breaths. 'Why?' he gasped at last and stared at Screed in horror. 'What kind of a monster were you?'

But he had no answers left to give. Twig pulled himself to his feet. As he turned away, the white ravens were already gathering. It was only then that he looked at the gauntlet.

## ·CHAPTER NINETEEN·

# SCREED'S
# LOOTY-BOOTY

With his sword cutting a swathe through the growing flock of scavenging birds, Twig hurried towards the Stone Pilot's body. The inside of the glass eye-panels set into the hood were misted up. Did this mean the Stone Pilot was still breathing? Could he still be alive after the savage blow that Screed had dealt him?

'If only I could get these things off,' Twig muttered as he tugged in vain at the set of bolts which held the hood and gloves in place. He knelt down and pressed his ear against the heavy coat, searching for a trace of a heartbeat. A broad grin spread over his face, for there it was – faint, but regular – the Stone Pilot's beating heart.

'Now, don't you worry,' Twig said as he leapt to his feet. 'I'll soon have you back at the shipwreck. It's cool there.' He slipped his hands under the Stone Pilot's arms and round his chest. 'You're going to be ... *wheeoo!* ...'

he groaned as he lifted the shoulders off the ground, '. . . just fine!'

With every gruelling step, Twig's body cried out for rest – yet he did not ease up, not even for a moment. If the Stone Pilot died, then Twig would have lost his entire crew and that was something he would not allow to happen.

'Almost there,' he muttered breathlessly. 'Not long now.'

The Stone Pilot made neither a sound nor a movement, but Twig knew that his heart must still be beating, for the white ravens were leaving them alone. The moment it stopped, they would attack in an instant.

At last, he found himself bathed once again in the long shadow cast by the shipwreck. Twig gazed up at the merciless white sky and offered silent thanks.

'Professor,' he called, looking about him. 'Professor?'

'In here,' came a weary voice from inside the shipwreck. Twig turned. To his left was a large hole in the side of the hull. 'In here,' the professor said again, his voice little more than a whisper.

As Twig dragged the Stone Pilot through the broken entrance, he was struck by the breathtaking smell of decay. He laid the Stone Pilot down beside the far wall and found the professor propped up against a fallen beam on the opposite side. The branch at his back was still keeping his neck poker-straight. He was alive – yet even in the gloom, it was clear that he was in a bad way.

'He killed him,' the professor was groaning. 'He murdered him.'

'No,' said Twig. 'He's injured – and perhaps badly, but he's still alive.'

The professor sighed weakly. 'Not the Stone Pilot,' he wheezed and swept his arm round. 'This ship,' he said. 'I found the name plate. It's the *Windcutter*. It was captained by Screedius Tollinix. Screedius Tollinix!' he wailed. 'A fine and valiant knight.' His eyes burned with rage. 'Until that loathsome guide got his hands on him, that is,' he added and collapsed in a fit of coughing.

Twig stared back at the professor. Of course! When the professor called out, Screed had recognized his own name. That was why he'd paused . . . And Twig had killed him. He hadn't the heart to tell the professor that Screedius Tollinix and their guide were one and the same.

He crouched down beside him. 'Try to get some sleep,' he said.

'No, no,' the professor said agitatedly. 'There will be time for sleep soon enough. There are things we must elucidate, explain: things we must discuss . . .' For a second his eyes went blank. When they focused again, they looked bewildered, frightened. 'Twig, my boy,' he said, his voice low and breathy. 'You must listen. And listen well. I must tell you about stormphrax.'

'But . . .' Twig began.

'After all, that is why I am here,' the professor went on. 'That is why your father insisted I travel with you all. For I know everything there is to know about the sacred crystals. Their value. Their properties. Their power.' He paused. 'Since stormphrax is too heavy to move when in darkness and too volatile in direct sunlight, we must . . . *you* must engineer a constant but dim light to accompany it until it has reached its resting place at the heart of the floating rock of Sanctaphrax. And when *that* happens . . .'

'But what's the point of all this?' Twig blurted out. 'We haven't got any stormphrax. We weren't able to retrieve any from the Twilight Woods. Or had you forgotten, Professor? We failed.'

'Twig, be quiet!' the professor insisted. He raised his arm and pointed to the far end of the hull. 'Over there,' he wheezed.

Twig turned. His eyes had grown accustomed to the darkness by now and, as he stared into the shadows, he saw a large chest half sunk in the mud. 'W . . . what is it?' he asked.

'Go and see,' said the professor.

As Twig crossed the oozing floor towards the chest, the smell of rotting flesh grew stronger. 'Woaagh!' he gasped, and gagged at the sight of the thousand miniature trophies nailed to the wooden walls. 'Bwwwoorrgh!' he heaved again, as the huge sloping pile in the corner revealed itself to be countless thousands more of the amputated toes.

'What in Sky's name?' he muttered, and looked back at the professor for some explanation.

The professor waved him on impatiently.

Twig stopped next to the glass and ironwood chest and looked down. The top was closed, but not locked. He hesitated. What if it was full of more body parts? What if Screed also had a thing for eyeballs, or tongues?

'Open it!' he heard the professor insist.

Twig leaned forwards, took a deep breath, and threw the lid open. A silvery light gleamed from within. Twig stared down and trembled with awe at the sight of the multitude of flashing, sparking crystals. 'Stormphrax!' he gasped.

'And more than enough for all our needs,' said the Professor of Light.

'But how?' said Twig. 'I . . .' He cut himself short. 'The toes!' he exclaimed.

'Precisely,' said the professor. 'As the hapless goblins, trolls, trogs or what have you set off from the Deepwoods for Undertown, their journey took them through the Twilight Woods. There, particles of storm-phrax collected under their toenails and claws, do you see? Then, when they reached the Mire, they encountered Screed – that most foul of individuals – who stole their money, slit their throats and took their toes.' He sighed wearily. 'Though why?' he moaned. 'That is the question. What use could such a degenerate soul have had for so wonderful a substance?'

The words of the sepia knight popped back into Twig's head. *A quest is a quest for ever.* And he shuddered with horror as he realized what must have happened.

Even though Screedius Tollinix had wrecked his ship, he had not been able to abandon his quest. After all, like Garlinius Gernix and Petronius Metrax before him and Quintinius Verginix after, he would have pledged to dedicate his life to the finding of stormphrax and sworn never to return to Sanctaphrax until and unless he had completed that sacred quest.

Unable to return to Sanctaphrax empty-handed, Screedius Tollinix had single-mindedly pursued his goal no matter what that involved. The noble Knight Academic, whom Twig had glimpsed at the moment of death, must have been driven insane by his desire to fulfil the promises he had made at the Inauguration Ceremony – no matter how much he amassed, it could never be enough.

'And I wouldn't like to guess how many had perished to satisfy the wicked creature's hideous lust,' the professor was saying.

Twig stared down at the glittering crystals. Each one, he now knew, had been paid for in blood. Trembling almost uncontrollably, he reached forwards, seized the lid and slammed it shut.

'It's not fair!' he stormed. 'I dreamed of returning – successful and victorious – with enough stormphrax to stabilize the floating city of Sanctaphrax for a thousand years.'

'But you still can,' the professor wheezed.

Twig rounded on him furiously. 'Not like this!' he shouted. Behind him, the Stone Pilot muttered drowsily. 'I wanted to discover new stormphrax, pure storm-phrax,' he continued. 'Fresh from a Great Storm. In the Twilight Woods. Not this . . . this evil treasure-trove scraped from the toes of the dead.'

'Ah, Twig,' the professor groaned. 'Twig, my boy . . .' He began coughing again, a low rasping sound that rattled in the back of his throat. 'Ends and means,' he wheezed. 'Ends and . . .' The racking cough returned, more heart-rending than ever.

'Professor!' Twig ran towards him. His face had turned a pale shade of yellowy-grey. His eyes were sunken, his cheeks hollow. Every breath was an effort. Twig took his hand. 'Professor, are you all right?'

The professor stared at Twig's gauntleted hand. Weakly, he drew his finger across the metal knuckles. Sepia dust clung to his fingertip. 'Of course,' he whispered, barely audibly. 'Phraxdust . . .' He paused.

'Yes,' said Twig, 'when Screed's blood touched it, it turned to pure water.' He bent down until his ear was all but pressing against the professor's quivering lips. The warm breath in his face smelt of decay.

'The secret . . .' the professor whispered. 'I know how to produce phraxdust. Safely.' He gasped and brought his hands to his throat. 'The Twilight Woods were telling us all the time.'

'Go on,' said Twig, and swallowed away his tears. 'In your own time, Professor.'

A smile played over the professor's lips. 'Time!' he croaked. 'Time . . .' His eyes rolled in his head. 'Stormphrax breaks down in the twilight of the woods. The twilight, Twig! Not darkness, not light – but twilight. Slowly it crumbles over the centuries, ground down by the pressure of twilight. Ground down, Twig, for hundreds upon hundreds of years, into dust. Phraxdust. The phraxdust that coats the armour of those poor lost knights – that coats the glove you wear.'

Twig looked down at the gauntlet and the fine layer of sepia dust. 'But the secret?' he whispered. 'I don't understand.'

The professor sighed and summoned up the last of his strength.

'Don't you see, Twig? What it takes hundreds of years for the Twilight Woods to do naturally, we can do with a single crushing blow. But that blow can only, *must* only, fall at the very moment of . . .'

'Twilight!' gasped Twig.

The professor let out a long, pitiful sigh. 'Tell . . . Professor of Darkness,' he whispered. 'You can . . . trust . . . him . . .'

He fell silent. The warm breath ceased. Twig straightened up and looked down at the wise old face.

The Professor of Light was dead. Already, the white ravens were screeching noisily outside. Twig heard them scrabbling overhead, scraping at the wood; he saw the boldest of them poking their heads through the hole in the side of the hull and peering round with their beady scavenging eyes.

'Be gone with you!' he cried.

The birds retreated, but only for a moment and not very far. Twig knew he would have to bury the professor's body at once. As he dragged it outside, the white ravens flocked round him, screeching with rage.

'You shan't have him!' Twig screeched back.

With the sun now low in the sky, he followed his lengthening shadows across the path, towards a circular patch of quickmud. There, at its edge, he lay the professor down. The white ravens flapped and fluttered in a frenzy of excitement. Twig tried hard to think of some words to mark the solemn occasion.

'Professor of Light,' he murmured. 'Venerable academic of Sanctaphrax. A wise and noble individual. This place is not good enough for your final resting place . . .' He faltered, then took a deep breath. 'Rest in peace.'

And with that, he pushed the body forwards. The feet went into the sinking-mud first, followed by the legs and the torso. The white ravens, beside themselves with rage, were swooping, diving, yet unable to get at the dead body. The mud crept up the professor's chest. His arms. His fingertips. Tears streamed down Twig's face.

'Farewell,' he whispered, as the head disappeared from view.

For a moment, all that could be seen to mark where the professor had been, were the uppermost twigs of the branch that Twig had secured to his neck. Then they too slipped down out of sight. A bubble of air plopped on the surface. Then stillness. Calmness. Peace.

Twig knelt on one knee, reached forwards with his gauntleted hand and dipped it into the pool of warm sinking-mud as a mark of respect. As he did so, it abruptly changed. Twig gasped. Before his very eyes, the thick white mud turned to water, as crystal clear as the babbling brooks which meandered through the

Deepwoods. Far below him, he could see the professor's body spiralling down deeper and deeper in its watery grave.

Twig sat back on his haunches and stared at the heavy gauntlet. The sepia dust, so fine it moved like liquid, was still slipping over the polished silver.

'Phraxdust,' he whispered reverently, as he picked himself up and looked around.

Far, far away in the distance he could make out the lights of Sanctaphrax, twinkling in the air. Below it, the squalid sprawl of Undertown squatted under its blanket of filthy brown smoke. The inhabitants of both places would benefit from the contents of the glass and iron-wood chest. The stormphrax would restore equilibrium to the floating rock, while the phraxdust would purify the festering Edgewater River.

Ends and means, the professor had said. Twig was unsure whether the lives that might be saved in Sanctaphrax and Undertown by the crystals could ever justify Screed's massacre of so many individuals. What he did know was that if he failed to return with the chest of stormphrax, then they would certainly all have died in vain.

'I must try,' he said to himself. 'For the sake of the living. For the sake of the dead.'

Just then, he heard a troubled groaning coming from inside the hull of the shipwreck. It was the Stone Pilot. He was finally coming round.

# ·CHAPTER TWENTY·

# THE STONE PILOT

The first thing Twig did on re-entering the shipwreck was to light the lantern which Screed had hanging on a nail by the opening. A warm honey-like glow filled the gloomy interior, and Twig saw that the Stone Pilot was sitting up.

'Thank Sky you're still alive,' he said.

The Stone Pilot nodded. 'But only just,' came a timid, muffled voice from inside the heavy suit. There was a pause. 'I can't feel my right leg at all.' Twig stared back in shocked silence. 'I was attacked by that so-called guide of ours,' the Stone Pilot went on. 'Must have knocked me senseless. I don't know how I ever got here.'

'I . . . I brought you here,' Twig explained.

The Stone Pilot nodded again. 'And Screed?'

'Screed is dead,' said Twig. 'By my sword. He . . . I . . .' He crouched before the Stone Pilot, confused. 'You can *speak*,' he said.

'I can.'

'But, I didn't know ... I mean, forgive me, but I always assumed you were dumb.'

'I don't waste my words,' he said. 'The world is wide and treacherous. These clothes and my silence are my protection.' He paused. 'Your father understood this well.'

'My father?' said Twig, surprised. 'He knew you could talk?'

'He knew *everything*,' said the Stone Pilot and, with these words, began squirming and wriggling until he had manoeuvred his right arm up out of its sleeve. Through the glass panels, Twig saw the surprisingly delicate fingers fiddling with the inner set of bolts which secured the hood to the shoulders. One by one, the catches clicked open.

Twig was spellbound. Not only had the Stone Pilot revealed that he could talk, but now – for the first time – he was about to show his face. Twig held his breath. What horrible disfigurement or affliction could the poor creature be suffering from, that he had gone to such lengths to conceal himself? What terrible secret lurked within that cumbersome suit of clothes?

As the hood was lifted, a neck came into view, pale and slender. Twig bit into his lower lip. The next moment, a mass of thick orange hair cascaded over the face. The Stone Pilot raised a hand, and swept it away.

Twig gasped. 'You're ... you're ...' he blustered.

'A girl,' the Stone Pilot replied. 'Are you surprised?'

'Of course I am!' said Twig. 'I had no idea. I thought you were going to be some kind of ... monster ...'

The Stone Pilot scowled and looked away. 'Perhaps it would be better if I were,' she said quietly. 'The most deformed and hideously scarred creature in the Deepwoods cannot be as lost and alone as I, now that I have lost Cloud Wolf – and the *Stormchaser*. It was the only place where I felt safe, and even there I still needed this.' She tapped the discarded hood.

'Cheer up,' said Twig, trying to sound reassuring. 'We'll get out of this.'

'It's no use,' cried the Stone Pilot. 'We're going to die in this great wide place. I know we are.'

'You mustn't talk like that,' said Twig sternly. Then, trying to distract the distressed girl, 'According to a story my father once told me, you were there at my birth,' he said. 'On board a sky ship, it was – a sky ship captained by the notorious . . .'

'Multinius Gobtrax,' the Stone Pilot interrupted. 'I recall it well,' she said, her voice thick with tears. 'We were over the Deepwoods in the middle of a terrible storm when Maris, your mother, went into labour.' She shook her head. 'I've never known up-currents like it. The sky ship was sucked up above the forest before any-one had a chance to down anchor or secure the grappling-irons.'

'Yet you managed to save the sky ship,' said Twig. 'I remember Cloud Wolf telling me how you doused the buoyant wood-burners, released the balance-weights, and climbed over the side to chip away at the flight-rock itself.'

The Stone Pilot looked down. 'I did what needed

to be done,' she said quietly.

'And I'm glad you did,' said Twig. 'After all, if you hadn't, then I wouldn't be here now.'

The Stone Pilot managed a smile. 'And who would have saved me from Screed if you weren't?' she said. 'We'll call it quits, shall we?'

'Yes,' said Twig uncertainly.

'But?' said the Stone Pilot.

'Nothing,' said Twig. 'It's just ... Well, that was sixteen years ago. How come you ...'

'Look so young?' she said, finishing his question for him.

Twig nodded.

The Stone Pilot looked away; a pale and slender hand reached for the hood. Twig stared thoughtfully at the seemingly ageless girl with her pale, almost translucent, skin and her shock of orange hair. She looked so familiar . . . And then he remembered.

'Mag!' he exclaimed.

'I beg your pardon,' said the Stone Pilot, surprised.

'That's who you remind me of,' he said. 'Someone I met a long time ago. She was a termagant trog girl. She . . .'

'What do you know about termagant trogs?' the Stone Pilot asked hesitantly.

Twig shrugged. What *did* he know about the termagants? He knew that Mag – a similarly pale-skinned and red-haired girl – had caught him and kept him as a pet in their underground caverns. He knew that, when she'd come of age, Mag had drunk from the sacred roots of the bloodoak tree and been transformed into a hulking great beast of a woman like Mumsie, her mother. He knew, too, that if he had not escaped when he did, he would have been torn to pieces.

'A pet?' said the Stone Pilot.

Twig nodded. 'She kept me on a long tether. She pampered and patted me.' He winced. 'And she used to spend hours beading and braiding my hair.'

'Until she turned termagant?'

'Exactly.'

The Stone Pilot fell silent and stared down stony-faced at the ground. When she looked up, Twig saw the tears welling in her eyes. 'That was one good thing about wearing the hood,' she said, hugging it to her body. 'Nobody ever saw me cry.' She sniffed. 'As you can see, I never turned termagant.'

Twig nodded, relieved that she hadn't. Watching his sweet, loving Mag turning into the fearful, bloodthirsty creature had been one of the most distressing incidents of his entire life.

'When my time came and the Mother Bloodoak bled for me, I was not there,' she explained sadly. 'And those who miss their appointed moment can never turn, but are condemned to remain as you see me now, until the day they die.'

'But . . . but why did you miss it?' Twig asked.

The trog girl sighed. 'It was on the day before I was due to turn termagant,' she said. 'I was outside the cavern walking my pet, a prowlgrin pup, when I was surrounded by a pack of trained whitecollar wood-wolves. They tore my pet to pieces but left me to their master. A slaver from Undertown,' she said, spitting out the words. 'He shackled me along with woodelves, trolls, goblins, and marched us off to a Deepwoods slave market. That's where your father found me – filthy, ragged and half out of my mind.'

'He bought you?' said Twig, wide-eyed.

'He saw the state I was in,' she said. 'He seized that miserable slaver's whip from him and nearly flayed him alive. Then he took me by the hand and said, "Come, little one, Maris will fix you up." And I went.'

Twig crouched back down beside her. 'It . . . it must have been awful for you,' he said sympathetically.

The Stone Pilot nodded. 'I could never find my cavern home,' she said. 'Sky knows, I've searched over the years. But in due course Cloud Wolf even gave me a home.'

'The *Stormchaser*,' said Twig.

'Yes,' replied the Stone Pilot. 'And a trade. I'm the best Stone Pilot in the skies. Or was. Now I've got nothing.'

'You've got me,' said Twig, stretching out a hand.

The Stone Pilot looked up at him and, hesitantly, took his hand in hers.

'If we're going to stay here, then we'll need to find some food,' said Twig brightly.

'Stay here?' said the Stone Pilot.

'Of course,' he said. 'How else are we going to make the ship skyworthy again? We'll never get out of the Mire if we don't.'

Twig looked round at the broken hull of the wreck. Getting the sky ship airborne again would be a formidable task – particularly since the Stone Pilot's injured leg meant he would have to do the work on his own. Then again, what choice did he have?

'The repairs don't have to be perfect,' said the Stone Pilot, following Twig's gaze. 'So long as you can locate the flight-rock, I think I can get the *Windcutter* flying again. Cloud Wolf taught me well.'

Twig smiled. 'I don't even know your name.'

The Stone Pilot stared back at him for a moment, eyes narrowed in thought, her hands gripping the protective hood. Finally, she spoke. 'My name is Maugin,' she said.

*

On that first morning, the rising sun woke Twig early. He left the sleeping Maugin to rest and made a thorough inspection of the entire sky ship. It was soon clear that the sun would rise above the fetid Mire many times before the *Windcutter* was skyworthy again.

The hull was not only broken in places but also rotting on the starboard side that rested in the mud, the mast was cracked and, though several of the hanging weights were in place, many were missing. The flight-rock had split in two. One half lay trapped beneath a heavy beam in the warm mud. The other half was nowhere to be seen.

'First of all,' he said, 'I must see whether there are any tools on board. If I can't find a hammer and some nails then I won't be able to repair anything.' He hesitated. 'On the other hand, what's the point of doing that before I find the other half of the flight-rock.' He turned. 'Then again, if there are no supplies on board, we'll starve to death anyway.' And with that, he returned the way he'd come.

Yet wherever Twig looked, he drew a blank. The 'tween-deck store-room, stock-room and stowing-room were all empty. The cabins and steerage had been stripped bare. And he already knew there was nothing in the hold where he and the Stone Pilot had spent the night.

'We're done for,' he sighed. 'I'd better break the news to Maugin.' And he headed down the stairs that would take him back down to the hold.

On reaching the bottom, Twig frowned with confusion. Where was the Stone Pilot? Where was the chest of stormphrax and the gruesome display of toes? As his eyes got used to the darkness, he realized he was in a different part of the hold altogether – the forehold rather than the mainhold. He looked round, first gasping, then grinning, then whooping with delight.

'Twig?' came a voice from the other side of the wooden wall. 'Is that you?'

'Yes!' Twig shouted back. 'And I've found it. I've found Screed's store and sleeping quarters. And . . . and . . . there's everything here we need,' he said. 'Plates and goblets, knives and spoons. Oh, and here are his fishing-rods, and hooks and lines. Candles and lantern oil. And a large box of ship's biscuit. And a barrel of woodgrog. And . . . Oh, Maugin! He's been sleeping on the sails.'

'And ropes?' called Maugin. 'We'll need ropes to raise them.'

Twig poked around under the mattress of folded sails. 'Yes!' he exclaimed. 'Coiled up as a base underneath, all the ropes we could possibly want. And . . . here! A huge chest, full of tools. We'll be able to get started right away.' He paused. 'How's your leg?'

'Not so bad,' Maugin called back, but Twig could hear pain in her soft voice.

Twig set to work eagerly. Hour after hour, he toiled, carrying out the instructions of the Stone Pilot, who – although she would have denied it – was suffering constant pain from the angry gash on her leg. But the *Windcutter* really was a wreck. Every spar seemed rotten, every plank ready to crumble. Although he did the best he could, patching here, trimming there, the task seemed hopeless. When the sun sank down below the horizon, he looked round, dismayed by how little he had actually achieved.

'I'm never going to get this finished,' he complained.

'Don't worry,' Maugin reassured him in her soft, shy voice. 'Find the other half of the flight-rock and we'll make her fly.'

Twig shook his head. 'But the flight-rock is buoyant,' he said. 'Won't it simply have floated away?'

'I don't think so,' the Stone Pilot replied. 'As you know, cold rock rises, hot rock sinks. Assuming it landed

somewhere in the warm Mire mud, it should still be
there.'

Although the Stone Pilot had been badly injured when
descending from the *Stormchaser*, her leg had, thankfully,
not been broken. With regular cleansings in the phraxdust-purified water, the swelling went down, the
redness faded and the angry wound slowly began to

heal. They had been there ten days when she first climbed shakily to her feet.

'That's amazing, Maugin!' said Twig, and took her by the arm. 'See if you can put some weight on it.' The Stone Pilot stepped tentatively forwards onto her right leg. It wobbled. She winced – but persevered. 'Excellent!' Twig enthused. 'It'll soon be as good as new.'

'It'll never be that,' said Maugin, smiling bravely. 'But I daresay it'll serve me well for a few more years. Now how's supper coming along?' She looked up and sniffed the air.

'Supper!' Twig exclaimed. 'I forgot all about it,' and he dashed outside to seize the metal griddle from the fire. 'Just how I like them!' he called back.

'You mean, burnt,' said Maugin, smiling as she peered through the hole in the hull.

Twig looked up and grinned. The Stone Pilot's shyness was slowly disappearing. 'So you won't be wanting any?' he said.

'I didn't say that,' came the reply. 'What have we got today, anyway? No, don't tell me. Oozefish!'

'Hammelhorn steaks, actually,' said Twig. 'With fresh crusty bread and a nice side salad.' Maugin's mouth dropped open. 'Only kidding,' said Twig as he handed her a platter with her daily ration of three oozefish, a slab of hard tack and a handful of dried woodsap segments arranged upon it. 'The perfect diet,' he said.

'If you say so,' said Maugin with a smile. She eased herself down onto a rock and began nibbling at a corner of the rock-hard biscuit.

Far away in the distance, the massive orange sun sank down below the horizon and the sky glowed pink and green. Twig and Maugin watched the lights of Sanctaphrax appearing, one by one. Behind their heads, the stars were already sparkling and – as they sat eating in silence – the night spread across the sky like an opening canopy.

'I love the evenings,' said Twig as he rose to light the lantern. 'It's so peaceful out here, with nothing and no-one for miles around and only open sky above.'

Maugin shuddered. 'It gives me the creeps,' she said.

Twig did not reply. He knew that, despite her years as a sky pirate, being a termagant trog Maugin still yearned for her life underground. It was – like Twig's own desire to sail the skies – in the blood.

'By the way,' he said, 'I've got some good news.'

'What?'

'I found the other half of the flight-rock.'

'You did?' said Maugin excitedly. 'Where?'

Twig swallowed hard. He had found it in the purified pool where the Professor of Light was buried. The previous evening, he had gone there in despair to talk to the old professor. And there it was, bobbing in the clear warm water, just beneath the surface.

'Oh, not far from here,' said Twig. 'Do you think you can join it together?'

'I've mended worse,' said Maugin.

Twig looked across at her and smiled. 'We've been lucky so far, haven't we?'

'Luckier than I ever dared to hope,' Maugin admitted.

At that moment, far up in the twinkling depths of the night, a shooting star blazed across the sky with a soft hiss. Twig lay back and watched it. 'It's so beautiful,' he sighed.

'Shhh!' said Maugin. 'And make a wish.'

Twig turned and looked at her. 'I already have.'

# ·CHAPTER TWENTY-ONE·

# THE FLIGHT TO UNDERTOWN

For the next two days, Twig and Maugin worked harder than ever. Having completed the nauseating task of removing Screed's collection of rotting toes, Twig cleared the mud away from the bottom of the ship. Next, he bound the cracked mast, completed the repairs to the hull-rigging and, with wood taken from the redundant cabins, began sealing the largest holes in the hull. Maugin bound the two halves of the flight-rock together in an intricate latticework of ropes, bound in wet mire mud and baked hard into place in the sun. Then the two of them began the arduous business of dragging the ropes and sails from the forehold to the decks.

Although made of woodspider-silk the sails were cumbersome to manoeuvre and half rotted with age. Every gust of wind set them fluttering and flapping, and small tears appeared that had to be patched.

'Hold on tight!' Twig ordered below, as the studsail he was holding billowed out. He was halfway up the mast at the time, and struggling to attach it to a sliding-cleat. 'Do you really think these will get us to Undertown?'

'Have faith,' Maugin called up, 'and a light touch on the sail levers. The flight-rock will do the rest.'

Twig smiled. There was something in Maugin's calm manner that reassured him. He was beginning to depend on this quiet, serious girl more and more. 'Come on,' he said. 'Only the staysail and the jib to rig up, and we're done.'

As the setting sun signalled the end of yet another day, Twig checked the knots for a final time, balanced his way back along the creaking bowsprit and jumped down onto the deck.

'There,' he announced. 'Finished.' He surveyed his handiwork nervously. 'Shall we go for a trial run?'

'It's getting dark,' said the Stone Pilot. 'We should leave it until morning.'

'You know best,' said Twig, somewhat relieved. 'Let's go and have a tot or two of woodgrog to celebrate. We've earned it.'

The following day, Twig was woken before the sun had risen. 'Get up,' Maugin was saying as she shook him by the shoulders.

Twig opened his eyes and looked round groggily. His head was thumping. Too much woodgrog, he realized miserably.

'We must leave now, before the wind changes,' said Maugin. 'I'm going down below deck to see to the flight-rock. You take the helm. I'll call up to you when I'm ready,' she said.

Twig washed, dressed, drank enough of the phraxdust-purified water to quench his thirst and clear his head, and made his way to the helm. There by the wheel – freshly aligned and greased – Twig stared at the two long rows of bone-handled levers. 'Stern-weight, prow-weight, starboard hull-weights, small, medium and large,' he muttered, ticking them off in his head. 'Then, mizzensail, foresail, topsail,' he said, turning his attention to the second row of levers. 'Skysail . . . No, studsail. Or is it the staysail . . .? Blast!'

'Ready to launch!' came Maugin's calm voice, echoing up the staircase from the bowels of the ship. 'Raise the mizzensail.'

'Aye-aye,' Twig called back, his own voice sounding shrill and more nervous than he'd have liked.

With his heart in his mouth, he leaned forwards, seized the mizzensail lever and pulled. The sail billowed and filled with air. At first, nothing happened. Then, with a judder and a creak, the *Windcutter* lifted slightly, and almost imperceptibly began to right itself. The rotten timbers groaned horribly.

'Down the port hull-weights,' Twig muttered. 'Up the large starboard hull-weight a tad and . . . Whoa!' he cried as the ship listed sharply to port. The sound of tearing sailcloth filled his ears.

'Careful,' called the Stone Pilot steadily.

Twig tried to remain cool. He raised the port hull-weights a fraction, and compensated by lowering the stern-weight. The sky ship stabilized and, with a long and rasping squelch, it rose arthritically up from the sucking mud.

'YES!' Twig cried out. The wish he had made as the shooting star flew across the sky had come true. The *Windcutter* was skyborne. They were on their way back to Undertown.

'Easy as she goes!' the Stone Pilot called.

Twig nodded as he turned the wheel slowly to the left. 'Stay calm,' he told himself. 'Keep a steady course – and concentrate.'

The sky ship keeled to port. Twig's head spun. There was so much to remember. With the wind coming from the south, the starboard hull-weights needed to be raised higher than the port hull-weights – but not too high, or else the sky ship would go into a spin. His task was made no easier by the lack of the neben-hull-weights and the constant nerve-racking creaking of the old rotten hull.

'You're doing fine!' the Stone Pilot called up encouragingly.

Am I? Twig wondered. He hoped so. That last time he had tried to sail a sky ship, it had ended in disaster – and that was with his father there to take over when things got too difficult for him. Now there was no-one to come to his aid. Twig was on his own.

'You can do it,' he urged himself. 'You *must* do it!'

At that moment, he glanced up to see a dark cloud speeding towards them. As the *Windcutter* rose higher, the cloud descended. They were on collision course.

'What is it?' Twig gasped. Trembling with unease, he spun the helm to the left. The cloud, too, shifted direction. 'And what's going to happen when it strikes?' he shuddered.

Closer and closer, it came. Twig became aware of a curious noise – a squawking, squeaking, screeching noise – that grew louder, and louder still. All at once, he saw the cloud for what it really was. A flock of birds; all flashing wings and lashing tails. The ratbirds were returning.

As one, the flock wheeled round the sky ship once, twice, three times, darting between the sails in figures of eight, before swooping down out of view beneath the hull. Through the many cracks they flew, and into the base-hold of the ship where they took up residence. The familiar sound of twittering and scratching filtered back up to the deck.

'Ratbirds!' Twig whispered, his face beaming with delight. It was a good sign. Even if it was an old wives' tale about ratbirds abandoning a doomed sky ship, Twig was as glad to see them arrive as Tem Barkwater had been dismayed when they left. And, as he raised the remaining sails and the sky ship lurched forwards, his heart soared. Like his father, his father before him, and his father before him, Twig – *Captain* Twig – was in charge of his own sky pirate ship.

Far below him – and farther all the time – the shadow of the sky ship skudded across the glistening white mud of the Mire. Now and then Twig would lean forwards and adjust one or two of the hanging weights. It was coming more easily now. He was beginning, as Cloud Wolf had put it, to develop *the touch*.

On and on they sailed, running before the wind. Ahead, the horizon melted away in a bank of swirling mist and the distant floating city of Sanctaphrax vanished. Below, the shadow abruptly disappeared too, as clouds – real clouds this time – swept across the sun. All round him, the air was filled with the creaking and whistling of a gale-force wind as it tugged and strained at the sky ship. Every now and then, a plank would splinter and fall away. The *Windcutter* was slowly falling to bits, but still she flew on.

'Don't panic,' Twig whispered in a vain attempt to still his thumping heart. He fiddled feverishly with the levers. 'Lower the sails a little. Raise the hanging weights. Gently. Gently.'

'We should be there before darkness falls,' came a voice at his shoulder.

Twig turned. It was Maugin. 'Shouldn't you be tending to the flight-rock?' he asked anxiously.

'There's nothing to do for the time being,' Maugin assured him. 'Not till we come in to land. I've been checking round the ship. We'll have to take it slowly.'

'And the stormphrax?' said Twig. 'The lantern needs to be burning at a sort of twilight brightness,' he reminded her.

'The stormphrax is fine,' she said. 'Everything's fine.' She paused. 'Except . . .'

'What?'

'I'm not sure,' she said. 'But I have the horrible feeling the mast-bindings we secured are giving way. We must sail with the wind until we absolutely have to tack against it to make Undertown. Otherwise the mast will break. It means we'll be taken over the Edge. We must keep our nerve until the last minute.'

Twig tensed. His palms were wet and his mouth was dry. Just the thought of sailing over the Edge into the uncharted sky beyond, where even the sky pirates never dared to venture, filled him with dread. Yet, if the Stone Pilot was right about the mast, they had no choice. They would have to sail with the wind until they were level with Undertown, and then turn, dash back towards land – and pray.

'Is the Mire still below us?' he said.

Maugin went to check. 'Yes,' she called back from the balustrade. 'But the Edge is approaching. Keep the lights of Sanctaphrax in view.'

'I know!' Twig snapped as he raised the starboard hull-weights. The boat lurched and listed; the mast creaked ominously.

'Go with the wind,' said Maugin. 'Let her have her head.'

Twig nodded grimly. His hands gripped the helm, white knuckled; he drew blood biting into his lower lip. The sky ship listed even further. If he wasn't careful it would roll over completely.

'Easy!' Maugin called, as the ship dipped savagely. Twig lowered the stern- and prow-weights. The sky ship steadied momentarily. Twig sighed – but his relief was short-lived. 'Twig,' she said, her voice as calm and steady as ever. 'We've gone over the Edge.'

An icy chill coursed through his veins. The wind had taken them towards the mysterious nether-regions beyond the Edge where dragons and monsters were said to roam, where few had visited and none had returned. To a place known only for the weather it conjured up – Great Storms, of course, but also mad howling whirl-winds that warped the mind and filled sleeping heads with visions; thick, suffocating fogs that stole the senses; driving rain, blinding snow, sulphurous dust storms that coated everything in a fine layer of particles – now green, now grey, now red.

'Got to keep sight of the lights of Sanctaphrax,' he murmured. 'Wait till they're level with us. Keep your nerve, Twig. Keep your nerve!'

Tearing herself away from the mesmerizing mists which writhed and swirled beneath her, Maugin ran back to the helm. 'I'll take the wheel,' she said. 'You concentrate on the levers.'

The wind gathered force. The tattered sails screamed as it tore through the fresh rents in the sailcloth. The groaning timbers of the hull grew shrill with splintering.

Twig's hands danced over the levers. Lifting here, lowering there, steadying the mast jib. And all the while, the lights of Sanctaphrax drew nearer on the starboard bow, glinting tantalizingly from solid ground.

Beneath the crumbling hull of the *Windcutter* was the inky blackness of the void. Panic rose in Twig's throat. He wanted to pull the ship about, straight into the teeth of the gale that gripped them, and make a dash for the grey cliff face of the Edge. If they crashed over land, at least they'd stand a chance of surviving. But here, beyond the Edge, they could fall for ever.

His hand jerked out for the starboard hull-weight lever. He felt an iron grip. Maugin's slender hand held him at the wrist. 'Not yet,' she whispered, mouth close to his ear. 'Have faith. Wait for the lights to come level. Wait, Twig. Wait.'

Twig's panic receded. But he was drenched with sweat, and shivering violently – with cold, with antici-pation. All at once, a sickening crash split the air behind them and the aft-spar flew past, down into the darkness, dragging its sail with it.

'It's all right,' Twig shouted, as he steadied the rudder-wheel to bring the bucking sky ship back under control. 'I've got her.'

Maugin surveyed the horizon. 'Now!' she shouted.

Twig's hand immediately shot out for the starboard hull-weight lever for a second time. This time Maugin did not stop him. He pulled down with all his might. As the heavy boom swung about, the *Windcutter* jarred as if hit by a giant hammer, and tacked into a blast of icy wind.

The mast screeched under the strain, its sails ripping apart and flying past him like phantoms. Then, with an ear-splitting splintering, the entire mighty upright began to buckle.

'Don't break,' Twig implored. 'Not now!'

With an agonizing screech, the mast folded backwards. The teeth of the gale bit deep into its rotten centre and . . . CRASH! It split in two and the top half slammed past the bridge.

Twig threw himself on the Stone Pilot as the great column swished past their heads like Screed's evil scythe.

'We're done for!' he screamed as the sails fell limp and the *Windcutter* began to drop through the air. Abruptly, the lights of Sanctaphrax were snuffed out. 'We're lost!'

'No!' Maugin was screaming back. 'The flight-rock. The flight-rock will save us. Cool the flight-rock and we float. Twig, we float!'

They clawed their way to the stone-cradle, with the wind whistling through their ears as the ship fell in a vertical spin.

'Pull that iron ring, Twig!' screamed the Stone Pilot. 'Pull it with me. One. Two. Three. Now!'

Together, they hauled back the great iron ring of the stone cradle and a loud hiss spat out from the bars as cold earth fell on the stone encased within. The roaring in Twig's ears grew less. The *Windcutter* was slowing. It was steadying. Twig opened his eyes. The wreck of the sky ship was righting itself as, with growing buoyancy, the flight-rock strained at the bars of the stone-cradle and pulled them upwards.

'Listen now, Twig.' Maugin's voice was tense and urgent. 'When we rise above the Edge, we *must* have sail – any sail. To take us forwards; to take us back over land.'

'I'll give you sail,' said Twig. He was strangely calm. They hadn't come this far to fail now.

The glow of the stormphrax chest cast a ghostly light over the tangled mess of rigging and tattered sail. Twig scanned the wreckage. The mast was broken – but it would have to do. He threw himself into the task of raising a makeshift sail with feverish intensity.

They were rising with increasing speed when suddenly, yes, there were the lights of Sanctaphrax, and Undertown, straight ahead in the distance. Twig pulled on the sail ropes with all his might, the coarse fibres biting into his flesh, drawing blood.

Then the wind struck. The jolt ran through Twig's body. He gasped with pain – but the tattered sails billowed. The old *Windcutter* gasped with Twig, and dragged itself back towards the Edge.

'Raise the starboard hull-weights,' Twig instructed himself, as he dashed back to the helm. 'Lower the port weights. And align the stern- and peri-hull-weights. That's it. Now raise the studsail a tad – easy does it, gently, and . . .' The heavy boom swung wildly round. Twig looked up nervously. The broken mast was hanging on; the makeshift sails were holding.

They were going to make it. Limping, splintered; tattered, cracked and wind-battered. But they were going to make it.

# CHAPTER TWENTY-TWO

# TO THE HEART OF SANCTAPHRAX

Twig moved forwards in his chair. 'You have no choice!' he said. 'I have something you need – and you have something I need.'

Mother Horsefeather permitted herself a little smile. The youth was certainly bold.

'You are your father's son,' she said, and clacked her beak. 'Coming here in that creaking wreck of a sky ship, giving ultimatums.' Her beady yellow eyes glinted. 'Might I remind you that if it hadn't been for my backing, the *Stormchaser* would never have set sail in the first place.'

'I know that,' said Twig, 'but . . .'

'Now you tell me that it is lost. With Cloud Wolf aboard. Yet there you are, shouting out your demands. It is *I* who should be making demands of you, *Captain Twig*,' she said.

'No, I . . .' said Twig uncertainly.

'Fifteen thousand it cost, plus interest. As you know, I'm not in the business of giving money away. I want a return on my investment . . .'

At that moment the Stone Pilot who, back inside her protective disguise, had been standing patiently at Twig's shoulders, strode forwards. She slammed her gloved hand down on the table.

'Hold your beak, bird-woman!' she roared. 'Let the captain speak.'

Mother Horsefeather clucked nervously, and smoothed down the ruffled feathers around her neck. She fixed Twig with a fearsome glare. 'Your father,' she sniffed, 'was a gentleman.'

Twig nodded and swallowed noisily. 'This is what I want,' he said. 'One, all debts incurred by my father, Cloud Wolf, are to be written off. Two, you are to supply me with a new sky ship, packed with supplies and ready to sail. I shall call it *Edgedancer*.'

'*Edgedancer*?' Mother Horsefeather sneered.

'And three,' Twig continued without a break, 'you will pay for a crew of my choosing to sail her. I'll take a pouchful of gold now, as a sign of your good faith.'

Mother Horsefeather's expression darkened, 'you ask a great deal, Captain Twig,' she said, thrusting her beak towards him. 'And what do you offer in return that is worth so much?'

Twig sat back in his chair and twiddled with his hair. 'I thought you'd never ask,' he said. 'I will give you the secret of safe phraxdust production.'

Mother Horsefeather's jaw dropped. A curious chirruping sound rattled at the back of her throat. 'But but but . . .' she gurgled. 'You mean . . . But I'll corner the water market,' she squawked.

Twig nodded, and stared at the bird-woman in disgust as her face contorted with joy and villainy and naked greed.

'I'll control it all!' she cackled. 'I'll be more powerful than that glutinous Leaguesmaster, Simenon Xintax. *And* the odious upstart, Vilnix Pompolnius. I'll be more powerful than the whole lot of them put together.' She turned on Twig suspiciously. 'You are sure you know the secret?' she said.

'I am,' said Twig. 'And when you fulfil my demands I shall prove it to you. You shall become powerful. And rich beyond your wildest dreams.'

Mother Horsefeather ruffled her feathers and fixed Twig with cold unblinking eyes. 'You have a deal, son of Cloud Wolf,' she said, pulling a leather pouch of gold coins from the pocket of her apron and tossing it across the table. 'But remember this, Captain Twig. If you double-cross me, I shall personally see to it that the leagues hear of your impudence.' Her beady eyes narrowed. 'The League of Torturers will be particularly interested to hear that they have a new subject to study – and at such great length!'

It was late afternoon by the time Twig left the Bloodoak tavern. With the Stone Pilot, he returned to the boom-docks, lugged the heavy chest up from the hold of the *Windcutter* and, together, the pair of them set off through Undertown.

The narrow, dirty streets were hot and sultry, and many of the stall-holders and shop-keepers had shut up their premises and retired for an afternoon nap. They would open again at sundown. One establishment, however, had not closed and, as Twig and the Stone Pilot struggled past with the chest of Stormphrax, its fat and glistening owner emerged from inside.

'Oy! It's you!' Flabsweat cried, and made a lunge at Twig.

Without even thinking, Twig drew his sword. 'Back off,' he said calmly, 'or it will be the worse for you.'

Flabsweat retreated, fear in his eyes. 'I ... I didn't mean no offence ...' he blustered.

Twig stared at the frightened shopkeeper uneasily. Is this what the quest had done to him? Is this what he had become? He looked down, removed the gauntlet from his hand and held it out. 'Here,' he said. 'Take it.'

Flabsweat reached forward. 'Wh ... what is it?' he said.

'A trophy from the Twilight Woods,' said Twig. 'It is coated with phraxdust – enough to produce fresh water for you, your family and all your animals for the rest of your lives.'

Flabsweat traced his finger over the liquid-like sepia dust. 'Phraxdust,' he gasped. 'Why, thank you. Thank you.'

'I trust that you will now consider the matter with the caterbird closed,' said Twig.

'Oh, quite closed, absolutely closed, completely and utterly closed,' Flabsweat babbled. Twig turned to go. 'And if there's anything I can do for you,' he said. 'Any of the more *exotic* species you might like me to procure ... I can get hold of anything. As a gift. Just you say the word.'

Twig paused and looked back. 'I might hold you to that,' he said.

Twig and the Stone Pilot continued on their way and, as Sanctaphrax came nearer, Twig's heart beat furiously. He didn't know whether he was nervous or excited. Only when they were at last directly beneath the massive floating rock did Twig look up. He saw a large basket suspended far above his head. 'Is there anyone up there?' he called. 'I wish to visit Sanctaphrax.'

The small, angular face of a gnokgoblin appeared at the edge of the basket, and peered down. 'At whose invitation?' he said.

'We are to visit the Professor of Darkness,' Twig replied.

The gnokgoblin's eyes narrowed. 'The Professor of Darkness, eh?' he said. The basket began to descend.

Twig turned to the Stone Pilot and smiled. 'So far, so good,' he whispered.

The basket came to rest just in front of them and the gnokgoblin looked them up and down. 'I hope that chest's not too heavy.'

'Nowhere near as heavy as it will be,' Twig said. 'But we could do with a hand.'

Together, the three of them hefted the chest into the basket and jumped in beside it. Then the gnokgoblin bent down, grasped the winch-handle and began turning. The basket wobbled and lurched, and rose slowly up into the air.

'Interesting individual, the Professor of Darkness,' the gnokgoblin said, his voice nasal and whining. 'Never abandoned his opposition to the Most High Academe.' He looked askance at Twig, gauging his opinion before continuing.

Twig snorted. 'A usurper is a usurper,' he said.

The Stone Pilot shuffled about uneasily. There were spies everywhere in Sanctaphrax.

'Well, he *is*,' Twig snapped.

' 'Tis the mind of many in the venerable floating city,' the gnokgoblin said, nodding sagely. He looked up and met Twig's questioning gaze. 'I'm not one to listen to rumours, you understand,' he said, 'but word is that the days of Vilnix Pompolnius are numbered.'

Twig listened in silence.

''Course, it's his own fault. How did he expect the leagues to react when he cut off their supplies of phrax-dust? Eh?'

'Perhaps he has no more to supply them with,' Twig offered.

'Which is my point entirely. If he's no use to the leaguesmen *nor* the academics, then how much longer can he cling on to power? Eh? You tell me that.' He drew a deep breath. 'If you ask *me*, it'll be those leaguesmen who get to him first. Don't like being double-crossed, they don't,' he said, and ran his finger sharply across his exposed throat. 'If you take my meaning?'

Twig nodded, but offered no comment. It occurred to him that if Vilnix Pompolnius ever got his hands on the stormphrax in the chest, not only would his current problems be over, but his position of corrupt power would become unassailable.

They continued in silence to the top, where the gnok-goblin leaped onto the landing stage to help Twig and the Stone Pilot with their heavy cargo. 'Just follow that path to the very end, and then turn left,' he said. 'The old Raintasters' Tower is straight ahead. You can't miss it.'

'Th . . . thanks,' Twig said, and shook his head. The splendour of the city which spread out before him was overwhelming.

For a start, what the gnokgoblin had called a path was in fact a wide avenue, paved in intricate patterns with red, black and white tiles and bordered on both sides with towers that gleamed like gold in the light from the sinking sun. And what towers!

Each one was different yet equally as wonderful as its neighbour. Some had minarets, some had spires; some were domed with intricate mosaics of mirrors and semi-precious stones. Some had clock towers, others belfreys. One had large windows, paned with crystal; another had clusters of diamond-shaped openings. One was so slender it swayed in the wind; another was squat and robust.

The design of each tower, of course, depended on which faculty or school it belonged to. As did the various instruments and pieces of paraphernalia attached to the sides. There were pin-wheels and wind-socks and canti-levered scales on one; sun-dials, weather vanes, plumb lines and brass calibraters on another. While on a third, an intricate system of suspended bottles – each one a different shade of blue – tinkled in the breeze.

Twig stared round him, open-mouthed. The finery, the elegance, the perfect proportions – wherever he looked. It was too much to take in. A line of ornate pillars. An intricately carved portico. The statues, the fountains – how *did* you make water fly like that? The sweeping staircases. The curving passageways. The delicately arched bridges.

'It's incredible,' he sighed.

All round him, the gowned academics were scurrying this way and that. Over the bridges, up and down the stairs, in and out of the towers they went: some alone, some in twos, some in huddled, whispering groups – all

with their heads down, engrossed in their own concerns and as oblivious to the sumptuousness of their surroundings as they were to the presence of the youth and the hooded character who struggled slowly past them with the heavy chest.

Twig had expected Sanctaphrax to be a subdued place of learning, reserved and reverent – yet the professors and lecturers and readers were behaving anything but. Sanctaphrax was thronging. The atmosphere was charged with secretive intrigue, with furtive anticipation and, as the academics passed him by, he caught snatches of troubled conversation.

'. . . perilously near the end . . .' '. . . chains won't hold much longer.' 'Vilnix Pompolnius, he's the one to blame . . .' 'I shall put your suggestions to the Professor of Fogprobing, perhaps . . .' 'Open sky – for ever . . .' 'Something must be done . . .'

'Something *is* being done,' Twig muttered as he and the Stone Pilot finally made it to the end of the long, curving avenue. They turned left. Before them stood a dilapidated tower.

Untouched since that darkening evening when Vilnix, the then apprentice raintaster, had carried out his fateful experiment, the residence of the Professor of Darkness was all but in ruins. The right side of the tower had been blown clean away, leaving staircases exposed and chambers permanently open. What remained pointed accusingly up at the sky.

Twig and the Stone Pilot stumbled over the shattered paving-stones which led up to the door. They went inside and lugged the chest up the stairs. There was a light fanning out across the landing of the second floor. Twig walked towards it. A modest plaque nailed to the door confirmed that they had come to the right place.

Twig knocked softly.

'Oh, what is it *now*?' came a weary voice. 'I've already told you all I know.'

'Professor,' Twig called urgently.

'I am old and frail,' the voice complained. 'And so so tired. Just leave me alone.'

'Professor, we must speak,' Twig persisted and tried the door. It was not locked and, despite the professor's continued protests, he and the Stone Pilot entered. The moment she was inside, Maugin abruptly dropped her end of the chest and sat down on the lid with an exhausted grunt. Twig lowered his end, looked up at the person behind the desk – and gasped.

Apart from the fact that he was wearing black robes, rather than white, the Professor of Darkness was the Professor of Light's double.

'Who in Sky's name are you?' he demanded, and leaped to his feet. 'I thought it was the guards back again.'

Twig smiled. 'You don't seem so old and frail now, Professor.'

'Bwuh . . . bwuh . . . bwuh . . .' the professor blustered, totally at a loss for words.

Twig stepped forwards. 'I am Twig,' he said. 'This is the Stone Pilot. Together we have completed the quest upon which my father, Quintinius Verginix, was recently sent.'

The professor's jaw dropped. 'I . . . that is, you . . .' His eyes twinkled. 'You mean to tell me . . .'

'We have returned with stormphrax,' said Twig.

The professor leaped to his feet and hurried across the room towards them. 'Stormphrax!' he said. 'Are you certain?'

'Quite certain,' said Twig. 'Your colleague, the Professor of Light, confirmed it.'

'Bah, that old buffoon!' he said gruffly, but Twig noticed the wateriness in his eyes. 'What's the bally-buzzard up to, anyway?' he asked.

Twig looked down. 'I'm afraid the Professor of Light is dead,' he said gently.

'Dead!' the professor gasped.

'His dying words were that I should tell you about the stormphrax,' said Twig. 'That I can . . . trust you.'

'My old friend, dead,' the professor said sadly. He smiled weakly. 'Come, then. Let's see what you've got there.'

The Stone Pilot climbed wearily to her feet and limped to one side. Twig stepped forwards and raised the lid. The Professor of Darkness looked inside. 'Why, the old woodgoat!' he squealed with delight. 'It *is* stormphrax! This is wonderful! Quite wonderful! But how in Sky's name did you come by so much? And why are the crystals all so small?'

'It's a long story,' said Twig.

'And one I look forward to hearing,' the professor said. 'But first we must get the stormphrax to the treasury . . .'

'No, Professor,' said Twig firmly. 'First there is something else I must show you. It is time to put an end to this phraxdust madness, once and for all.' He glanced out through the window at the sun, already deep orange and low in the sky. 'But we must be quick. I'll need a mortar and pestle.'

'But . . .'

'*Now*, Professor,' Twig insisted. 'Please!'

The professor pointed him towards a marble work-surface at the far end of the chamber. 'You'll find everything you could possibly need over there,' he said. 'But . . .'

'Thank you,' said Twig.

He seized a metal beaker and hurried back to the chest. As he passed the professor, he nodded towards the window. 'How long to go until twilight?' he asked. '*True* twilight.'

'Ah, true twilight,' the professor said dreamily. 'That mystical moment between light and darkness. So fleeting. So fine . . . It was the only aspect of our studies about which the Professor of Light and myself could ever agree upon . . .'

'Professor!' Twig snapped, as he passed him on his way back. 'How long?'

The professor marched towards the window and performed a quick calculation in his head. 'One and a half minutes,' he said huffily.

'Less time than I thought,' Twig muttered. He hurried over to the bench and selected a mortar. 'Gently, gently,' he whispered to himself as he poured some crystals down into the bowl. Next, he picked the heaviest pestle from the rack, and raised it above his head. 'Professor,' he called out, 'you must tell me when that moment of true twilight occurs. Do you understand?'

The professor looked round. He saw Twig standing above the bowl of stormphrax with the pestle raised above his head.

'No,' he gasped. 'Are you mad? You'll blow us all to open sky!'

'Have faith, Professor,' Twig said. 'And keep your eyes to the sky. Remember, not a moment too soon and not a moment too late.'

The chamber throbbed with silence for what seemed

like an eternity. Twig's arm
began to ache – and doubts to
niggle. What if the Professor
of Light had been wrong
after all? The shaft of golden
light pouring in through the
window shifted a shade.

'Now!' the Professor of
Darkness cried out, shat-
tering the awful silence.

Twig held his breath
and brought the pestle
down as hard as he could into the waiting mortar. There
was a thud. A crunch. A sparkling brilliance. But no
more. And, as the golden light at the window turned to
amber, Twig looked down at the bowlful of sepia powder sliding round like liquid.

'It worked,' he whispered. He spun round to the professor. 'It worked!'

The Professor of Darkness trotted towards him, beaming with delight. He looked down into the bowl. 'First stormphrax! Now phraxdust! Wait, I must pinch myself to check I'm not dreaming.'

'This is no dream,' said Twig. 'The stormphrax will restore equilibrium to Sanctaphrax and the phraxdust will purify the drinking water once more.' He turned and stared boldly into the professor's eyes. 'And now I know it works, there is something else to do, Professor,' he said, his voice hushed and earnest. 'I have a plan to ensure that the secret of safe phraxdust production shall never fall into the wrong hands. But I'll need to ask for your help if it is to work.'

'Ask away, Twig, my boy,' said the Professor of Darkness. 'Ask and it shall be done.'

With darkness falling, Twig and the Stone Pilot followed the professor from his chamber. Back down the spiral stairs they went, grunting and groaning as the heavy chest bumped against the walls. At the bottom, instead of going out through the door, the professor took them down a further flight of stairs, through a narrow archway and on into a tunnel. It was dark and dank there, with only the dim light from the lantern in the chest to show them which way to go.

'Daren't risk lighting the torches in case it destabilizes the stormphrax,' the professor called back.

On and on they walked. This way, that way, down stairs and ramps, gradually making their way to the very centre of the floating rock. Behind him, Twig could feel

the Stone Pilot getting slower and slower. He knew that
she was nearing the end of her strength.

'Is it much further to go?'
asked Twig.

'We're almost there,' said the professor. 'Just round this next corner and . . .'

'HALT! WHO GOES THERE?'

The professor stopped in his tracks. Twig – who was finding it difficult to see the black robes in the dark tunnels anyway – walked slap-bang into him. Maugin grunted with alarm and dropped the chest – onto her foot – and grunted again, this time with pain. Out of the confusion came the professor's frail voice.

'Is that you, Bogwitt?' he said. 'It is I, the Professor of Darkness. I must have access to the treasury.'

'Can't,' came the surly reply from the guard.

'I . . . I . . . I beg your pardon,' the professor spluttered. 'Do you dare to deny me entrance?'

'By order of the Most High Academe.'

'What?' exclaimed the professor. 'But both you and I know that our worthy leader, Vilnix Pompolnius, would never *dream* of including me in such an order. So let me pass. At once.'

'No-one is to enter the treasury,' said Bogwitt with sudden ferocity. 'Neither leaguesman nor academic.' He lifted his lamp to the professor's face. 'And especially not you. Those was my orders from Vilnix Pompolnius himself. What's more, you're to surrender your key.'

'Surrender my key? Over my dead body!' the professor huffed.

'If that's what you want, so be it,' came the chilling response.

The lamp was placed on the ground with a clatter, and

Twig heard the *swoosh* and *thwip* of a sword and dagger being unsheathed. He peered round over the professor's shoulder at the guard blocking their view.

'A flat-head,' he muttered to himself. 'I might have known.' As he stared at the swaggering goblin – all glinting ear-rings, gold teeth and blades – fury and loathing rose up in his throat. How dare this barbaric flat-head goblin stand in their way when they had come so far and achieved so much – when they were so near to their final destination?

'My dear Bogwitt,' the professor was saying. 'This must all be some kind of a misunderstanding. If you could just let us inside the treasury for a moment. No-one would ever know and . . .'

At that moment Twig's rage exploded. He wrested his own sword from its scabbard and leaped forwards.

'Let us pass, curse you!' he roared.

For a moment, the flat-head looked surprised – but only for a moment. With a leering smile playing over his lips, he squared up and lunged abruptly forwards, his sword thrusting towards Twig's neck. Twig stepped sharply back, and parried. The two swords clashed ferociously and – stunned by the awful force of the blow – Twig reeled backwards. Bogwitt was on him in a trice, sword thrusting and dagger slashing.

Twig trembled before the onslaught of wild, thrashing blows. Panting with effort, he staggered backwards, defending himself as best he could, but weakening with every second. Suddenly, the flat-head jumped to the right and swung his heavy sword in from the left. Twig was caught unawares. He stumbled to the side and struck his elbow on the wall.

'Aaaoow,' he howled, as searing pain shot up his arm and down his spine. His sword clattered to the stone floor.

Bogwitt stepped forwards, eyes glinting. He raised his own sword. 'Silly little fool,' he hissed. 'Did you really believe that you could defeat me – personal bodyguard to Vilnix Pompolnius himself – the fiercest and most feared guard in Sanctaphrax?' He gripped the hilt of his sword till his knuckles went white. A glistening purple tongue flicked across his thin lips; his eyes gleamed. 'I shall enjoy this.'

'Stop!' Twig cried out. 'Do not strike.'

The flat-head sneered. 'So the big brave bear was a

timid wee woodmouse all the time, was it?' he said, and laughed unpleasantly.

'Hear me out,' said Twig, and reached inside his jacket.

'What treachery is this?' the flat-head roared. 'Remove your hand at once, before I pin it to your heart.'

Twig slowly pulled out his hand, bringing with it the pouch which Mother Horsefeather had given him. He jingled it lightly in his palm. 'Gold, Bogwitt,' he said. 'Ten gold pieces could be yours.'

'Of course it could,' said Bogwitt. 'Or I could slit your pretty throat and take it all.'

'You could,' said Twig, standing his ground. 'But it wouldn't do you any good.'

The flat-head hesitated for a moment. 'What do you mean?' he asked gruffly.

'He to whom you have pledged your allegiance is about to be dethroned,' he said.

'What, Vilnix Pompolnius? Don't make me laugh!' said the flat-head. 'The Most High Academe?'

'The scurrilous usurper,' the Professor of Darkness muttered under his breath.

'The leaguesmen are against him,' Twig continued. 'The academics are against him.'

'But . . . but why?' demanded the flat-head.

'Why?' the Professor of Darkness broke in. 'Because he has run out of both the phraxdust which secured his alliance with the leaguesmen and the stormphrax which holds the floating city in place.'

Bogwitt looked confused. 'But there is stormphrax in

the treasury,' he said. 'That is what Vilnix ordered me to guard.'

'Why don't you take a look then?' suggested the professor, and handed him a heavy key.

The flat-head goblin's eyes narrowed. 'If this is some kind of a trick . . .?'

'Just look!' snapped the professor.

With his sword still raised, Bogwitt picked up his lamp and crossed over to the treasury door. There, he turned the key in the lock, twisted the handle and pushed. He stuck his head in and stared round in disbelief. Anger rose in his throat.

'Empty,' he snarled. 'The lying, cheating, no-good . . .

It's completely empty!'

'Vilnix lied to you,' the professor said simply. 'As he lies to everybody.'

'You backed the wrong side, Bogwitt,' Twig said, spelling it out for him. 'And now there can be no place for you in Sanctaphrax. However . . .'

'But I didn't know!' Bogwitt blurted out. 'I was only doing my job. I . . .'

'*However*,' Twig repeated, 'there is one possible way out of all this.' He paused. 'You are a good fighter, Bogwitt.'

'The best,' he nodded.

'And clearly loyal,' said Twig.

'I am, I am,' the flat-head agreed eagerly.

Twig nodded. 'Then this is what I propose,' he said. 'You join the crew of my sky pirate ship. But not as a slave. There will be no bondmen or galley-slaves on board the *Edgedancer*.' He glanced down at the leather pouch. 'What do you say?'

For a moment, the flat-head goblin remained silent. Then, slowly, a smile spread across his broad face. He met Twig's gaze. 'I says yes,' he replied.

Twig slowly counted out ten pieces of gold into his hand. 'But if you try to cross me, Bogwitt, it will be the worse for you,' he added threateningly. 'There are many, both in Undertown and Sanctaphrax, who would like to get their hands on Vilnix Pompolnius's former body-guard.'

'You can rely on me, Captain Twig,' said Bogwitt.

'I believe I can,' said Twig, and he slapped the coins down into the palm of his hand. 'Welcome aboard, Bogwitt,' he said.

The professor, who had been watching the exchange

with some confusion, stepped forwards. 'Come,' he said, 'let us complete our task.'

Twig nodded. 'Bogwitt,' he said, 'will you take the other end of that chest.' The flat-head did not move. 'Bogwitt!' Twig snapped. 'I trust that this is not the first indication of a mutinous nature.'

'No, no,' said Bogwitt, and approached the chest. 'Not at all, sir, but . . .' He shuddered. 'Why does the box glow so strangely?'

'Stormphrax,' Twig answered. 'We have brought stormphrax. Equilibrium is about to be restored to the empty treasury of Sanctaphrax.'

A minute later, the treasury was no longer empty. In the middle of the circle which had been carved at the very centre of the chamber, stood the chest of stormphrax.

'But why has nothing happened?' asked Bogwitt.

'Only when it's in darkness, pure and absolute, does the stormphrax attain maximum weight,' the professor explained. He raised the lid of the chest and removed the twilight lantern. 'Come,' he said. 'It is time.'

In a line, with the professor in front and Twig bringing up the rear, the four of them made for the door. As they went, the lantern and the lamp swung, sending dark shadows swooping round the chamber and across the chest. The stormphrax grew heavy, then light again – then heavier than ever. And as *that* happened, so the floor of the treasury rocked and trembled.

'Quick!' the professor cried, and broke into a run.

The others followed, stumbling and staggering as the

floor continued to judder. When he reached the door, Twig glanced back for one last look. The chest seemed absurdly small in the centre of the enormous chamber. Could it really be enough to stabilize the mighty floating rock?

'Twig!' said the professor sharply.

Twig stepped outside, seized the heavy iron handle and slammed the door shut behind him, the sound echoing back along the dark tunnels. At the same time, the floor beneath his feet abruptly dropped away.

His stomach lurched. His heart leapt into his mouth. Terrified, he cried out.

The next instant, the movement jerked to a halt. There was silence. There was stillness. Twig turned to the Professor of Darkness.

'Is that *it*?' he said.

'That is it,' the professor confirmed. 'The perfect amount.'

Twig shook his head in disbelief.

'Trust me,' said the professor. 'Deep down here at the centre of the rock, the effect is minimal. Up on the surface, however, in the city itself, the consequences will be cataclysmic. In fact, you must believe me when I say to you that Sanctaphrax will never ever be the same again.'

# ·CHAPTER TWENTY-THREE·

# SHOWDOWN

Vilnix Pompolnius was waking from a deep dreamless sleep when the floating rock first trembled. He opened his eyes, glanced round the luxurious Inner Sanctum and smiled a self-satisfied smile.

'How wonderful this all is,' he muttered. 'And how exquisitely clever I am to have made it mine.'

He threw back his covers, climbed out of bed and walked to the window. The sun – large and red and wobbling like an immense bowl of dellberry jelly – had just risen up above the horizon. Pink, feathery light spread across the sky. Vilnix yawned and rubbed his hand over his stubbly scalp.

'The start of yet another delightful day,' he said, and threw the window wide open.

A blast of refreshingly dewy air struck him in the face, snatching his breath away. Behind him, the glass

droplets of the crystal chandelier tinkled like wind-chimes. Vilnix leaned out and pulled the window shut again – he didn't want them to shatter. But the chandelier continued its insistent jangling music.

Vilnix frowned and looked round, puzzled. 'What in Sky's name . . .?' he muttered.

At that moment, the rock lurched and the mirror – the second mirror, the mirror which was leaning up against the wall – abruptly slid back, over the thick white carpet and down to the floor. Vilnix sighed. At least it hadn't smashed. But what had caused it to fall in the first place? The weight-fixers and chain-clampers weren't due to start work for another two hours and anyway, the float-ing rock was now gripped by judders and jolts far more severe than anything their drills could cause.

Horrified, Vilnix Pompolnius clung on to the window sill as the Inner Sanctum shook more violently than ever. Priceless objects were crashing to the floor all round the chamber – the porcelain vases and ivory figurines, the ornate carvings and the time-pieces, the leatherbound books.

Is it a storm? Vilnix wondered. Or an earthquake? Or has the floating rock finally become so buoyant that it is tearing away from its moorings?

At that moment, there was a loud cracking sound and the chandelier abruptly broke free from the ceiling moulding and hurtled to the floor. It landed with an almighty crash – on the mirror. Shards and splinters of crystal and glass flew all over the chamber, embedding themselves in the panelled walls.

'What is going on?' Vilnix screamed. 'Minulis! MINULIS!'

But, on this occasion, the personal manservant to the Most High Academe failed to appear.

'Minulis, where are you?' stormed Vilnix, and strode furiously towards the door of his servant's spartan antechamber. He'd show the impudent wretch that he wouldn't be kept waiting!

Vilnix hadn't got more than half-way across the glass-strewn carpet when, all at once and with no warning, the entire chamber dropped down. He stumbled and fell to the floor. Above his head, a crack opened from one side of the ceiling to the other, and a massive section of gold-embossed plaster came crashing down about him.

When the dust settled Vilnix raised his head, stood up and shook the powdery fragments from his robes. Sanctaphrax, he realized, was now steady again. Rock steady. 'And yet for a moment we were falling,' he whispered. 'Which can mean but one thing . . .' His sallow face reddened with fury. 'That odious sky pirate must have returned with the stormphrax undetected.'

His head spinning with decisions and imperatives, Vilnix pulled his gown of office over his hair-shirt, fixed the spiked steel skull-cap into place and swept from the chaos of the chamber.

'I'll show him,' he muttered furiously. 'I'll show them all! They'll see what happens to traitors who meddle in the affairs of the Most High Academe.'

It wasn't only the Inner Sanctum which suffered damage. In every corner of every room of every tower of

Sanctaphrax, the story was the same. Instruments slipped from worktops; books fell from shelves. Walls cracked, windows broke, stonework and plaster tumbled to the ground as the vibrations had grown more violent.

Shrieks of terror and howls of pain rose up above the rumbling, crashing roar, and the citizens of Sanctaphrax – young and old, venerable and lowly – spilled out from the towers and into the squares and streets. For a moment they stood there, at a loss to know what to do as minarets and castellations came crashing down around them.

'What's happening?' 'What's going on?' they screamed at one another. ''Tis the end of Sanctaphrax!' Then someone called out, 'To the Great Hall!' and, as one, they all surged along the main avenue towards the oldest and most solid building in all of Sanctaphrax, the place where they always took to in an emergency.

The crowd arrived at the hall, angry and loud. They poured inside and were outraged to discover that even this ancient place of sanctuary had not been spared the consequences of the terrible shaking that had gripped their floating city. Fallen blocks of stone littered the cracked marble floor; a pillar lay on its side while a second one looked ready to topple at any moment. And, as they watched, a jagged crack zig-zagged its way up across the back wall from the foundations to the roof.

'Not here,' they cried out. 'Not the Great Hall!'

By the time those at the back of the crowd were at last entering the building, the rock was once again still – yet no-one's rage had abated. Not a jot. From the academics, crushed together at the front of the hall, to the servants and guards, packed in around the walls, the cries were the same.

'Where's Vilnix?' they demanded. 'He's the cause of all this.' 'That sanctimonious scoundrel!' 'That accursed usurper!' 'That treacherous villain who cannot see beyond the lining of his own pockets!' 'Where *is* he?'

Then, as two figures strode out on to the podium, the questions abruptly changed. 'What's the Professor of Darkness doing up there?' 'And who is that with him?'

The professor raised his arms and appealed for quiet. 'Friends,' he cried. 'Friends.' A hush fell. 'I understand your distress. I share your pain that our beloved Sanctaphrax has been so sorely wounded. And yet,' he went on, 'there was no way that it could have been avoided.'

A growl of discontent rumbled round the room. This wasn't what they had come to hear. Twig stared at the sea of angry faces before him and trembled. If the professor wasn't careful, the crowd would rip them apart first and ask questions afterwards.

'What about my laboratory?' demanded the Professor of Windtouchers.

'And who's going to replace the windows of my observatory?' added the Professor of Cloudwatchers.

'Buildings can be repaired,' the professor continued, undaunted. 'And now there is no further need for chains, there will be hands enough to effect those repairs.'

An anxious muttering started up. 'No chains?' everyone was saying to everyone else. What madness was this? Of course they needed chains!

'No chains save the one ancient Anchor Chain which keeps us from drifting,' the professor explained.

'Clarify!' called the Professor of Cloudwatchers.

'Elucidate!' demanded the Professor of Windtouchers.

'What do you mean?' a gruff voice shouted from the back.

'I mean this,' the professor said. 'That the crisis which has been hanging over our heads for so long is, at long last, over. Sanctaphrax is once more in equilibrium.'

His words were greeted with absolute silence. Could it be true? they all wondered. Could it *really* be true?

'But what about all that jolting and juddering?' asked the Professor of Cloudwatchers.

'And the shaking and shuddering,' added the Professor of Windtouchers.

'That,' said the professor, turning to them, 'was the rock being weighed down by the cargo of stormphrax.' He looked up. 'It will not happen again for as long as any of us shall live. Of that, I give you my word.'

A murmur went round the hall; a murmur which grew louder and louder, until everyone seemed to be talking at the same time. Then a solitary cheer went up from the back. Others joined in. And the next moment, the entire hall was resounding with the exultant whoops and cries of unbounded joy.

'To the Professor of Darkness!' someone yelled.

'Yes, to the new Most High Academe of Sanctaphrax!' cried the Professor of Cloudwatchers, waving his arms in the air.

'Or should that be, to the *old* Most High Academe?' said the Professor of Windtouchers.

'Old or new, I would be honoured to resume my responsibilities as the Most High Academe,' the Professor of Darkness announced, to rapturous applause. 'And yet,' he continued, 'it is not I you have to thank for all that has taken place. I was not the one who ventured forth to the Twilight Woods and who risked all to return to Sanctaphrax with a cargo of precious stormphrax.'

'Then who? Who?' the crowd called out. Surely not the bony youth who hovered by his side.

The professor took a step towards Twig, seized him by the wrist and raised his arm high in the air. 'Professors, academics, citizens,' he announced. 'I give you Captain Twig. *He* is the person you must thank.'

Twig turned as red as a woodsap as the crowd whooped and whistled and cheered, overwhelmed by the waves of gratitude that washed over him.

'Thanks to this brave and valiant youth, we will no longer have to lie in our beds, quaking with fear that the floating-rock might break its moorings and fly up into open sky,' the professor said, raising Twig's arm still higher.

'Hooray!' cried the delighted crowd.

'Thanks to him, we have been freed from our dependence on the greedy leaguesmen for our well-being.'

'*Hooray!*' they bellowed, louder still.

'By all that is wise, he served us with heart and mind, forswearing all loyalties other than to Sanctaphrax,' the professor announced.

Twig trembled at the words. Where had he heard them before? he wondered. Why were they so familiar?

'He dedicated his life to the finding of stormphrax. He chased a Great Storm and did not return until he had completed his sacred – aye, Twig, your *sacred* – quest.' The professor smiled. 'Kneel my boy,' he said.

That was it! Twig remembered. They were the words used at his father's Inauguration Ceremony. 'But . . . I . . . you . . .' he blustered, and swallowed hard. Then, lowering his eyes to the floor, he dropped down onto his knees.

The crowd fell silent as the Professor of Darkness walked towards the back of the hall and removed the ceremonial sword from the cracked wall. Twig was trembling; he was trembling so badly he was sure every-

one must be able to hear his teeth chattering. The next
moment, the professor returned with the sword and
stood before him. Twig looked up to see the great gold
blade coming down slowly through the air as it dubbed
him, first on his right shoulder, then on his left.

'I pronounce you to be an honorary Knight Academic,'
the professor said. 'Arborinus Verginix be your name.
Arise!'

For a moment, Twig did not move. He could not. His
legs had turned to jelly. Only when the professor
reached down and took his hand did Twig manage to
climb shakily to his feet. A mighty, clamouring din was
echoing round the Great Hall, so loud it made his head
spin.

'Hooray! Hooray! Hooray!' the assembled company yelled, and they skipped and jumped and danced for joy, academics with servants, professor with professor, each putting away their grudges and grievances – at least for this one wonderful moment.

'We shall be able to engage in our lofty pursuits once more,' the Professor of Cloudwatchers exclaimed, and slapped his old rival on the back.

'We shall be able to indulge our intellect again,' the Professor of Windtouchers agreed. 'To calibrate the infinite subtleties of the wind . . .'

'And clouds,' the Professor of Cloudwatchers put in.

'From the whisper of a zephyr to the roar of a mighty hurricane . . .'

'Cirrus, stratus, cirrostratus, cumulonimbus . . .'

The Professor of Windtouchers drew breath sharply. 'If it wasn't for the wind,' he snapped, 'your clouds wouldn't even move.'

'It is only because of the clouds,' the Professor of Cloudwatchers replied hotly, 'that we see the wind blowing at all . . .'

But the Professor of Windtouchers was no longer listening to his colleague and rival. 'Look!' he gasped, and pointed to the front of the hall.

All around the Great Hall, his action was being repeated until the chamber was silent and all eyes were on the tall menacing figure who stalked across the stage and up the steps to the raised pulpit.

There he stood, stooped and angular, his hands gripping the sides of the wooden support. All round him

were his personal guards: a dozen hulking flat-heads,
legs astride, arms folded. Vilnix tugged at his sleeves,
readjusted his skull-cap, and slowly surveyed the
gathering from under hooded eyes. His lips curled with
contempt.

'What is the meaning of this?' he said, his voice soft,
yet threatening. 'Can I not turn my back for a moment?'

The crowd shuffled about uneasily.

Vilnix sneered and leaned out over the pulpit. Then, with his back arched and the skull-cap gleaming, he pointed accusingly at the Professor of Darkness. 'Will you listen to the lies of this false prophet?' he roared. 'This senile old fool who brought Sanctaphrax to the very brink of ruination before, and now seems intent on finishing the job off?'

Twig shook his head. No, no, that wasn't how it was at all. Yet, with every word Vilnix spoke, the crowd was becoming more restive.

'In cahoots with renegade sky pirates he was,' Vilnix said, spitting out the words.

The murmuring in the Great Hall grew louder, more insistent as the mood turned uglier. Eyes glinting triumphantly, Vilnix returned his gaze to the crowd.

'He and those he has duped into believing in him are traitors, collaborators, knaves. Guards!' he screamed. 'Seize him – seize them both – these verminous bugs that must be crushed . . .'

Two of the flat-heads strode towards them.

'It takes one to know one,' a shrill voice called out from the back. It was followed by a ripple of nervous laughter.

Vilnix spun round and peered furiously into the shadows. His heart began to pound. 'Who said that?' he demanded. 'Come on, who was it?' A servant, dressed all in white, stepped forwards. 'Minulis!' Vilnix gasped. 'Is that you?'

'The Professor of Darkness spoke the truth,' Minulis

shouted defiantly. A muttering went round the walls of the Great Hall. 'Unlike you!'

'How *dare* you!' screeched Vilnix. 'Guards, seize him too!'

Two more of the flat-heads jumped down off the stage, and began wading through the crush of bodies. But they didn't get far. For once the academics worked as one, linking arms, pushing back – allowing Minulis to continue.

'Many's the whispered conversation I overheard. The crooked deals you struck with the Leaguesmaster. The bribery. The corruption. *You* are the traitor!' he cried boldly. 'I am only sorry that when I was shaving your scurvy head I had not courage enough to slit your scrawny throat!'

White with rage and shaking, Vilnix screamed at him to be silent. 'Will you let your Most High Academe be slandered in this way?' he demanded of the crowd.

'You are not our Most High Academe,' came a voice. It was the Professor of Windtouchers.

'Not any more,' added the Professor of Cloudwatchers.

Vilnix's jaw dropped. Could he, who prided himself on his manipulation of a situation, have gauged the mood so badly?

'Guards, guards . . .' he cried. Two of the flat-heads took a step forwards, but then stopped. The crowd jeered and booed and hissed. 'Go on, then!' Vilnix screamed. But the flat-heads were having none of it. What was more, now that the natural reticence of the academics had been broken, their taunts and accusations came thick and fast. That he had abused his power, colluded with criminals, poisoned the river, desecrated the stormphrax – that he had threatened the very existence of Sanctaphrax.

'He wants stringing up!' someone screamed.

'Hanging's too good for him!' shouted another.

Vilnix didn't wait to hear any more. As the crowd surged towards him, he suddenly spun round, hitched up his robes and sped off.

A furious cry went up. 'After him!'

Down the steps at the edge of the stage, Vilnix ran, with Twig hard on his heels. The crowd raced to meet him.

'I'll cut him off,' someone shouted.

'Oh, no you won't,' Vilnix muttered as he dodged out of the way of the reaching arms and sped to the side wall. Behind a tapestry was a door. Vilnix was through it before anyone even realized it was there.

'He's getting away!' an angry voice shouted.

Twig was first through the door after him. He looked left. He looked right – and there was Vilnix, gown still up around his waist, tearing away down the central avenue. 'Stop!' he yelled. 'Stop!'

Faster and faster Twig ran, with the furious crowd following closely behind. Up an alley, over an arched bridge, through a tunnel and on, they ran. Vilnix Pompolnius knew Sanctaphrax like the back of his hand and, time and again, Twig lost precious seconds as he took a wrong fork or ran past a turning. Yet he was gaining. Slowly, but surely, he was catching up.

'You can't get away,' he bellowed, as Vilnix abruptly jumped down off an overhead walkway, and made a dash for the edge of the rock.

'Just watch me!' Vilnix cried, and cackled with laughter.

Twig looked up to see the gnokgoblin from earlier standing next to his basket and beckoning at Vilnix. 'This way, sire,' he said. 'You'll be down in a trice, so you will.'

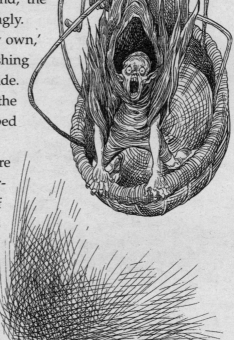

Twig groaned as Vilnix strode to the end of the landing stage. He *was* getting away, after all.

'Let me give you a hand,' the gnokgoblin said obligingly.

'I can manage on my own,' Vilnix said gruffly, pushing the gnokgoblin to one side. He put his hand on the wicker side and jumped into the basket.

The next instant, there was the sound of tearing. Twig saw a look of horror flash across Vilnix's face. Then he, together with the basket, disappeared and hurtled down to the ground below.

'AAAAaaarggh!' Vilnix screamed, halting everyone in their tracks. Desperate, frenzied, chilling, the cry faded – then stopped abruptly.

Far, far below on the ground, the body of Vilnix Pompolnius lay draped across a knife-grinder's wheeled stall. His arms were outstretched, his legs akimbo, the skull-cap so badly dented it would never be prised from his shattered skull. Millcrop, the knife-grinder, looked into the lifeless face of the former Most High Academe.

'Well, well,' he said. 'If it isn't old Villy. Should have stuck to knife-grinding, like me.'

Back up in Sanctaphrax, Twig reached out for the rope which had broken. Although a few of the strands were frayed, the rest had clearly been sliced through with a knife. He turned, and his gaze fell on the dagger tucked in at the gnokgoblin's belt. 'You,' he said.

The gnokgoblin shrugged. 'I told you the leaguesmen would see to him.' He jingled a pouch of coins in his hand before slipping them inside his jerkin. 'And good payers they are, too,' he smirked.

Twig climbed to his feet and walked past the gnok-goblin. 'Vilnix Pompolnius is dead,' he announced to the crowd.

A shout of joy and derision went up. 'He's gone! He's gone!' they all cried. 'And good riddance!'

Twig looked away uneasily. He was as relieved as anyone else that Vilnix Pompolnius was gone, yet the manner of his death disturbed him. It had been an underhand execution, and all the more dishonourable for that.

'*There* you are, captain,' came a voice.

It was Bogwitt. The Stone Pilot was standing beside him. Twig nodded to them. 'Come,' he said. 'Let us leave this place.'

# ·CHAPTER TWENTY-FOUR·

# THE *EDGEDANCER*

In the event, their departure was delayed by the Professor of Darkness who, catching up with them at one of the alternative baskets, tried everything he could to persuade Twig to stay.

'Where will you go?' he said. 'What will you do? There could be such a fine and venerable future for you here, my boy, if only you would take it.'

But Twig shook his head. 'I can't,' he said. 'I . . . I am a sky pirate captain. Like my father, and his father before him. It's in the blood.'

The professor nodded regretfully. 'But if you ever change your mind . . .' he said, 'the title of *Professor of Light* would sit comfortably on so valiant a pair of shoulders.'

Twig smiled.

'Ah, well,' the professor sighed. 'One can but try. Now

about the matter we discussed in my study,' he said. He stepped back to reveal two bulging sacks on the ground behind him. 'I think you'll find everything in order. Envelopes. Instructions. Crystals. Just as we agreed. And I will see to it that the bell rings every evening. It's always good to have a new tradition.' He smiled. 'Officially, it shall be in honour of your return from the Twilight Woods.'

Twig reached out and shook the professor's hand warmly. 'Until the next time, Professor,' he said.

Back in Undertown once more, Twig found that they had come down within spitting distance of the Bloodoak tavern. Yet a further two days were to pass before they crossed Mother Horsefeather's threshold. It took that long to assemble a crew.

That first morning, they paid Flabsweat a visit. Unfortunately for the fat, glistening proprietor, a fresh consignment of creatures had just arrived from the Deepwoods. If Twig had been alone, he might have withdrawn his offer, but the presence of the fierce flat-head and the ominous hooded creature persuaded him to honour the promise he had made.

Just as Cloud Wolf had taken on the Stone Pilot all those years ago to give her back her freedom, so Twig left with three individuals who should never have been in a pet shop in the first place.

The first was Spooler, an oakelf with wide eyes that twitched nervously. Although a fragile-looking specimen, Spooler had valuable experience of skysailing.

The second was Goom, an adolescent banderbear who still bore the wounds of the spiked pit it had been trapped in. As Twig looked the creature up and down, it leaned forwards and touched the banderbear tooth around his neck.

'Wuh?' it said questioningly.

'Wuh-wuh,' Twig explained.

'T-wuh-g?' it said.

Twig nodded. Even though the banderbear was young, it knew all about the boy in the Deepwoods who had once cured a banderbear of toothache.

And the third crew-member . . . Twig would not even have noticed the scaly creature with its reptilian tongue and fanned ears had it not spoken. 'You are looking for crew-members,' it hissed. 'How useful it would be to have someone aboard who can hear thoughts as well as words – Captain Twig.' It smiled and its fan-ears snapped shut. 'I am Woodfish.'

Twig nodded. 'Welcome aboard, Woodfish,' he said as he handed him his ten gold pieces.

Six strong, they were now. With a couple more the crew would be complete. Yet with Woodfish now amongst them, the finding of two suitable crew-mates proved difficult.

Every time Twig approached and talked to likely-looking characters in the inns and markets, Woodfish would listen in to their deepest thoughts, and was soon tutting critically and shaking his head. This one was too cowardly. This one, too careless. This one had mutiny in his heart.

It wasn't until late afternoon on the second day that they stumbled across the next crew-member in a seedy inn. At first he looked the least likely of them all, a stocky red-faced slaughterer, drunk at the bar and weeping into his woodale. But Woodfish was adamant. 'There is sorrow in his head, but his heart is good. What's more, he understands the rudiments of skysailing. Go and speak with him, captain.'

In the conversation that followed Twig discovered that the slaughterer's name was Tarp – Tarp Hammelherd – and that he had come to Undertown in search of his brother, Tendon, who had run a small lucky-charm business. That evening, not two hours since, he'd learned that Tendon was dead, blown up in some stupid accident with stormphrax – because he was thirsty.

'And it's not right,' he wailed.

Woodfish was correct. Tarp Hammelherd's heart *was* good and, having calmed him down, Twig offered him ten gold pieces and a place on the *Edgedancer*. Tarp accepted.

'Forgive me,' came a strident voice from behind them. 'But am I correct in understanding that you are looking for crew-members. If that is the case, then look no further.'

Twig turned round. The person before him was thin yet wiry, with a pinched and pointed face, a hooked nose and small, sticking-out ears. 'And you are?' he asked.

'Wingnut Sleet,' he replied. 'The finest quartermaster this side of the sky.'

Twig glanced at Woodfish, but the scaly eavesdropper merely shrugged.

'I have a head for heights, a mind for numbers and an eye for a bargain,' he announced, his restless blue eyes glinting behind steel glasses.

'I ... I ... Wait a moment,' said Twig, and took Woodfish aside. 'Well?' he whispered.

'I'm not sure, captain. Certainly, every word he spoke was the truth. And yet. I don't know ... there is something. Something pent-up about him. Something that might snap at any moment – or never at all.'

Twig sighed, exasperated. 'We could go on searching like this for ever,' he complained. 'And this Sleet character sounds good. If we take him on then we've got ourselves a complete crew.' He glanced out of the window. 'We could go to Mother Horsefeather at once.' He tipped the final ten pieces of gold from the pouch and turned to Woodfish. 'I'm going to take a chance on him.'

Woodfish nodded. 'Your decision, captain,' he said. 'Your decision.'

'The *Edgedancer* is ready and awaits you somewhere safe,' Mother Horsefeather said. 'But first, the secret.'

'Ah, yes,' said Twig. 'The secret.' Mother Horsefeather drew closer as Twig pulled a crystal of stormphrax from his pocket and placed it on the table before him. 'A mortar and pestle, if you please,' he said.

'But ... but ...' Mother Horsefeather clucked anxiously. 'This is what everyone tries – and you know what happens.'

Twig drummed his fingers impatiently. Mother Horsefeather fetched the mortar and pestle.

'Thank you,' he said. 'Now, observe. I place the crystal in the bottom, so. I raise the pestle and I wait.'

Feathers rustling, Mother Horsefeather stared at the youth as he whispered strange words under his breath.

'What are you saying?' she demanded. 'Is it some kind of incantation?'

Far above them, the sonorous bell of the Great Hall tolled. Twig brought the pestle down. The stormphrax turned to phraxdust with no more than a fizz and a glimmer.

'Yes, oh, yes!' Mother Horsefeather exclaimed and wrapped her huge padded wings warmly around Twig. 'Excellent. Excellent. But what *were* the words. You must tell me.'

Twig laughed. 'I was counting off the seconds,' he explained. 'The secret is that stormphrax can only be turned safely to dust at the exact moment of true twilight. Not a moment before. Not a moment after.'

'Twilight is twilight as far as I'm concerned,' said Mother Horsefeather. 'And it lasts a whole sight longer than a moment.'

Twig smiled. 'To you and me,' he said. 'And yet to the Professor of Darkness, that fragment of time which separates light from darkness is as plain as . . . as the beak upon your face.'

Mother Horsefeather clacked with irritation. 'And how am *I* to determine that fragment of time?'

'The Professor of Darkness will sound a bell every evening at the precise moment,' he explained. 'All you have to do is be ready.'

The bird-woman's eyes narrowed. 'The Professor of Darkness?' she said, suspiciously.

'It's not what you think,' said Twig hurriedly. 'He is doing it in celebration of my return from the Twilight Woods. He . . .'

'If you have breathed a word of this to him, then our deal is off,' Mother Horsefeather snapped. Her eyes glinted. 'In fact,' she said, 'since you have already told me so much . . .'

Twig stood up abruptly from the table. 'Consider how awful it would be if, one day, the bell rang either a moment too early or a moment too late,' he said coldly. 'I have kept my side of the bargain, Mother Horsefeather. My crew are waiting outside. Now I want my gold and my sky ship.'

Mother Horsefeather pulled a key from her apron and tossed it down on the table. 'The boom-docks,' she said. 'Wharf 3. The gold is on board.'

'Are you sure?' said Twig. 'Remember the bell.'

Mother Horsefeather clucked miserably. 'It will be by the time you get there,' she said.

The new crew fell in love with the *Edgedancer* the moment they clapped eyes on it.

'She's a beauty,' Tarp Hammelherd gasped, 'and no mistake.'

'A diamond,' murmured Sleet.

Twig beamed proudly as he stared up at the broad, white sails and criss-cross of spotless rigging. Together, they pulled the sky ship down the ramp-rollers, out of the ramshackle building and into the night. A full moon gleamed down on the polished masts and hull, on the silver lamps, on the burnished instruments and bone-handled levers.

'All aboard,' cried Twig, as he had heard his father cry so many times before. 'Take to your posts.'

The sky pirates leaped to obey. Twig went to the bridge, gripped the helm and waited for the Stone Pilot to signal that the flight-rock was ready.

The signal came.

'Unhitch the tolley-ropes,' Twig shouted. 'Raise the mainsail. Steady on the boom.' The *Edgedancer* began to rise. Gently, Twig realigned the stern- and prow-weights. The bow rose and the sky ship soared up into the air.

Twig laughed for joy. The sky ship handled like a dream. Unlike the *Windcutter*. He lowered the port hull-weights and adjusted the mainsail a fraction. And yet, he thought as the sky ship glided obediently round to the left, had it not been for that perilous journey across the Mire and over the Edge in the crumbling sky ship, he would never have learnt to master the controls. Now, with the experience of the *Windcutter* behind him, flying the *Edgedancer* was a piece of pie.

As they swooped down low over the Bloodoak tavern, Twig saw Mother Horsefeather peering up at him from the doorway. 'Tarp,' he called. 'Spooler. Start emptying the sacks.'

'Aye aye, captain!' they called back and, leaning over the back of the aft-deck, began throwing handful after handful of the envelopes to the air, where they fluttered, flapped and floated down to Undertown below. The sky pirates watched as the Undertowners ran this way and that in the oily, yellow lamplight, seizing up the curious folds of paper which had appeared as if from nowhere.

'Begging your pardon, captain,' said Tarp, as they circled the town for a second time. 'But what exactly are we doing?'

Twig grinned as the Bloodoak tavern came back into view. 'We are ending a monopoly.'

'Captain?'

'Each envelope contains a crystal of stormphrax and instructions for the safe production of phraxdust. It was the only way I could make sure that *everyone* would have access to pure, clean water once again.'

'Oh, I like that, captain,' Tarp cried. 'I like that a lot. That's fair, that is. My brother, Tendon, would most definitely have approved.'

'Which is more than can be said for Mother Horsefeather,' Sleet observed. 'She looks fit to explode.'

Twig laughed and replied to her clenched and shaking fists with a wave. 'It was high time for that avaricious bird-woman to get her come-uppance,' he said. 'She's ruled the Undertown roost for far too long.' He glanced round. 'How are those sacks coming along?'

'Nearly done, captain,' came the reply.

Twig smiled. He too was nearly done. With the storm-phrax in place, the chain-building would cease, the pollution would stop and the Edgewater River would, once again, run clean enough to drink. The vicious circle gripping Sanctaphrax and Undertown was almost at an end.

As the last envelopes fluttered down, Twig turned the helm to port. It was time to sail away from Sanctaphrax, from Undertown. He raised the sails and lowered the stern-weights. The *Edgedancer* leapt forwards. And, with the wind gathering strength and singing in the rigging, Twig closed his eyes and threw back his head, giddy with elation.

He had done it! He had achieved what his father, Quintinius Verginix, had set out to do all those years earlier. Perhaps that was the way it was always meant to be . . . Who could tell?

Whatever, Twig had chased a Great Storm to the Twilight Woods in search of stormphrax and, although he had ultimately come by the sacred substance in a different place, come by it he certainly had. Having departed as a stowaway, he had returned as a captain – victorious and triumphant. A hero.

The wind caressed his face and tousled his hair. Could there be anything more exhilarating than soaring across the endless expanse of blue? A broad grin spread across his face. No, nothing, he realized. Nothing in the world. After all, he had been born to it.

And at that moment Twig felt himself to be the most fortunate person who had ever lived.

'Skysailing in my own sky ship,' he murmured, his chest bursting with pride. 'The *Edgedancer*.'

All at once, the air around him became loud with a great wheezing and flapping of wings. He heard the sky pirates cry out in fear and alarm. Twig opened his eyes.

'You!' he exclaimed.

'Indeed,' the caterbird replied, as it shifted round on the balustrade and thrust its beak forwards.

'Are you all right, captain?' came a voice. It was Tarp Hammelherd. 'Or should I sink an arrow in the creature's scraggy neck now.'

Twig spun round to see Tarp's crossbow lowered and pulled. 'Avast!' he screamed. 'All weapons down.'

The caterbird's eyes swivelled round. 'A fine welcome, Master Twig,' it sniffed. 'Yet perhaps it is in order, for I bring bad news.'

'News? What news?' Twig asked uneasily.

'It is Cloud Wolf,' it said. 'Your father is in grave danger.'

'Danger?' said Twig anxiously.

'The Great Storm never released him from its terrible grip,' the caterbird explained. 'When I last saw him, he was being carried off. I followed as far as I dared . . .'

'Where to?' said Twig.

'Far from here. Too far.'

'Not . . .'

The caterbird nodded. 'Over the Edge, Twig. Farther than anyone has ever been before, deep deep into uncharted sky.'

Twig stared ahead, heart thumping wildly. His father, out there, lost in the monstrous, misty wasteland beyond the Edge – it was too appalling even to consider.

'I must try to rescue him,' he said resolutely.

'It will be a perilous undertaking, Master Twig . . .' the caterbird began.

'*Captain* Twig,' Twig interrupted stiffly. 'And there are no perils great enough to keep me away. The *Edgedancer* is ready. The crew are ready. And so am I.'

'Then we will set forth at once,' said the caterbird.

Twig started with surprise. 'We?' he said. 'Do you intend to travel with us?'

'You were at my hatching,' the caterbird reminded him. 'I am bound to watch over you – always.' It sighed. 'Sometimes I wish it were not so . . . But enough of all this. We must make haste. Find a rope. Tether one end to the bowsprit, the other round my belly. I will track your father across open sky.' It paused and shuddered. 'It will mean flying further than even I have been before – but I will lead you to him. Sky willing we will not be too late.'

'Sky willing,' Twig repeated softly. Then, without another word, he lowered the starboard hull-weights and shifted the rudder-wheel.

'All set,' cried the caterbird. It leapt up from the balustrade and flapped off ahead. As the tether grew tighter Twig pulled down hard on the helm. The *Edgedancer* leapt forwards.

With the caterbird in front, the sky ship sailed closer and closer to the Edge. Below it, the water of the Edgewater River fell abruptly away and cascaded down for ever through dark sky. The wind blew, the sails billowed and the *Edgedancer* soared out – *over* the Edge and beyond.

'Sky protect us,' Twig whispered. 'Sky protect us all!'

# ABOUT THE AUTHORS

PAUL STEWART is a well-established author of books for young readers – everything from picture books to football stories, fantasy and horror. Several of his books are published by Transworld, including *The Wakening*, which was selected as a Pick of the Year by the Federation of Children's Book Groups.

CHRIS RIDDELL is an accomplished graphic artist who has illustrated many acclaimed books for children, including *Something Else* by Kathryn Cave (Viking), which was shortlisted for the Kate Greenaway Medal and the Smarties Prize and won the Unesco Award. *The Swan's Stories* by Brian Alderson (Walker) was shortlisted for the 1997 Kurt Maschler Award and, in 2000, *Castle Diary* (Walker Books) was also shortlisted for the Kate Greenaway Medal.